Praise for *The Coroner's Lunch*

'Siri's greatest assets are his charm, persistence and dry humour, qualities that also make Cotterill's first novel an unexpected pleasure ... it portrays a credible fictitious world that is vivid and beguiling, a kind of oriental Mayhem Parva. A refreshing antidote to hi-tech crime busting'

Guardian

'Colin Cotterill's witty novel sharply captures the confusion after the revolution, and its hero, at turns cynical and humane, is an absolute diamond'

Daily Telegraph

'An exotic mix of superstition, ineptitude, and corruption – makes a refreshing change from the usual forensic investigation'

Sunday Telegraph

'The story is good, the characters interesting, the hero delightful and the setting fascinating: a find'

Literary Review

'*The Coroner's Lunch* has been likened to the Botswanan series of books by Alexander McCall Smith, but I would say it is, on the evidence of this first instalment, vastly better'

Euro Crime

'This intriguing mystery is made more enjoyable by the charming Siri, whose self-effacing nature is complemented by a resourceful mind and a determination to find the truth, however awkward it may prove. An enjoyable debut for a character who looks set to attract a keen following'

Big Issue (London)

'Cotterill's debut crime novel is an unusually refreshing cut above the average; peppered with dry humour, occasionally laugh-out-loud funny and thoroughly readable'

Buzz (Wales)

'One of the most unique and intriguing detectives you will find on paper. Colin Cotterill has outdone himself with this novel, his writing is full of humour, wisdom, and beautiful imagery, and leaves us eagerly waiting for the next instalment of this series'

RTE Guide

Praise for *Thirty-Three Teeth*

'The characters are as endearing, and the exotic setting as interesting, as in the first episode'

Literary Review

'Colin Cotterill shows in *Thirty-Three Teeth* that his engaging investigator Dr Siri Pariboun, an elderly coroner with shamanic gifts, should be much better known'

Sunday Times

'The National Coroner of Laos is an endearing, energetic seventy-something, with a lively sense of humour ... The mystical elements in their investigations are an unusual touch, but in the setting seem hardly less bizarre than the incompetence and unsuitability of the officials running the new democracy ... Fascinating background, engaging characters and witty dialogue'

Sunday Telegraph

'With its endearing cast of characters and some nifty plotting, *Thirty-Three Teeth* is occasionally surreal but always charming'

Guardian

'Foreign location, quirky detective, ironic tone, fundamental decency: check, check, check and check ... He [Siri] has Sherlock's logic, Quincy's forensic skills and Rumpole's ability to stick to the letter of the law, when expedient so to do. What makes Cotterill more than just a clone of previous experiments is the attention to detail, history and language ... It's a quick, easy read, which needles your ignorance, and makes you want the next one sooner'

Scotland on Sunday

'*Thirty-Three Teeth* by Colin Cotterill offers up a pleasantly mystical atmosphere that jives nicely with the tropical humidity emanating off the pages'

Time Out

'... a series of amusing set pieces, including a vivid account of the authorities' chaotic and misguided attempts to ban all spirits from the Communist state ... *Thirty-Three Teeth* provides a thankful opportunity to become reacquainted with the varied characters ... *Thirty-Three Teeth* is mainly about our interconnectedness ... The Buddhist context of the book is far more developed than in the previous book'

Euro Crime

ANARCHY AND OLD DOGS

Colin Cotterill

Quercus

First published in Great Britain in 2008 by Quercus

Quercus
21 Bloomsbury Square
London
WC1A 2NS

A CIP catalogue record for this book is available
from the British Library

ISBN 978 1 84724 576 2 (HB)
ISBN 978 1 84724 577 9 (TPB)

10 9 8 7 6 5 4 3 2 1

Printed and bound in Great Britain by Clays Ltd, St Ives plc.

I would like to thank my dedicated team of readers who, I'm delighted to say, have no hesitation in insulting me. Thanks to David, Lizzie, Dtee, Kye, Cathy, Geoff, Tony, my lovely Jess, and the marvelous John Cotterill, aka Dad.

FORM A223-79Q

ATTENTION: Judge Haeng Somboun
           C/O: Department of Justice,
           People's Democratic Republic of Laos

FROM: Dr Siri Paiboun

RE: National Coroner

DATE: 13/6/1976

RESUME:

1904   Plus or minus a year - years didn't have such
       clear boundaries in those days. Born in Khamuan
       Province, purportedly to Hmong parents. I don't
       recall it myself.
1908   Whisked off to live with a wicked aunt.
1914   Dumped in a temple in Savanaketh and left to the
       will of the Lord Buddha.
1920   Graduate from the temple high school. No great
       feat.
1921   Buddha investment pays off: shipped to Paris by
       kindly French sponsor intent on making something
       of me. The French make me start high school all
       over again just to prove it wasn't a fluke the
       first time.
1928   Enroll at Ancienne Medical School.
1931   Meet and marry Bouasawan in Paris and join the
       Communist Party for a lark.
1934   Begin internship at Hotel Dieu Hospital. Decide I
       might want to become a doctor after all.
1939   Return to Laos.
1940   Frolic in the jungles of Laos and Vietnam.
       Reassemble broken soldiers and avoid bombs.
1975   Come to Vientiane hoping for a peaceful
       retirement.
1976   Kidnapped by the Party and appointed national
       coroner. (I often weep at the thought of the great
       honour bestowed upon me.)

Sincerely,

Dr Siri Paiboun

CONTENTS

1

A NOTE TO A BLIND DENTIST

The post office box was eighteen across, twelve down, and it had a loop of wool wound around the door so Dr Buagaew wouldn't miss it. He traced the keyhole with his left hand and inserted the key with his right. From inside the wooden chamber came the scent of bygone correspondence: of brown-paper parcels and glue, of old parchment and secrets. His hand fell upon a thin envelope. He knew it would be there and he knew what it contained because only one other person was aware of the post office box address.

He relocked the door, folded the envelope, and, having put it in the inside pocket of his jacket, turned back in the direction of the exit. The Bureau de Poste was crowded. It always seemed to be so. He could hear the unruly scrum of ignorant villagers fighting their way to the counters. There were the sounds of pencils tapping urgent messages on postcards and the crinkle of the thirty-*kip* wrapping service. On the far side of the room, people shouted loudly into the long-distance telephones, sharing their most intimate stories with half of Vientiane.

It was all part of the hubbub of the city that Dr Buagaew disliked so much. If it hadn't been for the letters he wouldn't have travelled there at all. It was his habit to get off the bus beside the morning market, cross over Khu Vieng Avenue, collect his mail, and return on the same bus. He had no other business. In the capital of the People's Democratic Republic of Laos in August of 1977, traffic wasn't a fitting word to describe the infrequent passings of motor vehicles. Only those with familial or professional connections with the socialist government could afford to tantalize their tanks with petroleum. Two cars passing at the same time would be considered a traffic jam. Even midmorning, dogs stretched out on the warm asphalt and motorists had no qualms about going around them.

That might be the reason Dr Buagaew had never considered the road to be a potential danger. It could explain why he didn't stop at the broken stone kerb or take a great deal of notice of the engine sound. Once his bamboo cane had negotiated the cracks and potholes of the pavement, all that remained was to find the wire-mesh fence on the far side and follow it to his bus stop. The onlookers later concurred. They'd never seen anyone hit by a truck before, and it was such an unlikely event a man would almost have to throw himself beneath the front wheels for it to happen. Even then, the vehicle would probably be travelling slowly enough to slam on the brakes and avoid any embarrassment.

It was therefore agreed the old blind man must have been in deep karmic debt to have stepped in front of the runaway logging truck. What were the odds? A large Chinese vehicle? A stuck accelerator? A young driver bailing out in panic some twenty yards earlier? The truck had careened past the post office and crushed Dr Buagaew before slamming into the wooden public-address-system pole at the corner of Lan Xang Avenue. The latter stood defiantly for several seconds before swaying and crashing down onto the empty street.

This tragedy was a talking point that afternoon but very few tears were shed for the anonymous blind man. The locals didn't have room in their souls for someone else's misfortune. Vientiane had a certain mood about it these days. The government was starting to look like a depressingly unloved relative who'd come to visit for the weekend and stayed for two years. These were uncomfortable times in a country not unused to discomfort. The drought had wrung every last tear of moisture from the sad earth. The seasonal monsoons had held off, and a few brief mango flower showers were quickly sucked into the ground and forgotten. The World Bank was donating rice, but with few trucks and little petrol, most of it hadn't found its way beyond the cities.

It would be a good time, one would imagine, for a novice socialist government to ease up and give its downtrodden population a break from petty regulations. The Pathet Lao had come to power in 1975 and even the prime minister admitted they hadn't achieved too much since then. But the jungle-trained administration adopted a policy of disguising its lack of ability by baffling the populace with red tape. No fewer than six signatures were needed for permission to ride a bicycle from one prefecture to another. The death of livestock, even from natural causes, had to be accounted for in writing. And heaven help a family intent on adding an extension to its hovel. A small copse of trees' worth of paper and an entire octopus of ink would be used up by the ensuing paperwork.

Some fifty thousand former Royalist officials were now

in re-education camps, and the positions they once occupied had been either left empty or filled with Party cadres unqualified for the work. They all did their best, but best doesn't always amount to competent.

2

THE FOOTPATH FORTUNE-TELLER

Dr Siri Paiboun, the country's one and only coroner, was in the morgue rolling a testicle between his thumb and forefinger. It was a peculiar sensation. He held it up to the light to catch its opaqueness and took a photograph of it. He then placed it beside its comrade on the table in front of him and took one more snap of the couple together.

'You know? They're marvels, really they are,' he said.

'How so?'

Nurse Dtui was rummaging impatiently through the drawer for a suitable bag to put them in. She was a pretty girl in her twenties with a smile that won hearts. Her ice white uniform stretched across her solid block of a body, giving her the appearance of a large standing refrigerator, albeit a very happy one.

'They don't look like much,' Siri said, 'but these little fellows are the powerhouse of every sexual event that takes place in a man's body. They pump out testosterone to advertise virility and attract the female, they stimulate an erection, and they produce sperm to fertilize the ovum. And with all that responsibility, there isn't even a place for them inside. They have to dangle there like afterthoughts. Damned inconsiderate of the Maker if you ask me.'

'I doubt these'll be making any more contributions to the procreation of the species, what with having been fried and all,' Dtui said and smiled as she held up an envelope of stapled paper that had once contained banana fritters. 'This'll do.'

'You seem to be in somewhat of a hurry, Nurse Dtui.'

'It's Wednesday. Don't want to miss my fortune-telling appointment.'

'Aren't you supposed to be tending vegetables for the republic or some such after-hours nursing duty?'

'I can do that after my reading. It doesn't take half an hour.'

'I'm disappointed in you, really I am. Surely you don't believe all that clairvoyant bunkum?'

'That's good, coming from you.'

'Meaning what?'

'Let me just make sure I've got this right. A man who hosts the spirit of a thousand-year-old Hmong shaman – a man who's being pursued by the malevolent spirits of the jungle – a man who is regularly visited by the ghosts of murder victims …'

'This sounds like one hell of a man.'

'… a man who has no fewer than thirty-three teeth crammed together in his magical mouth, which positively proves his connections to the spirit world, believes that fortune-telling is bunkum?'

'Absolutely. It's a load of rot. The future's a pimple on your nose. No matter how fast you run, you'll never catch up with it. Nor should you try to.'

'That sounds suspiciously like one of Judge Haeng's Party slogans.'

'Not at all. It's mine. Nobody can profess to know the

future. Those fortune-teller charlatans make a living out of telling gullible folks what they want to hear.'

'Well, I certainly didn't want to hear that my study tour of the Soviet Union would be cancelled.'

'He told you that? See what I mean? Rot! Nothing can prevent your going to Moscow. It's all signed and sealed. That's why fortune-tellers are so dangerous, Dtui. They plant these weed-seeds in your head that take root and gnarl and prickle. It all confuses you so much that you act in ways that make the predictions come true. You think the fortune-teller has seen the future but in fact he's altered your flight path. He's sent you off in a direction that will converge with his prediction. You actually believe yourself into his fantasy.'

'Poop!'

'Poop? Poop? That's charming. It would appear the principle of respecting one's elders has gone down the toilet with all the other niceties of this planet.'

'Sorry. But poop's poop, elder or not. Auntie Bpoo's legitimate. I'd bet my socks on it.'

'Auntie Bpoo? Now there's a name to conjure with. Where's her office?'

'Well …'

'Well?'

'The footpath in front of the Aeroflot ticket agency.'

'Oh, Dtui. You surely don't mean the transvestite?'

'Yes.'

'Then I rest my case. It's a sorrier story than I could have imagined. You can see for yourself what a successful business he's built up. Such a splendid location. If the man could actually see the future, don't you think he'd be well off by now? Do you think he'd need to daub himself in garish makeup and sit on a straw mat? Goodness, if I were clair-voyant I'd be in Bangkok by now, drinking morning coffee and cognac with other respectable retirees.'

'She isn't allowed to use her gifts for personal gain.'

'Are you saying she … *he* doesn't charge?'

'Not one *kip*.'

Siri was only briefly bumped off the track. 'Oh, I see. They have a code of ethics. In that case, those ethics should extend to not giving out irresponsible predictions like your not going to the Soviet Bloc. I think this Auntie Bpoo chap would benefit from a good talking-to.'

'Go on then.'

'What?'

'Go chat with her.'

'This is the kind of thing you'd normally try to talk me out of.'

'No, I think the old dog might learn a few tricks.'

'I very much doubt that.'

'Then I dare you to go and see her. But be nice. Just ride out the bizarre stuff and she'll win you over. I guarantee it.'

'It appears she specializes in negatives.'

'Not always. She likes to cheer you up every now and then. She said I'd be married by the end of the month.'

Siri laughed. 'Who's the lucky man?'

'I didn't get a name.'

'Well, you'd better pull your finger out. It's already the fifteenth.'

Dtui bagged and labelled the testicles for the samples storeroom. 'Severed scrotum. Mr Tawon. Aug. 1977.' They wouldn't be joining the body on its trip to the pyre. Mr Tawon had wandered from the sanctity of marriage on regular occasions. After two decades of his infidelity, his loyal and patient wife had reached the end of her tether and decided it was time to bring him to the end of his. Across the river in Thailand, after an appropriate period of rehabilitation, Mr Tawon might have hoped to continue his philandering. Thai wives were more inclined to slice the carrot than the onions. If the cuckold was able to find his errant member and limp off to a surgeon, there was a thirty per cent chance of the organ's being successfully reattached.

But Mr Tawon's wife had done her homework. As her husband slept off a rice-whisky binge, the smell of cheap perfume still on his skin, she'd taken a razor to his scrotum. To be sure he wouldn't be tempted to reoffend in the afterlife, she'd deep-fried the detached ovoids in sesame oil. While trying to rescue them, Mr Tawon had bled to death. As Dr Siri remarked, this was a tale to bring tears to even the most insensitive of males.

'A lesson to all of us,' he'd called it.

Dr Siri Paiboun never failed to absorb wisdom from the departed. Even at seventy-three years of age, even after a life of studying and war and politics and love, he still conceded he had a lot to learn. Many Lao half his age bragged of being experts. They could have benefited from just a smidgen of Siri's humility because a true expert was one who admitted there weren't always answers. Oh, it's certain many of the other fellows weren't as ornery as the old man, but he'd earned the right to be stubborn and argumentative just by staying alive as long as he had. He hardly ever flew into a rage or insulted anyone who didn't absolutely deserve it. And he was certainly patient. He'd been compared to the Vietnamese Thousand Year Plant, which waited its entire life for the off chance that some forest deer might brush against its one and only spore and carry it off to more fertile ground.

And like the Thousand Year Plant, the good doctor was well preserved for a man his age. His hair was thick and white like the feathers of a newborn bantam. His peculiar green eyes still sparkled as bright as a raja's emeralds. His short frame was solid with muscle and his mind was as sharp as it had ever been. Only recently had things begun to go wrong. His lungs took longer to fill since the night his collapsing house had filled them with dust. And he had to admit that over the past few months he'd begun to lose his senses. Not those senses that prevent a man from betting on a cockfight or bedding his best friend's wife. No, the senses slowly draining away from Siri were those that gave colour and flavour and scent to the world. He could have blamed the drought for the greying of the blossoms or the dulling of their fragrances. But nature couldn't be faulted for the blandness of the spices that had once invigorated a recipe for him. The more intimate Dr Siri Paiboun became with the supernatural, the flatter became the natural world around him.

As the brothers of the postmortem eunuch once known as Mr Tawon were carrying him off to the temple, they passed the crumpled body of a truck-accident victim. It was being borne on an old Halls Menthol Cough Drop advertising billboard, used as a litter, by two young policemen. The billboard had also been a victim of the truck. The officers wore unmatching, ill-fitting uniforms. As they entered, Siri looked at their boyish faces and noted how narrow the gap was becoming between puberty and authority.

'Hey, Uncle,' one of them said, resting his end of the

placard on his knee. 'Where d'ya want this?'

Siri walked up to him and stared into his calf-like eyes. 'Seeing as I'm an only child,' he said, 'and as I haven't been sexually active for fifteen years, it's rather unlikely that you and I are related. In that case, I think you'd be safer off calling me "sir", don't you?'

'You what?'

'Sorry, Doctor,' the other policeboy interrupted. 'He's new. Just down from the country. Is there somewhere we can put this down? It's getting a bit heavy.'

Siri led them through to the cutting room and pulled open the single freezer door.

'Perhaps you could put him in here for me,' Siri said. 'What happened?'

'He got hit by a runaway truck in front of the central Bureau de Poste.'

'How unusual. I take it he didn't see it coming.'

'He didn't see anything, Comrade. He's blind. Or at least he used to be.'

Siri pulled back one of the corpse's eyelids to reveal the cataracts that had expanded the man's pupils and turned them cloudy like opals.

'Quite right. Any idea who he is?'

'Not a clue,' said the first officer, '… sir. I thought that's what you were supposed to tell us.'

'Well, boy, unless he's got his name tattooed on his backside, your guess is as good as mine. I'm a coroner, not a fortune-teller.'

3

A STICKY-RICE POLICEMAN

Auntie Bpoo wasn't one of those transvestites who fooled the eye from a distance. Even on the darkest of nights she wouldn't be mistaken for anything other than a middle-aged man in women's clothing. In daylight, viewed from the opposite corner of Samsenthai Road, she was a luminous beacon – and definitely a buoy. Her broad shoulders held up the spaghetti straps of a shocking pink halter. Her white stomach hung over the elastic waistband of her leopard-skin leggings like a floe of ice oozing from the freezer of a cheap refrigerator. The rouge on her cheeks and the purple around her eyes were redder and more purple than even the most flamboyant bird of paradise. But her hair, black and cut military short, set off a cream hibiscus blossom tucked behind her ear.

Siri stood in front of the closed-down coffee stand opposite and pretended to be manoeuvering a misplaced paving stone back into its spot with his foot. But only the black stupa hunched in its island of overgrown grass took any notice of him. Even through the film of dust that hung over the city's main street like a hazy hangover, Auntie Bpoo was an overstatement. Siri turned and headed back to his motorcycle. What was he thinking? What on earth had crawled into his head? He should have gone straight home like he'd planned. But no. Here he was contemplating something quite foolish. Perhaps he'd just wanted to see for himself what could possess an otherwise rational nurse to fall for an obvious confidence trick. And who was feeding this roadside duchess? She didn't accept payment but she obviously wasn't starving to death. It was his inner detective that turned Siri around once more and sent him across Vientiane's busiest street. On normal days he would have just launched himself into the road, but, given the day's events, he decided to stop at the kerb and look both ways before crossing.

A minute later he was sitting cross-legged on a banana-leaf mat beneath the long evening shadow of the Aeroflot sign. He watched Auntie Bpoo shuffle cards, just shuffle and shuffle, until he was sure the noses of the kings and queens had been scoured completely from their faces. She hadn't looked up at him, not even when he arrived. She hadn't so much as acknowledged his presence. When she spoke at last she began with a poem. At least Siri assumed that's what it was. He'd heard bad poetry before, but Auntie Bpoo's had a depth all her own.

'First a sheep (she began)
  Cheap start. Turns into four
      Then a boar
  A lion, chimpanzees
  Perfect clones
    Our own anomalies
  A hundred me
    We, thee
All the same.'

Siri wondered whether to comment. Was he supposed to ask what it all meant? Applaud? But, before he could speak, the clownish face of the transvestite looked up at him and smiled – an ugly betel-nut gash.

'Dr Siri,' she said. 'I've been expecting you.'

Siri felt oddly disconcerted that she should know who he was. They'd never met. Perhaps Dtui …? He coughed to jog the surprise from his voice.

'I'm actually here to tell you—' he began.

'That you think my predictions are a pile of poppycock,' she said.

Siri was impressed. Those were the exact words he'd chosen to complete his hijacked sentence. It was either a grand trick or an amazing coincidence.

'Well done. Perhaps you could tell me what I had for dinner yesterday evening,' Siri suggested.

'No. I couldn't,' Auntie Bpoo growled, and returned her gaze to the cards. 'If you want a cabaret, go to Bangkok.'

'But I thought that's exactly what you were – an elaborate parlour trick,' Siri managed, although he was lacking his usual bravado.

When she looked up at him again, her eyes were the dull silver grey of ball bearings. They seemed to bore into him. 'Before the second equinox, Dr Siri Paiboun, you will have betrayed your country.'

'I will what? Don't be ridiculous.'

'You came to me. I didn't pursue you.'

'I just came to—'

'And hang on to your lucky charm, Doctor. The *Phibob* are lurking. They're waiting for their opportunity.'

'Who … who told you about them?'

Siri felt a cold shudder rise from the pavement and climb his spine. This fortune-teller had access to facts she couldn't possibly have overheard. Dangerous knowledge. The spirits of the forest had hounded Siri to a ledge overhanging the valley of death. They'd hunted down the spirit of the thousand-year-old shaman, Yeh Ming, who'd chosen Siri as his host. But in order to destroy the one, they had to eliminate the other. Siri was in constant fear of them. He reached for his chest where the charmed white amulet, his only protection from the *Phibob*, lay warm against his skin. It was beneath his shirt, impossible to see.

'I don't see what's here and now,' the transvestite told him. 'I see what's to come. But often the future explains the present.'

Suddenly and inexplicably, she began to giggle shrilly. A dog in the gutter fled in panic. It seemed to Siri, amidst a sudden atmosphere of foreboding, that the monster sitting before him might have swallowed a young girl whole.

'Oh, my. It's late,' the little girl said in her tiny voice. 'Just think of little me walking home through the dark streets. I have to scamper.'

She quickly gathered her cards and her bag and shooed Siri off the mat so she could roll it up. All these actions she completed like a ballerina on heroin. Auntie Bpoo had turned into a silly feminine thing that Siri wanted to slap the senses back into, but naturally he didn't. She still outweighed him by some eighty pounds. Instead, he stood back in the Aeroflot doorway and watched her escape, stepping mincingly, hurriedly, past the black stupa. Siri was breathless and dumbfounded. There were few living beings that could make him feel inferior, but Auntie Bpoo, the transvestite fortune-teller, had joined their ranks.

*

One hand protruded stiffly from beneath the white sheet. It lay, palm upward, on the side table, as if begging for the return of its life. Mourners in all white or all black filed past the body in disorderly fashion. One by one they dipped a tin cup into a clay water pot and trickled a little onto the ash gray fingers. They begged forgiveness from the corpse just in case there were any forgotten misdemeanors they had committed. Four monks sat to one side, chanting behind their ceremonial fans like shy table-tennis players. The *sai sin* string circled them and looped down to the body, a karmic telegraph, passing their messages through to the deceased. Dtui stood at her mother's feet and thanked the visitors for coming. They smiled. She smiled. They joked. She laughed. There was nothing to be gained by turning a funeral into something depressing.

In the yard of the little temple there were drinks laid out on a long trestle table under the shade of a scrambled egg tree. There guests could sit and remember their nice friend Manoluk. They'd probably get rowdy and raucous after a few glasses of rice whisky and tell bawdy stories of her youth. If they didn't know any, they'd make them up. Certainly, they'd talk of the eleven children she'd borne, and their thoughts would come to rest on Dtui, the only one she'd been able to keep alive, the one she'd spoiled and toiled to provide an education for. They'd raise their glasses to the big soft nurse and shout 'Good luck' and play a few hands of cards before staggering off home. They would shed no unlucky tears to jinx Manoluk's journey to Nirvana. Only in their dreams would their true sorrow show itself.

At 6 a.m., Siri had awakened in a sweat with the image of Auntie Bpoo still in his head. He'd dreamed of slow dancing with her in a French bordello. Her makeup had smeared onto his cheeks, giving him the appearance of a Comanche warrior. Members of the Lao People's Party politburo were sitting around him at low tables wearing French berets. They cast circumspect glances in the direction of the dance floor. Siri looked over the hairy shoulder of his partner and counted them off, one by one. The president, of course; the prime minister; the heads of education and of agriculture. He'd located seven of the eight members but had no time to work out who was absent because a bomb – albeit a black, ball-shaped cartoon bomb – came flying through a window. It exploded and blew them all to kingdom come.

There was pitch-blackness and the pungent odour of fried bodies, and that was when Siri emerged from his dream. He recalled how bright the colours had been there compared to the washed-out hues that surrounded him in his room. How fruity the bordello wine, how sweet the Gitanes' smoke that hung in the air. All that flavour had gone and he was left with drabness and the monotonous sobbing of a young woman. It took him some minutes to identify the sound as coming from Dtui in the next room.

He found her lying beside her mother's body on the single mattress. For many painful years, Manoluk had tolerated the pain of cirrhosis as she provided for her girl. Once Dtui graduated, the roles had been reversed, and the larger part of the daughter's wages had gone towards expensive medication that had never actually performed the miracles claimed. They'd merely kept her mother alive and in pain – until now. As Siri looked on from the doorway he wondered whether Dtui's tears were of grief or relief. Her mother had finally stopped suffering. If the mattress had been wider, or Dtui and Manoluk narrower, he would have joined them there. He would have held Dtui's hand and absorbed some small part of her sadness.

In the stuffy heat of August, there was little time to lose. During the day, the housemates joined together to prepare for the bathing rites and the initial ceremony. Siri's household was a menagerie of misfits. Mrs Fah and her children delivered the hastily written announcements. Mr Inthanet, the puppeteer, drove his fiancée's old truck to the temple. And Comrade Noo, the renegade Thai forest monk, was already addressing the body's spiritual needs on the flatbed behind. Dtui had taken the day off to arrange the catering. Lao funerals gave people a hearty appetite, and the problems of feeding the guests kept her mind from feeling sorry for itself.

They'd all chipped in the few *kip* they had to spare for whatever happened to be available at the fresh market. Shopping in Vientiane had become a lottery. Fruits and vegetables had vanished one by one from the stalls. Farmers were allowed to feed their families but were taxed heavily for anything they produced for sale. It was one more astoundingly silly policy. Far from filling the markets with fresh produce and the treasury with much needed revenue, it succeeded in reversing history to a time when the Lao traditionally produced no more than was absolutely necessary to survive. Nobody could accuse the rural Lao of rising to a challenge. Attempting to piece together a menu from the stalls of brown legumes and flyblown buffalo meat had certainly kept Dtui's mind off her mother.

Only Dr Siri had made it to work that day. He'd paid the bulk sum of the funeral expenses; they'd agreed at least one person should be at work to earn next month's humble salary. He'd spent the day with the crumpled body of the blind man. Performing the autopsy by himself had made him realize how much he'd come to depend on his morgue team. He missed Dtui's concise note taking and sharp observations. He missed Mr Geung (presently convalescing from a near death encounter with a mosquito), who manhandled bodies and sawed through bones apparently without effort. By the late afternoon, Siri slumped, exhausted, on a stool beside the body. He'd somehow managed to fold it into one of the brand-new red PVC body bags so generously provided by the Soviet Union.

All that remained was to sign the death certificate and to trace the deceased's family so they could be notified. Siri was rummaging through the dead man's clothes for clues when he looked up to see a neat fellow of around forty-five walk into the cutting room. He had the slim build and good looks of a man who took care of himself, but the frayed shirt of one who didn't.

'Are you looking for something that'll fit you?' he asked Siri.

'Aha, Phosy. The capital's only middle-aged policeman. How are you, son?'

'Undernourished but otherwise happy, thanks. You?'

'Sparkling. Just sparkling.' Siri peeled off one rubber glove and shook his friend's hand enthusiastically. Inspector Phosy smiled and returned the enthusiasm. 'What brings you to my morgue?' Siri asked.

'Your traffic accident, of course.'

'Why? I thought you only handled cases with government connections.'

'Right you are. And the weapon in question was an army logging truck, was it not?'

'Of course. Well, I don't suspect foul play, if that's what you're after. You might be able to charge the driver with negligence if he hadn't fled the scene and vanished. Poor fellow's probably scared out of his wits they might execute him. But I believe they found the accelerator had stuck. You might stand a better chance of suing the Chinese for selling us their crappy old army surplus vehicles in the first place.'

'I'll bear that in mind. How about the victim?'

'No idea where he's from. Blind chap.'

'He didn't have his name and address written inside his shirt in case he got lost?'

'In braille? No such luck. But he did have this with him.' Siri held up a fawn-coloured envelope addressed to 'Mr Bounthan, Vientiane Central Post Office, PO Box 53, Vientiane Prefecture.' The stamp had been postmarked twice: once, six days earlier in Pakse – the largest city in the south – and once, the previous day in Vientiane.

'Well, that's good,' Phosy said. 'We know he has a first name that matches thirty per cent of the male population, and no surname.'

'Doesn't help much, does it?'

'Let's have a look inside.'

Siri slit open the envelope with a scalpel and pulled out a single sheet of paper. It was white, lined, and folded in half. Siri opened it and glared at the paper.

'Now that's odd,' he said.

'What does it say?'

'Nothing.'

'Nothing at all?'

'Take a look.'

Phosy held up the paper by one corner and looked closely at both sides. It was blank.

'What do you make of it?' Siri asked.

'I suppose it makes sense. Him being blind and all.'

Siri laughed. 'Ah, nice to see crime prevention in such good hands.'

'All right. So why would anyone go to the trouble of sending an empty sheet of paper?'

'We have to assume it meant something to the deceased. I don't suppose …?' He took the paper from Phosy and held it up to his nose. He sniffed lightly and shook his head. Then he took a deeper draft. 'Eureka. What does this smell like to you, Inspector?'

Phosy sniffed. 'I don't know. Sulphur?'

'Almost right. Copper sulphate to be exact. It's a common pesticide, very effective poison on humans, too. And it has to be damned strong or, given my present condition, I wouldn't be able to smell it at all. So what does that suggest to you, my crime-fighting friend?'

'It was sent by an assassin who hoped the blind man would eat it, thus killing himself without leaving a trace?'

'Phosy, I don't think you're taking this investigation seriously. Take your active imagination on a walk though the field of espionage.'

'Siri, I did all my training in the north-east of Laos. I'm a sticky-rice-and-raw-fish policeman. You know that. I've never been inside a crime laboratory in my life. I rely on earthy logic and gut instinct to solve my cases. Don't try to baffle me with exotic scents and all that CIA hocus-pocus.'

'Very well. In that case, I suspect what we have here is a message written in invisible ink.'

Phosy raised one eyebrow. 'And how would an old bush surgeon know a thing like that?'

'Inspector Phosy, allow me to reintroduce you to

Inspector Maigret of the Paris Palais de Justice. I became very involved in a number of his cases as they were outlined on the pages of his *L'Oeuvre* while I was in France. Unlike ourselves, Inspector Maigret has the very good fortune to be fictional, and thus can dispense with such human annoyances as inefficiency and budget restraints. He always gets his man. In one particular case, a junior minister wrote to his mistress on laundry tickets in invisible ink so her husband wouldn't be suspicious. Naturally, the husband found out and dispatched the blackguard, but the point is, Maigret described the constituents of the ink and its reagent in great detail. Being of a scientific bent, I retained that information and carry it to this day in my remarkable mind. If this is indeed a hidden message, all we need is sodium carbonate – common washing soda – to be able to read it.'

'I'm impressed. And all this time I thought there was nothing positive to be gained from reading mysteries.'

'You'd be surprised.'

'Got any?'

'Washing soda? Not on me. But I bet our Mr Geung has a supply in his broom closet.' Siri vanished into the store-room and emerged a few seconds later with a large jar. 'I'd say this is it.'

'And where is Mr Geung today?'

Siri began diluting the washing soda with water. 'Right. You don't know about our recent adventures. We have a lot to catch up on. We almost lost Geung to dengue fever last month.'

'Damn. Is he all right?'

'He will be. I admit he's dragging out his convalescence. Pretty nurses waiting on him hand and foot. If I were a cynic, I'd say he's milking it for all the attention he can get.

Meanwhile, I'm left doing all the unskilled labour myself, which is exactly when you realize there's nothing unskilled about labour.'

He used a fine brush to dab the weak solution onto the note. 'Well, what do you know?' The characters on the paper materialized slowly as if they were waking from a long sleep. None were immediately recognizable as words. It was more of a list than a message. Siri knew the individual letters from French but could understand nothing. It was apparent that the note he held was not written in a language he'd ever had cause to learn.

'So, what does it say?' Phosy asked.

'Haven't got a clue.'

'Hmm. Remarkable mind.'

'What was that?'

'Nothing.'

'I'm inclined to believe this is written in code, but I think we should check it with an English speaker just to be sure. What do you say we do a little investigating?'

4

UKQ'HH JARAN CAP PDEO

At the lycée, Siri and Phosy found teacher Oum emerging despondently from a classroom. She was in her early thirties, short and usually jolly. But today she had an expression on her face as blank as a glazed bun. The thirteen-year-olds trailing behind her had that same iced-over look.

'Oum!' Siri said.

She looked at him for a second or two before coming round.

'Comrade Siri. Comrade Phosy. Thank heaven.'

'What's wrong?' Phosy asked.

'A new-history lesson. I'm comatose.'

New history was one of the subjects inflicted on schools by the Department of Education, along with Russian and Marxist-Leninist theory. It intimated that life on earth had begun in the caves of Huaphan, where the Pathet Lao had orchestrated its takeover. Whereas in old history, centuries of Lao royal heritage and world events had taken centre stage, new history seemed to suggest that fifty years was an inordinately long time, and that the West was a small outer suburb of Vientiane – a place no self-respecting person would want to venture into on a dark night.

'But you're a chemistry teacher,' Siri reminded her.

'I was, Doctor. I was. And I shall be again on Thursday. But we're all being encouraged to diversify.' She glanced at Phosy, whose politics she wasn't completely sure about. One had to be careful in this day and age. 'It's a marvellous system. I teach physical education on Mondays. Can you believe it? The pupils saw me in shorts for the first time last week and half of them have been off sick since.'

'What do you know about new history?' Siri asked.

'Don't need to know anything,' she said and held up a thick ring binder crammed to bursting with notes. 'It's all here. I just write today's lesson on the blackboard and the kids copy it.'

'And today's lesson was …?'

'The great victory at Sala Phou Khoun.'

'Is that so? I was there, you know. It wasn't that great,' Siri told her. 'If I'd realized, I could have come earlier and given your class a few insights.'

'Sorry,' she said, as she led them to a bench on the school grounds. 'We aren't allowed to stray from the curriculum. Each class has a spy – sorry, I mean a monitor – who reports back to the school political officer. The kids aren't even allowed to ask questions. But that's just as well, considering I don't have any answers.'

She plonked herself down on the bench as if the lesson had doubled her weight. 'Now, what can I do for Vientiane's two most eligible bachelors? You know I don't have any chemicals. They're still stuck at customs. I hear the Department of Interior people have been sniffing them to see if they're hallucinatory.'

Siri and Phosy sat on either side of her. Siri took out the blind man's note.

'In fact, it's your English we're after,' he said.

25

Oum had been in the middle of her postgraduate study in Australia when the communists took over Laos. Her time in Sydney had been marked by two incredibly bad decisions. The first was to let herself be impregnated by a ginger-haired Aussie lad who skipped town shortly after. This error of judgment led to the birth of Nali, one of a very limited edition of redheaded Lao babies. The other bad decision was to cut short her studies and return to her homeland. The authorities had hounded her from the moment she arrived at Wattay Airport. Certainly she had to be a spy. With tens of thousands of people heading out of the country, why else would she want to go against the flow? And, to make matters worse, she spoke English – a decadent Western tool created to spread propaganda and lies. Teacher Oum was a marked woman.

'I'd be delighted,' she said and took the paper from Siri. She perused the list.

'What does it say?' Phosy asked.

'Haven't got a clue. It's not English,' she said. 'But you knew that, didn't you, Doctor? You aren't here because of my language skills.'

'What on earth do you mean?'

'Siri, you know as well as I do that this list is written in code. It could just as well be French or any other language that uses the Roman script. You're here to see whether I can crack it. You think I'm a spy, too.'

'I don't think any such thing. I just know you have a very advanced scientific mind that could probably make short work of such a simple puzzle as this. Your being a spy is irrelevant.'

'Siri, I am not …'

'I'm sorry. Could you just take a look at it for us?'

Reluctantly, Oum copied the note out on the back of one of her history sheets. It looked unfathomable:

22
xesaaghu iaik bnki qhb

oo ykjbeniaz bkn 24li
jk kxf bnki ll

jas lhwuano
x26a/ywxo ykjbeniaz
x28a/iwoo ykjbeniaz
iwzx ykjbeniaz
x24oa/cjgl ykjbeniaz
x28o/cjol qjzayezaz
ywgg ykjbeniaz
ywlg ykjbeniaz
x30o/ykzg qjzayezaz
x32o/iwog ykjbeniaz
iwgg ykjbeniaz

z zwu lnklkoaz wqc52
nalhu zenayp

pda zareh'o rwcejw

'I'll take a look at it tonight,' she said, still obviously miffed that Siri thought she was a spy. 'But I can't promise anything. I don't have any formal training in this kind of thing.'

'Oum, dear,' Siri smiled, 'if you can turn your mind to history and physical education, I'm sure this will present you no difficulty at all.'

*

Dong Bang was twenty miles from Vientiane. If the road had been better, Siri's old Triumph motorcycle would have made the trip in twenty minutes. As it turned out, it took them almost twice that. Phosy's knuckles were welded together in front of Siri's chest when finally they arrived at the little wooden pavilion where the long-distance bus picked up and dropped off passengers. Like most other places in Laos this year, the little village wore sixteen shades of brown dust. Two small wooden houses with shops out front abutted the road but there were no people to be seen. A pair of dogs slept in the shade of the bus shelter, growling at each other in their dreams.

Siri and Phosy had been to the morning market bus station in Vientiane and asked around about the blind man. People had to have noticed him. It hadn't been long before they were directed to the Dong Bang–Ban Nathe service. The country bus had sat idling like a big duck in a nest of exhaust smog. They talked with the driver. It wasn't he who'd brought the blind man into town the previous day, but this fellow had done so on two, perhaps three, other occasions. The most recent he could recall was about two weeks earlier. The driver remembered the old blind man waiting in the Dong Bang pavilion with a woman. She'd waved down the bus and handed the money to the driver. She never travelled with the blind man and didn't meet him on his return. Once the bus reached the morning market, the blind man climbed down with everyone else and crossed the road to the Bureau de Poste. He'd be back on the bus in time for the return journey.

So this wasn't the blind man's first trip and the note was probably not the first he'd collected at the post office. Thus, with nothing better to do, Siri and Phosy had taken a ride to Dong Bang. All they needed was to find the blind man's house and break the news to his family. But it was no longer just an exercise, a matter of filling in the details on the death certificate and closing their respective case files. They had a mystery on their hands. Who would send notes to a blind man, and why would they go to the trouble of writing them in invisible ink and in code? Neither Siri nor Phosy could resist such a conundrum.

They left the motorcycle behind the pavilion and walked to the nearest open-front shop. It was a noodle restaurant and wholesale compost outlet. Hoes and spades homemade from slices of war shrapnel were also for sale. The chef-cum-shopkeeper was sprawled on a hammock strung between the two beams holding up the roof of the store. When Siri coughed, she opened her eyes reluctantly and seemed disappointed to have customers.

'Yes, my loves?'

'We're trying to find the home of a blind man we believe lives here,' Phosy said. 'His name's Bounthan.'

'No, dearie,' she said. 'There's only the one blind chap here and that's Dr Buagaew.'

Siri and Phosy looked at each other. Phosy said, '*Doctor* Buagaew? A physician?'

The woman scratched between her breasts. 'No. In fact, he's a dentist. We all just call him "Doctor".'

'But he's blind,' Phosy exclaimed.

'He wasn't always, love,' she replied, now scratching her big backside through the thick canvas hammock. 'He was a damned good dentist till the cataracts got him. People used to come from all around these parts to have Dr Buagaew fix their teeth. The worse his sight got, of course, the more mistakes he started to make, until he couldn't do it no more. People said they didn't mind that he was blind; it was still better than going all the way to Vientiane. But he felt bad about pulling out the wrong teeth and that. Changed his character completely, it did. It was a bit like he turned reclusive. Stopped talking to everyone.'

'How did he make a living once he went blind?' Siri asked.

'No idea, love. Best ask him, eh? He lives across the way. It's the only two-storey place in the village. Can't miss it.'

Siri and Phosy crossed the quiet main street and headed in the direction she'd indicated. Obviously, news of Dr Buagaew's demise hadn't reached the village. This was the part of his job Dr Siri hated: informing the next of kin. But, as it turned out, the white-haired, chopstick-thin wife of the blind dentist already knew she was a widow. When her husband hadn't come back on the returning bus, or on the subsequent one, she'd become concerned. She'd headed into the city to look for him. She'd learned about the accident from the pen sellers in front of the post office. She told her visitors it was a very sad thing but there seemed to be little feeling in her words. The three of them were sitting on pieces of a tightly woven rattan lounge suite in a well-furnished living room. A large brass fan circled overhead. The doctor and his wife obviously hadn't fallen on hard times since his retirement.

'We were wondering why you hadn't come to claim the body,' Siri said.

'Nobody knew where he'd been taken,' she replied. Her voice was slight, almost inaudible beneath the whir of the fan. Her skin was dark and rutted like ripples on a night pond. She hadn't offered her visitors a drink.

'But the morgue would have been the logical place to

look,' Siri continued. Normally, he wouldn't have pursued the point with a bereaved wife but there was something about her demeanour that suggested she wasn't particularly heartbroken.

'I suppose so,' she said. 'I don't really know about things like that.'

'About cremations and burial ceremonies, you mean?'

'About the rules of death in a socialist state. I assumed the government would take care of everything. I'm a bit of a novice when it comes to communism, I'm afraid. I just know the new system is very efficient. Well, yes, look. You two are here already.'

Neither man was of a mind to refute that observation, and neither wanted to point out the rarity of the service they were performing.

'Comrade,' Phosy said, 'perhaps you could help us clear up a little mystery.'

'I'll do my best, of course.'

He took the folded note from his shirt pocket and handed it to Dr Buagaew's wife. 'We were wondering what this is. Your husband apparently collected it at the post office before he was killed.'

Siri observed that she didn't flinch or change her expression when she took the paper from Phosy. He wondered whether she had any muscles at all in her face. She took a long time to read down the list, then she looked up at Phosy. To Siri's surprise, she managed a smile of sorts.

'Why, it's nothing at all,' she said.

'We were just curious,' Siri told her. 'We made a sort of bet as to what it might be.'

She looked from one man to the other as if attempting to weigh their collective intelligence. Finally, she pointed her chin at a small antique table behind their seat. Siri had noticed it when they first entered. On it lay a fine wooden chessboard whose expensive jade pieces were poised midbattle.

'Do you know what that is, gentlemen?' she asked. Siri was about to reply but she didn't wait for a response. Her assessment had obviously classified the men as unworldly. 'It's an old-fashioned game called chess. It's very compli-cated. My husband did try to teach it to me once but I have no head for such trivial complications. Dr Buagaew loved the game but he didn't have anyone to play with in this rustic place. So, for a number of years, he maintained a long-distance chess-playing relationship with an old friend of his from school. He lives in the south. I believe there are players in other places, too, but I can't give you the details. They play via the mail service.'

'So, these symbols …?'

'… are a record of their moves. Had Dr Buagaew survived, he would have brought me this list and instructed me to read it to him as he sat at the table there.'

'You know the English alphabet?' Phosy asked.

'A little. My husband, on the other hand, was quite fluent in English.'

'And once you read out his friend's code, Dr Buagaew would understand and make the moves on this board?' Siri continued.

'And study the pieces with his fingers. It's one of the few tactile games a blind man can enjoy. Once he had his own move worked out, he'd read the code to me and I'd write back to his friend.'

'You also wrote in invisible ink?' Phosy asked.

'Invisible ink? Heavens no. Why should I do such a thing?'

'Because this note was originally unreadable. It was written with a special solution that needed to be treated to make it legible.'

'Oh, my. That sounds like another of my husband's friend's little tricks. He often played games like that to amuse the doctor. I remember one time he wrote all the characters in reverse. Another time he wrote in Chinese. I was up all night with the Chinese dictionary trying to work it out.'

'He sounds like a real card.'

'I think perhaps he was just trying to cheer up Buagaew after he lost his sight.'

'But usually they wrote in Roman script?'

'Yes.'

'Any idea why?'

'My husband and his friend both learned the game – chess, that is – from a British Quaker missionary when they were teenagers. So it was the natural medium in which to exchange information when they played.'

Phosy's interrogation seemed to have dried up. He appeared satisfied with the woman's explanations, but Siri had one more question of his own.

'Why did he insist on making the arduous trip into the city by himself? I mean, it would have been easier for you to go and pick up the letters.'

'Doctor, in your career you must have come across numerous men who have become disabled as a result of the wars. It's a question of pride for them to remain independent in spite of their afflictions. To the end, my husband insisted he could do everything without my help. Perhaps what happened yesterday finally proved him wrong.'

Back at the bus shelter, Siri's motorcycle had attracted a

coating of red ants. Phosy slapped away at them absent-mindedly with his cap.

'What do you think?' he asked.

'Well, I'd say we can be certain of two things,' Siri told him. 'One, that Dr Buagaew's wife didn't love her husband, and two, that the dentist was lying to her through his teeth.'

His thoughts were interrupted by an agonizing scream from his friend. While Phosy had been launching his frontal attack on the ants, a rear-guard unit had worked its way up his trouser leg and its troops were devouring him from the thigh up. It's hard to hold a serious debriefing with a man who's ripping off his trousers in the middle of a town's main street.

5

YOU'RE ONLY DEAD ONCE

It was somewhere between 2 and 3 a.m., and only Dtui, Siri, and Phosy still remained beneath the canopy of dark leaves in the temple yard. Twice, the abbot had risen, bleary-eyed, to remind them that his monks had to be up at five to collect alms, so could they keep the noise down? Twice, the mourners had apologized and continued their anecdotes in respectful whispers. But large quantities of rice whisky tend to play havoc with a body's volume control. It didn't take long before they were laughing and singing and shouting messages to Manoluk, who lay shrouded in cloves and tobacco leaves in the prayer chamber just behind them. You're only dead once, and the guests wanted this to be a good send-off for their old friend.

The last of the other mourners had staggered home before 1 a.m. and, although they were exhausted, the three comrades felt obliged to maintain a vigil. They were huddled together around the last inch of an orange candle. There was no breeze to disturb the flame or cool the sticky night.

'You'd tell me, wouldn't you, Doc?' Dtui said through lips she couldn't quite feel. Rice whisky doesn't numb, it anaesthetizes.

'Tell you what?'

'If she comes to see you.'

'Manoluk? Don't be silly. The spirits only contact me if they're restless. What's your ma got to be unhappy about?'

'Well, the fact that she's dead,' Phosy suggested.

When you're drinking with a corpse, there's no such thing as irreverence. Comments like that had them all rocking with laughter. They heard a loud cough from the abbot's hut.

'All right,' Siri whispered. 'I concede she might not be too delighted about being dead, but she certainly has no grievances about the way Dtui looked after her all those years. No mother could ask for more love and dedication from a daughter.'

They toasted to Dtui.

'Well, just in case she does,' Dtui said, 'even if it's to say hello and tell you what her new teak house in Nirvana's like. You'd let me know, eh?'

'I promise.'

Phosy staggered off to water the gooseberry bush beyond the temple gates. There was a blissful silence, which in Laos can incorporate a lot of noise. There's the humming and buzzing of insects and the distant howling of dogs. Somewhere a wind chime is disturbed by a lizard. House timbers stretch and groan. Water drips from a leaky tap into the huge stone temple pot. But, as any Lao would tell you, these are just musical accompaniments to make silence more interesting.

'I knew, you know?' Dtui confessed.

'Knew what?'

'That she was going.'

'Of course, we all had an idea.'

'No. I mean, I knew exactly when. Last night. I hurried

home to spend the last few hours with her. That's why I wasn't at the vegetable co-op.'

'Auntie Bpoo told you?'

Dtui smiled at her boss. 'You went to see her, didn't you? Didn't I tell you?'

'There was something disconcerting about her. I have to admit she may have certain … gifts.'

'She told me not to waste my time sitting there with her.'

'Just like that? She didn't force you to sit through a poem?'

'Oh, there's always a poem first. Nobody has the foggiest idea what they're all about. Yesterday was something about magic tinderboxes you can speak into and hear voices from faraway lands. Still, it makes her happy. She only asks that you listen. What did she tell you?'

'Me? Just a lot of bunkum.'

Dtui giggled. 'Really? So why do you suddenly think she's legitimate?'

'I didn't say that exactly. I just …'

Phosy had returned from his garden adventure and decided now was as good a time as any to fall across one of the trestle tables. It collapsed beneath his weight and its empty glasses and bottles crashed to the ground. If the rolling of eyes had a sound, it would certainly have been heard from the abbot's hut at that moment. Siri and Dtui helped Phosy back to his seat even though they were no more coordinated than he. They all agreed they needed a drink to calm their nerves after the excitement.

'It's a resounding pity Civilai couldn't be here tonight,' Phosy said. He sounded remarkably sober for somebody who'd just broken a dozen rented glasses and a previously untouched bottle of Vietnamese snake hooch. Civilai was

ANARCHY AND OLD DOGS

their only friend on the politburo and a kindred spirit. The fictitious date of birth Siri had conjured up for his official documents was May 21,1904. It coincidentally turned out to be two days after Civilai's actual birthday, so Civilai took delight in calling him 'younger brother.' They'd studied socialist doctrine together in Vietnam, had been there at the founding of the Pathet Lao, and each had alienated about the same number of senior Party members. They were undiplomatic old coots who were too stubborn to play the political game by the rules. For Civilai, who was on the Central Committee, this was a major disability. Nobody in any position of authority bothered to listen to him any more. He only had Siri to vent his frustrations on. That – and their love of food and a good stiff drink – was what made the two men so close.

'Where is he anyway?'

Phosy's question had already been answered several times throughout the course of the evening.

'He's back in the USSR,' Dtui reminded him. 'Like the Beatles.'

'Who?'

'He'll be back tomorrow or whenever the Soviets let him go. I'm not telling you again.'

'They have beetles in the USSR?'

'Never mind.'

'Poor old fellow's become a cocktail Party member,' Siri lamented. He shifted his chair backwards so he could see the sky but found there were no stars in the muggy soup above them. He wondered whether storm clouds might be gathering at long last and completely forgot his point.

'I don't think I understand that,' Dtui said.

'All right, just look at him. He's the one they send to

attend conferences but they don't let him speak. They put his name down for all the shows and concerts and he's always the first one up on the dance floor. He has to meet all the visiting big nobs and take them to dinner and on to whatever tickles their fancies. He's become so adept at small talk he's lost the ability to make big talk. He said he feels like the comedian who warms up audiences before the star comes onstage.'

'So why doesn't he retire?'

'Oh, Dtui. If they let us retire from the Party, do you think either of us would still be here? We're symbolic old relics. They need people like us around to impress the young fellows coming up through the ranks. A statue would do the job better because stone doesn't answer back. But we aren't enough of a threat to justify an assassination so they have to put up with us.'

Siri stared into his drink as he contemplated that point and suddenly felt sorry for himself. There followed another period of Lao silence during which he realized he and the abbot were the only ones still conscious. Phosy and Dtui lay with their heads on the bare wood of the tabletop, snoring back and forth. Siri smiled at the bodies. He felt victorious, like the last man standing in a battle. He took his glass of whisky to the prayer-hall steps and held it in front of his face.

'Manoluk,' he said. 'Looks like just you and me. These young folks today have no idea how to have a good time. Want to dance?'

There were always good arguments against going to work directly from an all-night drinking binge at a temple. One – perhaps the only one – in favour was that after opening the morgue doors to make it look as if business continued as usual, one could always retire to the Mahosot Hospital canteen, where they served the muddiest and most evil coffee in the country. On top of the congealed brown sediment sat barely a mouthful of liquid coffee. No sooner was it cool enough to drink than it was necessary to order another. But that mouthful would be remembered deep into old age and could cut through a hangover like a cyclone through a barn.

Siri, Dtui, and Phosy had defied a hundred deaths balanced on the Triumph and arrived at the morgue at five. Now, at seven, their minds were buzzing like hornets in a jam jar. They'd lost the ability to blink, and they had smiles painted across their faces just like those contented people in the propaganda posters: UNITED WORKERS ARE HAPPY WORKERS. Four Mahosot coffees could do that to a person, too.

Finally, they found themselves back at the morgue.

'I feel like bathroom mould,' Phosy said, his voice like a plough dragged over rocks.

'Never mind,' Siri told him, 'only ten hours and we can all go home and get some sleep.'

Dtui was squeezing her own wrist. 'I'm afraid there may be some blood left in my alcohol stream. We're medical personnel; we should know better. Stimulate my brain, someone, before it pickles. Give me a job.'

'I'm afraid the morgue is devoid of murder,' Siri told her.

'Then give me some old case to go over again. See if I can solve it quicker this time.'

'Perhaps you could help us with our dentist mystery,' Siri suggested. 'Our own investigation was somewhat lacking.'

'Lacking?' Phosy said. 'Didn't I find the house ... the wife?'

'Indeed you did,' Siri said. 'And brilliant detective work it was, too. But I fear the whole story we heard was as convoluted as the note.'

'You didn't believe her?'

'Have you ever played chess, Phosy?'

'Most certainly. Once we'd castrated the pigs and plucked the chickens, and as soon as we'd worn our hands raw digging ditches, me and the other orphans would rush home for a quick game of chess before stacking the rice husks.'

'A simple no would have sufficed.'

'Then no. But I take it you have.'

'It was one of the few distractions in Paris that didn't cost any money. They played in the parks. I started off watching, fascinated. Then I began to play myself. I didn't ever make it to the position of grand maître, but I won the odd game. The thing is, in the winter when we couldn't play outside, there were competitions in the newspapers. They'd plot out the game in symbols and you had to work out the next best move. So I know the abbreviations, and not one item on the dentist's list has any connection to chess.'

'So, the widow was lying,' Phosy said.

'Or her husband lied to her. She hadn't learned chess so he could have told her anything. And didn't the invisible ink story seem just a little too pat? His friend was playing a prank? Come on. He may have been able to con his wife, but not a team of hardened cynics like us. Let's take another look at the list and see what else we can come up with.'

Siri went to the cutting room and stood in front of the blackboard they used to chalk up weights and lengths. With one eye on the note, he copied the list noisily. The generously donated Chinese chalk snapped itself into fractions as he wrote, leaving him with a tiny stub between his thumb and forefinger as he scratched the last symbols. He stepped back between Dtui and Phosy like an artist admiring his work. They stood there studying the list before them: standing, studying, staring, swaying. The characters merged and curled together like clothes in a spin dryer and the three would probably have stayed there all day transfixed by the meaningless letters if they hadn't been interrupted by a shrill cough. They turned but there was nobody behind them. The sound had come from outside the morgue.

'Who's there?' Siri asked. But he had to wait for a reply.

'I have a note for Dr Siri Paiboun,' came a young voice.

'That's me,' Siri said. 'Come on inside.'

'Er, I think I'll just leave it here,' said the voice.

When Dtui went to the front step she found a white envelope on the welcome mat and saw a young girl in the black *phasin* skirt and white blouse of the lycée fleeing across the hospital grounds.

'Looks like the kids at the lycée still think this place is haunted,' Dtui said, handing the letter to Siri.

'Can't imagine why they'd think that,' said Phosy. He looked over the doctor's shoulder. 'Is it from Oum?'

'Well, I'll be ...' Siri smiled. 'Our Australian spy has cracked it.'

'Thank God for that. I was going giddy staring at this list.'

'She says it came to her in the middle of a geography lesson. She hasn't had time to work out the whole thing but she says she knows the key. It's here, at the top.'

'The number 22?' Dtui asked. 'I was going to say that.'

'Of course you were.' Siri retrieved another stick of chalk from the drawer and wrote 'Biweekly' beneath the first set of characters. 'Oum says that if we count back twenty-two places in the English alphabet from each letter in the note, words are spelled out. You go back twenty-two places with the numbers too. This is all she had time to establish. All we need is an alphabet and a little patience.'

Dtui copied out the English alphabet on a sheet of paper and taped it beside the blackboard. Letter by letter Siri wrote out the cipher as Phosy counted back and Dtui called out the correct characters. Once they'd reached the bottom, Dtui looked at the latest version of the note. It had three distinct parts. She translated the first.

> 22
> xesaaghu iaik bnki qhb
> BIWEEKLY MEMO FROM ULF
> oo ykjbeniaz bkn 24li
> SS CONFIRMED FOR 2PM
> jk kxf bnki ll
> NO OBJ FROM PP

'Well, if it's a message, it's still in code. It looks more like a laundry list. There aren't that many actual words here. It starts by saying this is a biweekly memo and it's from someone called Ulf. Or maybe it isn't a someone, could be a place. I've never heard of it. The first line is mostly abbreviations. "SS confirmed for 2PM" I suppose could mean something with the initials SS is due to start at two in the afternoon. Then it says, "No obj from PP". "Obj" could be *objection*, I guess. No objection from someone with the initials PP, unless PP's a place – Phnom Penh?'

She concentrated her attention then on the second part. 'After the first part, there's just a list of letters and numbers under the heading "New Players".'

jas lhwuano
NEW PLAYERS
x26a/ywxo   ykjbeniaz
B4E/CABS CONFIRMED
x28a/iwoo   ykjbeniaz
B6E/MASS CONFIRMED
    iwzx ykjbeniaz
    MADB CONFIRMED
x24oa/cjgl   ykjbeniaz
B2SE/GNKP CONFIRMED
x28o/cjol qjzayezaz
B6S/GNSP UNDECIDED
    ywgg ykjbeniaz
    CAKK CONFIRMED
    ywlg ykjbeniaz
    CAPK CONFIRMED
x30o/ykzg   qjzayezaz
B8S/CODK UNDECIDED
x32o/iwog   ykjbeniaz
B10S/MASK CONFIRMED
    iwgg ykjbeniaz
    MAKK CONFIRMED

'Could be some kind of game. After each set it says either
"confirmed" or "undecided". So, for example, this first
one says, "B4E/CABS confirmed". Mean anything to you
fellows?'

'Not a thing,' Phosy confessed. 'Is there any more?'

'Just the last bit.'

z zwu lnklkoaz wqc52
D DAY PROPOSED AUG30

' "D day?" '

Siri said, 'I believe it's the name the allies gave to the invasion of France in the Second World War.'

'We're about to be invaded by the Americans again,' Phosy said.

'I doubt they'd be bothered,' said Siri, and turned back to Dtui. 'What about the last lines?'

nalhu zenayp
REPLY DIRECT

'It says to reply directly to the name at the bottom.'

'And that is?'

A big Dtui smile spread across her face and her rosy cheeks puffed up like the bottom of an orang-utan. She read it aloud. 'Reply direct to the Devil's Vagina.'

pda zareh'o rwcejw
THE DEVIL'S VAGINA

'The what?'

'I just call them like I see them, boss,' she said. 'And that's exactly what it says.'

'What the hell is a devil's vagina? I don't understand any of it. It's even more confusing decoded. Can you make any sense out of the letters and numbers?'

'Let's see. Inspector Dtui can do this,' she said unblinking, still wired from the coffee and drained from the emotions of the past twenty-four hours. 'Focus. This might take some time. Bear with me. What do we see here?' She was talking to herself, as Siri and Phosy could see nothing. 'Almost everything on the list starts with a B. Only the third line that begins with B has two letters after the number. I get a feeling that's the way in. Always look for an anomaly.'

That was where she focused her coffee buzz and where, after five minutes of staring, she had her brain wave. She turned and raised her arms to the clueless men behind her.

'What?' Phosy asked.

'South-east,' she said. 'That's it. SE is southeast. The others are south and east. That's all it could be.'

Of course, that wasn't all it could be, but caffeine has a way of making a person see the obvious even if it isn't there.

'So,' Siri said. 'Something in the east, the south, and the south-east that has numbers. Roads? Postal codes? Mountain elevation?'

'Army units!' Phosy said. 'Could it be referring to military bases?'

Siri scoured his French vocabulary and came up with only one B.

'*Bataillon*. Dtui, is it the same word in English?'

'There wasn't a lot of military vocab in my medical textbooks, Doc. But I wouldn't put it past the French to steal words from English. Totally untrustworthy people the French.'

Siri nodded at the policeman. 'What made you think of army units?'

'Only that I know for sure the Eighth Battalion's in Sekong and the Sixth East is just outside Bolikham.'

'That's it,' Dtui said. 'It fits.'

Phosy was certain, too. 'It won't take much to match up the rest. I've got a feeling we're on to something. What about the letters after the slash?'

Dtui went down the list: MASS, MADB, GNKP, all the way to MAKK, but inspiration escaped her. She copied them onto a sheet of paper and went off to work on it at her desk. Phosy rode his lilac Vespa to temporary police headquarters on Sethathirat, where he could phone around to his old army colleagues. The word 'classified' didn't apply in friendly, for-old-times'-sake chats. A day that hadn't exactly started with a bang for them had suddenly dawned into something exciting. Inspired by the industry of his colleagues, Siri went directly to the ward of private rooms, found one empty, and lay back on the starched sheet for a brief rest. He woke four hours later. He considered this his contribution to the project. A team needs an alert, conscious leader. To make himself even more qualified for the job, he stopped off at the canteen for noodles. These were the leadership qualities he most admired in himself.

He reached the morgue at 1 p.m. to find his entranced colleagues swaying in front of the blackboard.

'What have I missed?' he asked.

They didn't even turn to look at him. He had the feeling neither had noticed his absence.

'We've got it, Siri,' Phosy said.

'What?'

'Your Dtui, she's a phenomenon, a genius in white. Tell him, Dtui.'

Dtui strode up to the blackboard with a fresh stick of chalk and drew a line between the first two and second two columns of letters.

CA | BS
MA | SS
MA | DB
GN | KP
GN | SP

47

CA	KK
CA	PK
CO	DK
MA	SK
MA	KK

'It was the military reference that did it for me,' she said. 'Like I said, the only English I know I got from my medical studies, so I had to spend some time with my nose in the dictionary. But I wondered whether the letters ...' She jabbed at the column too enthusiastically and snapped the chalk. 'Darn. I wondered whether the letters might have something to do with rank. So I looked up all the ranks and, sure enough, the first two letters in the column correspond: major, general, captain, and colonel.'

'Ho, well done,' Siri said, stepping forward.

'That leaves the other column, and I thought logically the letters could have been the initials of the person holding that rank.'

'And they were,' Phosy joined in. 'I spent the morning finding what battalions were stationed in what provinces. They all match this list. When Dtui told me her theory, I called back to get the name of the general attached to Southern Battalion Six. The army isn't big on giving out names but my contact owed me a favour.'

'And his initials just happened to be SP,' Siri said.

'Souvan Phibounsuk.'

'Goodness.' Siri sat on the sink unit and put his hands on his head. 'We have a confidential list of military placements and the names of ranking officers – sent in code and written in invisible ink. Are you two thinking what I'm thinking?'

'Some plot's being hatched,' Phosy said. 'This is a list of the officers they've talked into joining them.'

'D-day,' Siri said, half to himself. 'That's it. It's a coup d'état. August 30 is the date set for an uprising.'

'It has to be,' Phosy agreed.

'But this is enormous,' Dtui said. 'What do we do? Who do we tell?'

'Good question, Comrade Dtui,' said Siri, staring at the list on the board.

'Well, obviously the Security Division,' Phosy said. Unconsciously, their voices had dropped to whispers. 'They're responsible for things like this, aren't they?'

'It isn't that easy, Phosy. Look at the list. They have generals. We don't know how high this thing goes. If we disclose what we think we know to the wrong person—'

'They'll find the three of us tied to rocks at the bottom of the Mekhong. There'll be river crabs living in our—'

'Thank you, Nurse Dtui.' Siri smiled. 'A little dramatic but the drift is there. The fact is we don't know whom to trust. And, to be honest, we don't have any hard evidence that what we've found here is actually what it seems to be.'

'Come on, Doc. What else could it be? Birthday invitations?'

'I admit it looks ominous, but I think we should go at this delicately.'

'So what do you propose we do?' Phosy asked.

The policeman was still swaying like a palm tree in a strong breeze. Siri looked into his friends' faces, ceramic with fatigue.

'The first thing I suggest is that you two go home and get some sleep. We need all our wits about us and there's no urgency. If the note is to be believed, we have until the thirtieth. That's two weeks. Inspector Phosy, perhaps when you're refreshed we could take another trip out to Dong Bang tomorrow to see whether the dentist's wife has kept any of her husband's notes. Comrade Civilai should be back from Moscow later tonight. I want to run all this by him before we do anything rash. He'll know how to handle things and he can put us in touch with his inner circle. If nothing else, he knows which people are on his side.'

There were no objections from Phosy or Dtui. They collected their belongings and trudged to the door. Dtui stopped in the doorway and looked back at Siri.

'You know?' she said. 'I don't understand how you do it, Doc. Look at you. Older than Angkor Wat, up all night boozing, and you still look as frisky as a prawn on a hot plate. What's your secret?'

Siri considered telling the truth, but only briefly. 'What can I say? A life without impure thoughts,' he said. 'Look and learn, Dtui.'

It was an odd afternoon. The thick, puffy clouds squatting low over Vientiane weren't particularly convincing. They were like stage scenery clouds that could be pushed aside at any time to reveal the sun. What Laos needed was rain, not the promise of it. Siri had stopped by Civilai's office and been told by his typist that he'd be arriving at some unearthly hour the following morning. Siri figured it would be at least lunchtime before his friend was in any fit state to quash a coup. So he scribbled a quick note to say he'd made a lunchtime booking at their riverside log for 12:30 – and Civilai should bring enough packed lunch for both of them. He added, 'This is urgent so don't come up with any lame excuses.'

Siri's next stop was the Department of Justice, where he was hoping he'd be able to drop his reports on Manivone's desk before her boss, Judge Haeng, could railroad him into his office for a quick burden-sharing tutorial. There was no love lost between Siri and his much younger boss. Siri didn't take orders and Judge Haeng didn't do much of anything other than give them. The national coroner was the only man in the country remotely qualified to do the job, so dismissal wasn't a threat Haeng could wield with any conviction. Siri dreamed of retirement, of inactivity and peace. He would have loved Haeng to kick him out and the young man would have been delighted to do so. The judge, with his iffy Soviet qualifications, was consumed by the need to maintain face – and Siri had smashed that face to smithereens once or twice. But, as of this week, a shadow even darker than Siri had been cast over Haeng's department.

In July, Laos had signed an agreement of friendship and cooperation with the government of Vietnam. Although it was packaged as a way to facilitate trade and exchange information, in fact, it gave the Vietnamese a green light to station military units on Lao soil and to have an even greater influence over Lao policy making. Vietnamese 'advisers' had been billeted at Lao government departments, some even being bold enough to have their own desks moved into the offices of the department heads. Such was the case at the Department of Justice, and Judge Haeng didn't like it one little bit.

His office mate was a toothless but ever-smiling man who wore his hair greased flat on his head like a matinee idol. Although he sported a large, charcoal grey suit rather than a uniform, he was a colonel in the People's Army of

Vietnam and a senior lecturer in law at the new institute in Hanoi. To Haeng's chagrin, he could read and write Lao, and under the agreement, every document that passed over Haeng's desk, 'in' or 'out', had to pay a visit to Colonel Phat. Although the colonel hadn't yet made any direct comments, Haeng watched him out of the corner of his eye as the man shook his head and tutted repeatedly as he pored over the reports. As a result, the judge concentrated doubly hard on his grammar and spelling. He also tried to be out of his office whenever Phat was in, which was most of the time.

So, to make a long story no less long, that was why Haeng bumped into Siri at Mrs Manivone's desk in the typing pool that day.

'Ah, Siri,' Haeng said, as if he were actually glad to see the coroner.

'Judge Haeng.'

'What are you doing?'

'Just delivering my reports for the week. I was on my way to—'

'Good. Glad I caught you.'

'You are?'

'Absolutely. There's a little matter I might get you to take care of for us.'

'That depends. When?'

' "When?" That's hardly the reaction we expect from a soldier of the revolution, Siri.' Haeng cast a glance toward the clerks sitting around the room. He seemed to know instinctively they were hungry for some homegrown socialist wisdom. 'A true warrior would say, "Let me at it." '

'He would?'

'Yes, Siri. A dedicated socialist plunges headfirst into the troubled waters without testing the depth.'

'Isn't he likely to bump his head on the bottom?' Siri asked.

'What?'

'If it's too shallow.'

'I don't ... No. He wouldn't care. He would—'

'What if he can't swim? Like me.' Siri and Haeng both heard a muffled chuckle from behind them.

'It's not literal, Siri. It's a ... Look, never mind. Come with me. We have something to talk about in private.' He headed off toward the exit. Siri knew why.

'Isn't your office this way?'

'Yes, but it's ... occupied. We can talk outside.'

As he led them toward the door, Haeng grabbed a small red book from a large pile beside the souvenir cabinet. He didn't stop till he reached the edge of the basketball court. Once a happy after-work recreation spot for the American imperialists, the concrete rectangle was now in the process of being reclaimed by nature. Undernourished ivy and morning glories criss-crossed the backboards and curled wreathlike around the rims.

There came a belch of thunder from overhead that rolled languidly across the stodgy clouds.

'Looks like rain at last,' Haeng said. It was the first decorous comment Siri could remember hearing from the spotty young man. He was too surprised to respond. 'But, anyway,' Haeng continued, 'we've had a bit of an embarrassment in the south.'

'Souths are notorious for embarrassing their northern neighbours.'

'Quite. It appears a deputy governor has managed to get himself electrocuted in the bathtub.'

53

'Clumsy.'

'Yes, I suppose you could say that. But there are complications. I was on the phone with the governor for an hour this morning. He seems to think there are political implications.'

Siri laughed. 'About a man electrocuting himself in the bath?'

'Siri. Please restrain the levity. The deputy governor was up here recently paying a courtesy visit to the Soviet embassy. I'm sure you recall how their ambassador likes to give away those horrible Soviet-built appliances as souvenirs: irons, fans, soldering equipment, all that type of stuff. Most of it's built to withstand missile attacks – no removable parts. When any of it breaks down, you have no choice but to sell it for scrap and buy a new one. Well, the deputy governor got a water heater as a souvenir. You know the sort: thick wooden handle with a hook and a long metal element curled into a loop.'

'I've got one. You hook it onto the side of the bathtub, plug it in, and it heats up your water.'

'That's the one. It would seem the deputy governor was in the bath while the heater was still live. Stewed himself. I tried to convince the governor that it sounded like his deputy's own stupid fault, but you know what they're like down there. He's accusing the Russians of assassinating his deputy. He believes the heater was rigged, and he's threatening to write his accusations in a letter to the Soviet authorities if the case isn't investigated. We certainly can't have that. I just need someone to go down there and put his mind at ease.'

'Why me? And I don't need the warrior speech again.'

Judge Haeng had tried the line 'Don't question my

instructions' before, and knew it didn't work on a man like Siri. 'Because you're the national coroner, Siri. You're the only one who can convince him it was an accident. He'll have to believe you.'

Siri had become selective about the long-distance cases he accepted these days. They invariably got him into trouble. Travelling to the other end of the country for some ridiculous water-heater accident seemed pointless. There was only one thing that might entice him.

'What province?' he asked.

'Champasak.'

'I'll go.'

'You will?' As usual when Siri agreed to obey one of Haeng's directives, a look of astonishment appeared briefly on the judge's face. Siri enjoyed watching it arrive and his fight to erase it.

'Jolly good. Here, take this for the journey.' Haeng held out the book.

'What is it?'

'It's Chairman Mao's *Little Red Book*. We've had it translated into Lao.'

'What on earth for?'

Haeng stifled his frustration and forced the book into Siri's pocket.

'A good socialist is not a dustbin, with a closed lid. He is a letter box, always open to receive news.'

'Well, that explains everything. I'll do my best to keep my slot open.'

'Good man. Right. I'll book you on a flight early tomorrow morning.'

'No. Can't get away till the evening. Say six?'

'Siri, you know there are no scheduled flights at that time.'

'Judge, that's when I'll be free to go.'

'There's no way to—'

'Have you told the Soviet ambassador what they're accusing him of in the south?'

'Of course not.'

'Then I suggest you do. With the Soviets and the Chinese and the Vietnamese all jockeying for some kind of role in our humble land, it would surprise me if the ambassador didn't make his old Yak available for a special little trip south. You might mention that the Champasak governor's threatening to write to Moscow.'

'I don't—'

'Trust me, son. It's high time the puppet started pulling back on the strings.'

6

IN SEARCH OF A PROLETARIAT

Siri wondered what the hell he was doing there. He was aware of people walking along the far side of Samsenthai, looking in his direction. He was conscious of the clerk in the Aeroflot office staring out from behind the counter. Hers was one of only three glass-fronted shops on the block, and Siri could see his own embarrassed reflection in the office window. A cloud that had been threatening rain was purplish now, like an eggplant, and so close you could jump up and give it a squeeze. It complemented Auntie Bpoo's dress, which was crimson crepe and stopped just above her rugby-player knees. Once again, Siri sat in front of her like a schoolboy before the headmistress, waiting for her to deign to speak with him. At last, she stopped meshing her playing cards together and looked him in the eye. A poem.

> *Time will blow*
> > *Woe betide – when every man*
> > *And woman can*
> > *Have access to a world*
> *Of evil and of knowledge all unfurled*
> *Within a case*
> > *Face to face in every home.*

The transvestite's stare burned into Siri's face until he was forced to respond.

'Right,' he said. 'Thanks for that. I was just hoping to ask about your last—'

'Ten thousand *kip*.'

'Eh?'

'Ten thousand. Cash. I don't take bank drafts.'

'I thought you did all this for free.'

'I tell you your future for free. For interviews I charge.'

'I'm not interviewing you.'

'Then stop asking questions and give me a kiss.'

'What?'

'Just kidding. I wanted to see the look on your face. Now, Dr Siri. Dr Siri Paiboun. The lesser beasts around you seem to have settled down. Am I right?'

Siri didn't need clarification. For over a month, birds and insects and small animals near him had acted weirdly. But as of last week, things seemed to be back to normal. The most recent incident he could recall was when he awoke one morning to find a large gecko on the pillow beside him. It was on its back and appeared to be snoring. That had been the last. For some reason he wasn't surprised that Auntie Bpoo would know this.

'Yes.'

'Good. Just a little surge of energy. But don't ignore the animal kingdom completely. Pay special attention to waterborne creatures.'

'Fish, in particular?'

'Ten thousand *kip*.'

'Sorry.'

'You will suffer a loss of sensation.'

'It's started already.'

'This too will pass. Your body's going through certain changes.'

'Damn, I thought all that was behind me decades ago.'

The corner of Auntie Bpoo's mouth creased. It might have been a smile.

She continued. 'You have to expect ascents and descents. These are marvellous times.'

Quite unexpectedly, she raised the hem of her crepe dress and gave Siri a flash of her naked genitalia. Attached with pink plastic string to the usual goods were four or five additional baubles: one delicate silver globe, two ping-pong balls, and a seashell. At least that was all Siri was able to memorize in the time allotted him. He didn't recall seeing a penis but it might have been there somewhere among the flotsam. Auntie Bpoo lowered the dress and continued as if nothing had happened.

'One more thing, old fool. Do not forget this. At the back of every wicked man, there is a shadow. Is that shadow any less guilty than he?'

Siri sat on the familiar leather seat of his old motorcycle and marvelled: seventy-three years of age and still clueless, still a victim of impulse and irrational instincts. Dependent suddenly on a man in a dress who spoke in riddles and left him feeling as small as a head louse. But this grotesque man-woman creature knew it all. She knew what Siri was tuned in to and what was going on inside him. The doctor had no choice but to listen to her words and attempt to make sense of them. The life Siri had been cornered into was a lonely one that even his closest allies couldn't begin to understand. No matter how queer his new acquaintance might have been, he was determined to make a friend of her.

*

It was a dream that was black from beginning to end, but it was a dream. It was like a visit to the cinema when the projector breaks down and you sit in the darkness waiting for the projectionist to fix it, and you sit and sit, but the film doesn't return. Siri could feel himself alone in the viewing room, waiting. He could smell the stale popcorn crushed into the carpet, see the faint margin of light around the emergency exit doors. But there was no film.

He awoke in his government-supplied bungalow, the sun not yet backlighting the Mickey Mice on his curtain. His dream line to the afterlife was out of order. For some reason he'd become bound to the earth. He suddenly felt vulnerable, and mortal.

Siri and Civilai sat on their log, staring out across the sand, mud, and low waterline that made up a Mekhong desperate for a rainy season. The rains had come late in China and hadn't yet started to fill the river downstream. Nobody could recall the water course running so low this late in the year. It was a depressingly dreary view. Even affluent Thailand on the far bank looked impoverished. The ceiling of cartoon cloud continued to hang just above their heads, and the wrapped baguettes sat on the log beside them. The old friends had been silent for three minutes. If the Guinness people had been around, it would have qualified as a world record.

'Shit,' said Civilai.

'You're telling me,' said Siri.

'What on earth do we do about this one?'

'I was rather hoping you'd have something in mind. It's not as if you haven't been involved in a rebellion before.'

'True, little brother. But if you remember, we were on the side of the people doing the rebelling.'

'Then it's easy. All we have to do is put ourselves in the shoes of the tyrants we ousted. What would we do if we were the Royal Lao government?'

'We'd convert all our assets into gold and swim across the river to Thailand.'

'Perhaps that wasn't such a good example. What do you say we just pass on what we've found to the Security Division and let them sort it out?'

'Siri, you amaze me at times. We aren't exactly talking KGB here. What type of training do you think those boys have had? They're converted foot soldiers from the countryside. They're chicken counters. Their job is to make sure people are disclosing their incomes and paying their taxes. What type of high-level counterinsurgency operation do you think they could mount?'

'Surely there's a mechanism in place.'

'We're an eighteen-month-old administration. We're spread thin on the ground. We're barely hanging on as it is. We need several more years to have an infrastructure up and running for something like this.'

'All right. So we just let it happen?'

'You know I didn't say that.'

'How about at the top level? People we've known all the way through the campaign: military leaders, politburo people. Men with enough local support to put up some resistance. After all we've been through, I'm certainly not going down without a fight.'

'I'm shocked, Siri. I didn't think you cared.'

'I spent thirty-odd years crawling through the jungle for this country. My wife died for it. How can I not care? Do you know what last Saturday was? It was Free Lao Day. I went to pay respects at the Epitaph to the Unknown Soldier. People gave their lives for this independence. How can I let some opportunistic glamour seeker leapfrog an administration that struggled for thirty years to get where it is and … and steal our country from under us? Jesus. What was the point of it all if we just hand it over before we've even had time to get it right?'

'OK. I get it.' Civilai put his arm around his friend's shoulder. 'I'd been wondering whether there were any nationalist embers left burning in your grate. I was starting to think your cynicism had pissed them all out.'

'Me? Great, coming from a man who called the prime minister a toad.'

'That was an accident. I meant "slug". I just couldn't think of the word on the spur of the moment.' Siri laughed and his bout of gravity came to an end. 'We're both ornery old warhorses,' Civilai continued, 'but they need asses like us. If they refuse to put us out to pasture, they have to expect a kick every now and then.'

'So what do you say we put our asinine minds together and see if we can't come up with something to avert this coup.'

Civilai slowly began to unwrap the baguettes. 'I know people,' he said.

'Who?'

The first drop of rain landed on Siri's knee. It was as thick and heavy as a cow pat.

'I don't think I should tell you just yet.'

'Why on earth not?'

Civilai produced two perfect loaves – delights, works of art – but not even their splendour could cheer Siri's mood.

A second drop of rain smashed into the crispy leaves above their heads. Civilai handed a baguette to Siri, who just held on to it, still awaiting an answer to his question.

'Because,' Civilai said, 'when conducting a countercoup, one has to consider what the status quo would be if the coup was successful. The leaders would round up whoever was instrumental in the attempt to oppose them. They'd be the first to be liquidated. The fewer middlemen the better.'

'I'm not a middleman. Let them liquidate me. Or, what? You think I'd crumble under interrogation and implicate all your "people"?'

Large jellyfish-sized globules of rain were falling in countable drops all around them.

'No,' Civilai said, biting into one end of his lunch. 'All they'd have to do is offer you a decent supply of coffee and a carefree life and you'd squeal your guts out.'

'If the coup were successful I'd march up to the buggers and tell them what I damn well think of them.'

'That's the diplomacy that got you where you are today. If you—' A huge blob of rain somehow avoided the tree and landed with a smack in Civilai's face. Siri laughed and wiped his friend's glasses clean with a tissue from the lunch bag. The seriousness of politics quickly gave way to the seriousness of eating. The bread was fresh and the stuffing delicious. These were two men who appreciated a good baguette. And they knew exactly the drink with which to complement it. Siri offered his flask of pennywort juice to Civilai. No cabernet sauvignon could have enhanced a sandwich more. They ate without speaking and watched the heavy drops of rain land in the river, never gaining enough momentum to be called a shower.

Despite their present predicament, this was when Siri

was at his happiest, eating and drinking on the bank of the Mekhong beside his best friend. He turned to look at Civilai. When trying to describe him to others, Siri had worked his way through a long list of insects – ant, hornet, wasp – before finally arriving at the simile that suited him best. Civilai was undoubtedly like a grasshopper. His head was a large, skin-covered helmet of a thing, mostly posterior. At its front, on his pointy nose, sat a huge pair of black-framed glasses. His grasshopper body was all gangly bones and angular joints. As he ate, an enormous Adam's apple travelled up and down his long neck like an elevator.

'If you don't stop staring at me, I'll slap you,' Civilai said without looking at Siri.

'I can't help it. You're such a glamour-puss.'

'You obviously spend too much time with the dead, Dr Siri.'

Like Siri, Civilai had France to thank for his academic degree and to blame for his political leanings. Whereas Siri had found his way to Paris via a temple education and charity, Civilai had been groomed for excellence by his parents. His wealthy Lao-Chinese father had been selectively married into an even more affluent Vietnamese-Chinese family, and even before Civilai was born, there had been no doubt that Mr and Mrs Songsawat's son would be educated at the Sorbonne. They had mapped out a Francophile education for the boy in Saigon and invested a small fortune in contributions to ensure that he wouldn't be rejected. As it turned out, his grades alone would have secured him a scholarship. On the day he sailed on the *Victor Hugo* to Europe, the family expected their smart lad to return with first-class honours in law and commerce, and one day take over the running of their vast business interests in Laos.

But there was one factor they'd failed to take into consideration. Civilai had a mind of his own, a considerable mind at that. At the lycée in Saigon he'd befriended another son of the mandarins by the name of Hok Nguyen Truk. They were both idealists, and their curiosity had led them to a startling discovery. The poor in their respective countries were being squeezed dry by wealthy landlords, by the same families who'd raised the two boys to believe it was normal to have a man to trim one's toenails. This revelation resulted in a hatred of the class to which they belonged and a hostility toward their fathers. They detested them for fawning on the French imperialists and for growing fatter from their dealings with the French while the poor starved.

So there they were, two angry youths in search of a sympathetic doctrine. They found it in the Paris of 1923. They arrived at a Sorbonne that was a safe haven for liberals and members of the lunatic fringe. Although their classes were comparatively conservative, the student body was replete with left-wingers and radicals. At a rally one weekend they met a Vietnamese who was making a living on the docks during the day and proselytizing Marxism-Leninism at night. He'd given his name as Nguyen Tat Than. He was a lean, hungry-eyed man in his early thirties who wore French suits elegantly and spoke with passion. His philosophies and hopes so closely matched their own that they soon shared his dream to take socialism to Indochina and free their downtrodden brothers and sisters from the repressive yoke of colonialism.

In this idealistic state, Civilai had chosen to ignore the absence in Laos of one of the fundamental components for a successful communist revolution. There was no rebellious Lao proletariat. There were no factories in which to organize unions, and hardly any working class. Eighty per cent of the people grew rice on small plots of land. All their energy was invested in survival. The farmers were so resigned to their fate that a great deal of agitation would have been needed to convince them they were dissatisfied at all.

But by the time the two young men arrived back in Asia in 1929, the seeds of revolt had been sown in their fertile minds. Communism would save their repressed countrymen whether they liked it or not. In Siam they reunited with their guru Nguyen Tat Than, who by then was calling himself Quoc and posing as a Buddhist monk. The French had a death warrant out for him in Vietnam for his agitation in rural areas. Quoc was one of the many pseudonyms adopted for his survival by the remarkable man, but it was the name on an identity card belonging to a deceased Chinese merchant that would ultimately provide the sobriquet the world most associated with him: Ho Chi Minh.

Civilai and Hok travelled with Ho to Hong Kong, where, in 1930, they helped establish the Communist Party of Vietnam. As the only Lao in the group, Civilai took responsibility for organizing his own people to rise up against the French tyrants and reclaim their homeland. But therein lay one more potentially insurmountable problem. Laos only existed as a geographical entity because, to cut down on paperwork, a French administrator had inked a national border around some thirty diverse tribal groups and posted an announcement that this was now officially a country. Ethnic Lao constituted no more than sixty per cent of this brand-new, custom-built colony.

This posed a quandary for Civilai and his cadres as they wandered from village to village stirring up national pride, building a national identity from the ground up. The villagers quite logically argued that they hadn't wanted to be Lao in the first place. Why should they fight for the right to be so? That was perhaps why the Vietnamese revolution had taken shape so efficiently and why Civilai had aged rapidly over the years.

The rain shower had exhausted itself even before the baguettes. They'd finished their lunch, these purveyors of frustrating politics, and sat still and silent on their log. Crumbs lay at their feet like wood shavings around a completed carving. Neither wanted to voice his feelings but Siri could tell what his friend was thinking. Avoiding a well-organized coup at this juncture in history could very well prove impossible. If that weren't the case, he knew Civilai would have headed straight off to his office to set wheels in motion. Instead he stared dully at the river.

'I'm off to Pakse this evening,' Siri said.

'Why?'

'Some fool electrocuted himself in the bath.'

'Hmm. Well worth travelling four hundred miles to see, I'd say.'

'Two birds, one stone.'

'The dentist's letter?'

'It was postmarked Pakse.'

'You want to get your hands on the Devil's Vagina.'

'Who wouldn't?'

'You're interfering in something that could get you killed, you know?'

'I've dodged bullets, escaped exploding buildings. I've even eaten in the hospital canteen for over a year. If I can survive that, I can get through anything. I'm starting to believe I'm invincible.'

'You're not.'

'Then I'll go down kicking and screaming. One day, during this or the next junta reign, they'll remember me as a hero and put my face on a stamp. I'll meet Boua in Nirvana and have something to boast about. I might even make her proud of me, at last.'

'Your wife was always proud of you, little brother.'

'You think so?'

'I know she was.' A glorious yellow caterpillar had lowered itself from the tree on a web rope and come to rest on Civilai's knee. Siri watched him gently run his finger along its back. 'Of course, she always preferred me to you. But she was quite fond of you.'

Siri laughed and shook his head.

'Being perfect must have made your life miserable at times,' Siri said.

'The Lord Buddha says all existence involves suffering.'

'Is that right? Didn't he have a thousand concubines before he saw the light?'

'Exactly. So he knew what suffering was all about. I have just the one and I suffer interminably.'

'Next time I meet Nong for one of our secret afternoon trysts I'm going to tell her you called her a concubine.'

Civilai didn't rise to the bait.

'I'm coming with you,' he said.

'To meet your wife?'

'To Pakse.'

'Really? Don't you have meetings to go to? Hands to shake?'

'They owe me a break. You're a doctor. You can diagnose me with some disease, recommend I take a few days to recover from it.'

Siri was delighted. 'All right. Any specific requests?'

'Nothing disfiguring. Something that doesn't stop me drinking.'

'Syphilis would put you down for a day or two.'

'No. I don't think Mrs Nong would see the funny side of that. How about something internal and painful but non-life threatening?'

'Chronic haemorrhoids?'

'Perfect.'

Siri was just completing Civilai's medical certificate when Phosy stopped by the morgue. He wore a layer of dust and looked like a shift worker at the snuff factory.

'How did it go?' Siri asked. As Siri had to prepare for his trip south, they'd decided Phosy should go by himself to revisit the dentist's wife.

'It was a lot faster on *your* bike.'

'I said you could use it.'

'I know, but regulations. We have to use the department scooter on official business.'

'Even if it's a pink Vespa?'

'It's lilac. At least it was until today.'

'I'd hate to think of you giving chase to a criminal on that.'

'Come on, Siri. You know there are no criminals in the PDR Laos.'

'You saw the widow?'

'I saw what was left of her.'

'What do you mean?'

'Well, I got there at about eleven. The door was ajar and when I called out, there was no answer. I went inside and it was obvious there'd been some kind of struggle. The table was on its side and the pieces of that game thing had been scattered. There were cups and papers lying all around. Then I saw the blood.'

'Oh, my. Poor woman.'

'There was a pool of it near the couch, and a trail leading to the back door. I went through the place. Clean as a flute. No rifled drawers or cupboards. No overturned mattresses. Whoever hit the old lady hadn't gone there to rob her. At least I don't think so. There were odd pieces of jewellery upstairs but I didn't find any money. And no personal documents for either of them.'

'No identity cards, house documents, licenses?'

'Not a one. But they might have had them stashed away somewhere else for safety. I didn't find a purse or handbag, so whoever it was might have taken that stuff when they dragged the old woman's body out.'

'You think she was dead?'

'There was a hell of a lot of blood, Doctor. I'm not sure she could have survived a wound like that. I brought you some.'

'Some what?'

'Some of the blood.' Phosy produced a small sauce bottle from his shirt pocket. 'I think I cleaned the sauce out pretty thoroughly.'

'What in hell's name do you expect me to do with that?'

'I don't know. You're a coroner. I thought you might be able to tell me something from it.'

'Like how she died? What she had for breakfast on the morning of her attack?'

'I don't know. You're the expert.'

'I'm a very little expert, and certainly not a magician. And I'm an expert only in the absence of real professionals who have the benefit of a laboratory and technicians and years of training – people who might know what they're actually talking about. This isn't Hollywood. There, I believe, they can tell you a victim's shoe size from a sample of blood. Given my present state, I can barely tell you what colour it is.'

Siri took the bottle from Phosy and shook it.

'How did you get it into the bottle?'

'Just scooped the bottle through the puddle.'

'It was that deep?'

'Deep enough.'

'Then I imagine your old lady hadn't been gone long.'

'Why so?'

'In this heat, on a parquet floor, blood would dry in – I don't know – an hour at the most.'

'That means they must have taken her body out in daylight. That's odd. I asked around. None of the neighbours remembered seeing anything. In a little place like that, you'd notice a body being removed.'

'That's one more thing that doesn't make sense,' Siri said. 'Let's look at motive. Say someone wanted to keep the messages a secret. They knew we were nosing around and that she'd seen the contents of the notes. They couldn't risk her disclosing what she knew. So killing her I can understand. But what could be gained from taking the body away? Delaying the discovery?'

'Not likely.' Phosy began to wash his hands and face in the small sink in the corner of the office. 'If you're going to all that trouble, you'd clean up the crime scene. At the very least you'd shut the front door. Whoever did this wanted us to know that she'd been the victim of a violent assault.'

'That message would have been clearer if they'd left her

body there. They could even have made it look like a house-breaking.'

'But this way leaves us in doubt. Maybe she didn't die. It leaves us wondering what else they could be doing to her.'

'A kind of warning, you mean? To us?'

'Possibly. We might be well advised to spread around what we know to others. As long as we're the only ones privy to the information it wouldn't be that difficult to contain the damage by eliminating us,' Phosy cautioned Siri.

'I talked to Civilai. He thinks he has people he can trust. He'll spend the afternoon setting up a network.'

'Dtui and I will have to be in on it.'

'We've already discussed you two. You have your parts. But we can't arrange anything for certain until we've nosed around in Pakse.'

'We? Civilai's going with you?'

'He insisted.'

'Hell, Siri.'

'What?'

'He isn't exactly low profile, is he? Do you think you can root around discreetly in the south with a politburo member at your side?'

'Don't panic. He's going south to "convalesce after a minor operation". It'll be very hush-hush. It's just a coincidence we'll be there at the same time.'

'Who's going to believe that?'

'Phosy, he knows people down there. He can get us information I probably wouldn't have access to. He knows what he's doing.'

'I should go with you anyway.'

'No, son. You need to be here. If we can trace the letter,

we'll need someone here to follow up on it. I'll phone and leave messages at my house as to my progress. You can pick them up there via Dtui. That will avoid the official government phone lines and the official government phone tappers.'

'What makes you think your phone isn't bugged, too?'

'I'm sure we can put together a little jiggery pokery of our own, a simple code that will baffle the Security Division. It can't be that difficult. We aren't beyond a little espionage of our own.'

'Dr Siri, are you sure you know what you're doing?'

'As I believe I've told you before, I've never been sure of anything in my life. But it's worth a try. It's even a bit exciting, don't you think?'

7

THE NIGHT BRUCE LEE SAVED LAOS

As Siri had anticipated, the Soviet ambassador did indeed make the Yak 40 available for the trip south. It helped that a politburo member had also requested passage. Civilai was driven directly to the plane and made every effort to stagger bowlegged up the steps so anyone watching might sympathize. Haemorrhoids were no laughing matter.

Despite the short notice for the flight, there were eight other passengers on board. Siri sat on a wooden bench nurturing his paranoia. He looked at the men opposite and tried to match their faces with an identikit for traitors he carried in his mind. He dismissed the four Russian education experts on their way to the teachers college. The two forestry officials had been too vocal as they sat behind Siri in the waiting room. They'd spouted precise figures to demonstrate how many millions of *kip* per day the government was losing as a result of the Thai logging embargo. The two army officers, however, sat composed and apart amid the spin-dryer vibrations of the old Soviet war craft.

Just a coincidence? Siri wondered. They wore their uniforms proudly and sat erect, like men who had acquired their self-discipline in a place other than the jungles of Laos. He'd smiled at them when he'd first climbed on board and one of them had nodded back. The other, a thin man whose skin was stretched over his cheekbones like melted cheese, had looked away, pretending not to notice. In the din of the ancient Yak there was no conversation to be had, but Siri committed the stern sunburned face to memory. For the entire journey the soldier sat still, unconcerned by the discomfort of the seat, staring ahead at portholes too small to see through.

Civilai, being an aristocrat of the politburo, was seated behind the bored Ukrainian pilots. Not first-class accommodation, except that it gave the VIP a marvellous view of the lightning that slivered and danced above the low clouds. It was like a grand plot of the weather, secretly stirring up its storms, bringing its witches' brew of monsoons to the boil, holding back its life-giving rains till the last second. Civilai knew it would break someday soon. All this power would be unleashed, drenching the delicate earth below. His people, who for months had struggled to survive the drought, would find themselves struggling to survive the storms. Unfair really, but there was no more chance of stopping the weather than there was of ... He shuddered as he considered the enormity of the task ahead of him.

Pakse was a city without a centre. It sat in the armpit between the Se Don and the Mekhong rivers, its suburbs only recently venturing across their banks. It wasn't a place with a distinguished history. That mantle was held by Bassak, twenty-five miles downriver. That city, the old capital of Champasak, had been the seat of omnipotent and notorious regents: a place of legends. At one period in history it had been the heart of the southern kingdom, then one day it had ceased to beat, had lost the will to be great. Pakse, on the other hand, had always been a more logical base for trade because of the confluence of the rivers and its proximity to Thailand. The French had recognized this fact and made it their center of administration in the south. The only wonder was why it hadn't become the capital sooner. Once deserted, Bassak fell to ruin. As any good historian knows, nostalgia is always a poor relative to commerce.

So, as a city built on greed, Pakse was never likely to be a place one would visit just for enjoyment. There was nothing grand or spectacular to put on a postcard and impress people at home. Not even the ugly unfinished palace of the exiled regent warranted a photograph. The government buildings were practical and basic; the houses had been constructed for seeing out of. Even the temples were pale recent copies of their sisters in the north. The roads were yellow clay and what few plants had survived the development were camouflaged in its grime. If the northern capital of Luang Prabang was a jewel in the Indochinese crown, Pakse was the seat of the royal underpants.

Siri and Civilai obviously weren't occupying adjoining rooms on the second floor of the Pakse Hotel to partake in the joys of city sightseeing. Civilai had turned up there without his trademark glasses and wearing a monk's tight woolly hat. He'd checked in under the name of Sawan and was certain the night clerk had no idea who he was. Nobody knew or cared who Siri was, so he checked in under his own name. The two counter-revolutionaries sat on the edge of Civilai's bed staring at the amazing cross-stitch depiction of stags in a Nordic stream that had been framed and hung on the wall. A ceiling fan rocked perilously above their heads.

'Makes you want to go to Scandinavia, doesn't it?' Siri said.

'What time is it?'

'Eight.'

They'd left Wattay Airport early and made good time. There would be no knowledge gained with regard to their quest until daylight.

'Want to do something?'

They arrived at the little Pakse Cinema ten minutes after the film had started. It was a delight to be there. The Odeon, the only picture house in Vientiane, had been commandeered as a political lecture hall. The day that happened, Civilai and Siri's hearts had been deprived of oxygen. They'd been starved of one more breath of culture. The old boys were movie aficionados: addicts, some might say. Their habit had been nurtured in the smoky cinemas of Paris. In Hanoi, and in the caves of Huaphan, they'd attended every film projection, no matter how desperately awful the movie on offer promised to be. They were perhaps the only two in the audience to derive pleasure from such blockbusters as *Rural Sanitation in Southern Yunan* and *The Benefits of Oiling Your Weapon*. They'd left the cinema cave in tears after a showing of *The Public Humiliation of an Illiterate Goat Herder*. The films didn't matter. It was the atmosphere they loved, that truly social feeling of strangers sharing emotions, laughing together, being thoroughly depressed together, being moved as one, like passengers on a funfair ride. They missed it: that instant communism.

As they paid their hundred *kip* they heard gales of laughter emanating from inside the picture house. The cashier told them they should go through the heavy black doors and wait until their eyes were accustomed to the darkness. Then they could sit wherever they liked. The house wasn't full. Not too many people could afford a night out at the cinema these days. A hundred *kip* was almost forty cents, and money like that could be better spent.

They did as they were told, stood inside the thick curtain door and waited until their eyes could tell the difference between empty seats and laps. They settled into two seats close to the exit and stared wide eyed at the screen. It was a marvellous sight. A bare-chested Chinese – Bruce Lee, according to the poster – was standing bravely at the centre of a circle of evil-looking hoodlums. There was no soundtrack. At the front of the cinema, silhouetted against the bottom of the screen, sat three artistes. One was a man surrounded by a collection of musical instruments. He was well illuminated by a spotlight that cast a halo onto the film. The other two were actors. One male, one female, judging from their outlines. They had only small electric bulbs in front of them, illuminating their scripts. These were the interpreters of the film.

Bruce looked to one side and stared directly at the ringleader of the gangsters.

'You seem to underestimate the Lao Democratic Republic,' he said in a high-pitched voice. The mouth movement was far more economical than the words he spoke. The audience chuckled. Siri grabbed his friend's arm.

'Ha,' said the villain in a deep manly voice. 'We represent the oppressive West. You know we shall always be victorious over small fry such as you and the community farmers of which you are one.'

'You are a usurper of agronomic labour,' said Bruce. 'I shall teach you a lesson.' To the accompaniment of cymbals and something like a kazoo, he proceeded to beat the stuffing out of the attackers, no doubt appreciative of the fact that they approached him one by one rather than en masse.

Soon only Bruce and the evil Asian lapdog of colonial oppression remained standing. The latter's eyebrows suggested he felt helpless without his gang of handpicked henchmen, just as the Royalist regime would have felt without its American lackeys to hide behind. Bruce, the Lao Democratic Republic incarnate, flexed his bloodied biceps in the direction of his oppressor foe.

'So, it's just you and me,' Bruce said. 'Me, the representative of the honest people of the land. You, a capitalist who would gladly sell the soil beneath our feet to the foreign devils.'

The lips of the protagonist and antagonist had not actually moved during this altercation. Siri and Civilai were rocking in their seats with laughter, their cheeks wet with tears. They thought it couldn't get any better, but it did. To the gasps of the audience, the capitalist who would sell the soil from beneath their feet somersaulted backwards onto a roof, saying, 'We slaves of the Western money culture will always prevail, you common coolie.' And then vanished.

Bruce was devastated that the lower classes had once again become the victims of the idle rich, but a woman's voice from offscreen shouted, 'The Republic of Laos loves you, Somchit, for protecting us from foreign aggression. Our day will come.'

The audience cheered, and Siri and Civilai slapped their palms together, breathless with laughter.

'Now this,' Siri wheezed at last, 'is entertainment.'

Ten rows behind them sat the only man in the audience who wasn't enjoying the show. His military uniform now replaced by slacks and a short-sleeved sports shirt, the tight-cheeked passenger from the Yak flight kept his eyes firmly focused on the backs of his targets. A Type 77 Chinese pistol jutted uncomfortably into his belt.

8

THE 220-VOLT BATHTUB

After a disappointing breakfast of Vietnamese lentil soup and stale baguettes, Siri and Civilai walked from the Pakse Hotel into another overcast, steamy morning. The same type of stodgy cloud they'd left behind in Vientiane was hanging over them like soft bread. The whole country had become a sandwich. The town's reluctance to turn itself into a real city that welcomed visitors was evident in its lack of footpaths and its abundance of deep holes. The only buildings that didn't look like they might blow down in a strong gale were government departments housed in Franco-Chinese blocks with thick walls and gaping windows that threw forth their wooden shutters like bat wings. Nothing was really white – not the whitewash on the temple walls or the street signs, or the eyes or teeth of the dowdy people they passed. Bullock carts and small pony traps overtook them in the street, and both the drivers and the beasts they drove glanced back discreetly at the two old men. Civilai in a peaked cap and dark glasses looked like the undernourished older relative of a Cuban revolutionary. Siri bounded along beside him.

The Pakse Bureau de Poste was housed in a small concrete building covered in flaking grey paint. What had apparently once been a neat, well-cared-for garden hugging the wooden fence had grown wild and unlovable. Thorny sprigs reached out for the old men from between the palings. It was here Siri and Civilai parted company, Siri to fulfil his obligation to the Justice Department, Civilai to see whether the post office could shed any light on the origin of the dentist's letter. They agreed to meet for lunch at the ferry crossing, where they would pass on the morning's results.

When Siri arrived at the police station, he failed to disturb the duty officer from the delicate task of removing chin hairs with a pair of tweezers. The officer didn't even look up from the little round hand mirror he held in front of his face.

Siri said, 'Excuse me' and waited for a 'Yes, sir. I'll be with you in a minute.'

It didn't come.

'Well,' Siri said, 'either you have a hearing problem or I became invisible overnight. Which is it?'

The officer nipped and plucked once more before lowering the glass and glaring over it at the intruder.

'And who do you think you are?' he asked. His voice rasped like a man who'd consumed too much spirit the night before.

'I think I'm Dr Siri Paiboun from the Justice Department, but I confess I haven't checked my identification papers for a few days.'

There were places where a mention of the Justice Department would snap a government official into a respectful state of mind. Pakse was certainly not one of those places. The officer fished around under his desk for a wastebasket and swept his pluckings into it with the side of his hand. Having done so, he yelled at the top of his voice, 'Hey, Tao!'

A middle-aged man in police trousers and an off-white

undershirt poked his head out of an office three doors down. He was about Siri's height but three times his girth. His short grey hair had receded to a point beyond the crown of his head, leaving behind one small circular atoll of bristle at the front.

'What?' he said, apparently suffering from the same throat affliction as his colleague.

'Your Vientiane guy's here.'

'Good.'

There was no hello. Tao ducked back into the room and left Siri hanging there like crematorium smoke. They'd warned him in Vientiane that in Pakse he might not find the same poor standard of public officialdom that he'd become accustomed to in the capital. They'd told him he should lower his standards even further.

For any northern cadre, a posting to the deep south was the Lao equivalent of a Russian's banishment to Siberia. The south was still a hotbed of anticommunist feeling. After dark, the authorities could only guarantee security as far as the outer city limits. Beyond that, Royalist insurgents operated with impunity in the villages, spreading dissent and recruiting new troops for the guerrilla war against the socialists. It was an exact reversal of the situation six years earlier when the CIA and Royalists had barricaded themselves inside Pakse, and the Pathet Lao and Vietminh had ruled the roost in the countryside. Pakse always proved to be a burning pot handle for any faction that tried to hold on to it. So police officers transferred from the north had invariably offended somebody in authority or had shown themselves to be unfit for employment anywhere else.

Tao emerged from his office wearing a police hat that was too small for his head and a leather jacket twice his size. He obviously hadn't noticed how hot and clammy the day was. He strode past Siri and slapped him on the back.

'Come on, old fellow,' he said. 'Where's your car?'

'What car?'

Tao stopped and turned back with an angry look on his face. 'They didn't arrange your transport? I thought you were government.'

'I just work for them, like you.'

'All right. We can go on my bike but you'll have to pay for the petrol.'

He marched through the large open frontage of the building and out to the dust bowl in front. He'd reached his motorcycle before he realized the Vientiane guy wasn't following. Siri, smiling, was leaning on the counter.

The pudgy policeman called out, 'Oy. Come on. They're waiting for us. What are you, crippled or something?'

Siri took a small plastic jar of aniseed balls from his top pocket and slowly unscrewed the cap. Tao marched back inside already glossy with sweat. 'What are you playing at?'

'Your name's Tao, right?' Siri said, offering him a handful of aniseed, which was rejected.

'Yeah?'

'Well, Tao. You're probably the type of man who believes he's been sent to work in the worst place on the planet. Am I right?'

'I've got no time for this. What's your point?'

'My point is, this is far from the worst place on the planet. There are much worse places than this. Even in Laos there are worse hellholes. There are postings so horrible, Pakse would seem like the Tiger Balm Pleasure Gardens by comparison. And not only do I know where those postings are, I can arrange for people to be sent there.'

'I don't—'

'So here's the deal, Officer Tao. I'm going to be here for a few days. While I'm in town, you're going to call me "doctor" or "comrade" or even "sir", if you like. Because even though I don't wear a uniform, I outrank you about twentyfold. When there is a need, you will ferry me around on your decrepit motorcycle without any extortion attempts. It is your duty and you receive a budget to do so. By showing me respect, you'll see that I can be a very useful contact for you, Officer Tao. Do we understand each other yet?'

Tao looked over Siri's shoulder to see whether the duty officer had been a witness to his dressing-down, but they were alone at the front desk. He seemed to weigh the offer in his mind, but it really wasn't that difficult a decision to make.

'All right.'

'All right, what?'

'Doctor?'

'Very good. Shall we go?'

Once the roles were established, Officer Tao became a very jolly little man. He chatted amiably on their journey across town and made it clear to Siri that if there was anything he needed while he was in town, Tao was his man. It took only ten minutes to get to the deputy governor's house behind the sports stadium. A Land Rover was parked in front, and a large man in a safari suit was sitting cross-legged on the porch.

'You're honoured,' Tao said. 'The governor's here to meet you himself.'

They pulled up beside a lemon ghost tree and Tao removed his hat respectfully. 'Governor Comrade Katay, this is Dr Siri from the Justice Department.'

If he hadn't been told this was the governor, Siri would have mistaken the nervous-looking character for a janitor. When he stood, it was as if his suit were filled with crumpled newspaper rather than a body. He held out his hand to Siri, who shook it and smiled. There was no power in the governor's handshake and no confidence in his voice.

'It *is* you,' the governor said. 'I thought it might be. You don't remember me, do you?'

Siri stared at the large man, trying to place him. If they'd met, it must have been long ago and ... Then it came to him.

'The school at Tum Piu,' Siri said. 'You taught – what was it? – Lao language?'

Yes, Siri remembered him, a nervous, paranoid teacher, suspecting this student or that of having rightist sympathies. He'd been fed well since those days but the tic below his eye had followed him from the north-east. Siri had been the resident surgeon in the Piu cave hospital, a place now renowned for a Nomad Fighter rocket attack that had cremated all the staff and patients. The school further down the valley had housed the children of the hospital staff and the surrounding villagers. Overnight it became an orphanage. In one of the many quirks of fate that had saved Siri's life over the years, on the day of the attack he'd been called to Xam Neua to tend to the president.

By all accounts, Katay had been a competent teacher and a dedicated Party man, but Siri was shocked to find him here as governor. Of course, there had been numerous positions to fill around the country when the Pathet Lao took over and a limited number of trustworthy cadres to fill them. But he was hardly governor material.

'Lao language and ideology,' he said proudly as if that was the pinnacle of his career and things had gone downhill since. 'Now look at me.'

'You've come a long way, Comrade.'

Katay laughed with embarrassment and lowered his voice. 'No doubt they'll replace me soon enough. There are plenty of young chaps being trained in the Eastern Bloc.'

'Meanwhile ... ?'

'Meanwhile I'm running a renegade province and I have a limited number of workers under me whom I can trust. There are spies everywhere here, Siri, and assassins. That's why I was so glad when I saw your name on the telegram. I enjoyed our political debates at Tum Piu so much. I know you're a man after my own heart.'

Siri vaguely recalled that their 'debates' had been mostly him listening and Katay spouting a stream of conspiracy theories.

'So, what do we have here?' Siri asked.

Katay looked sideways at Tao, who was standing by the Land Rover talking to the governor's driver. He put his arm around Siri's shoulder and led him onto the front porch. There Siri detected a familiar odour. Katay's voice was almost a whisper now and he was leaning close into the doctor's face.

'I've had a suspicion for a long time,' he whispered, 'that the Soviets are trying to undermine the Vietnamese influence in Laos. I believe their ultimate objective is to overthrow our government and take over the country.'

Siri was afraid to ask why the hell they would want to. So he kept quiet and nodded.

Katay continued. 'Of course, they have to be discreet. Eliminate our key personnel one at a time. I was curious as to how they might go about it and then it happened – bam! My deputy, assassinated in his own bath.'

'You're positive it was an assassination and not, say, an accident?'

'Look at the facts, Siri. The facts. His first night back from Vientiane after meeting with the Russians. His first bath using that fiendish Soviet water heater. It had to be rigged to kill him. That's why I needed you here.'

'Actually, I'm more of a doctor than an electrician. You might need to bring some technical person in to prove something like that, comrade.'

'But you're the coroner now. You can tell whether he was murdered. Right?'

'Not always. But let's see. Where's the body?'

'Inside.'

'In his house? Still?'

'Right. I had them lock the place as soon as I heard. His wife phoned me when it happened and described the scene to me. I told her to leave and touch nothing. She brought me the key and went to stay with her mother.'

'So, the body is …?'

'Still in the bath, I presume.'

'What? After two days? My God. I hope she removed the plug. We'll have beef stock in there if she didn't.'

'I told her to pull the circuit breaker.'

'Thank goodness for small mercies. You have the key?' Katay held it up. Siri called to Tao and asked him if he'd like to join them.

'Not really,' Tao shouted back.

'Officer!'

'Coming, Comrade.'

The three men recoiled when the door shutters were

pulled back and the stench of death hurried to escape. Siri felt no spiritual presence. No hovering grievances looking for revenge. They walked through to the back kitchen where Deputy Governor Say lay naked in a zinc bath. Only his head remained above the surface of the now tepid water and it carried a peculiar frozen smile like that on the face of a ventriloquist's dummy. His body was pink and hairless.

'All right. I've seen it,' said Officer Tao. 'Think I should be heading back to—'

'Tao, it's your crime scene,' Siri reminded him. 'Take some notes.'

'Notes? Right.' Tao looked around for a pen and paper in the cluttered kitchen. Siri approached the bath and knelt beside it. The brand-new Russian water heater was hooked onto the side of the bath and its element hung below the surface of the water. The lead of the heater looped down to join an extension cord that snaked across the floor to another extension. This was a junction to which a dozen other cords were connected, an octopus of accidents waiting to happen. The skin of the corpse was unmarked.

Siri called to the governor, who remained in the kitchen doorway. He put a handkerchief over his nose and walked forward.

'Yes, Doctor?'

'I presume your deputy was a reasonably intelligent man.'

'Why, yes. He was an old student of mine. Quite brilliant. I recommended him for the position.'

'So we'd have to assume he wasn't the type of man who'd climb into a tin bath full of water in which dangled a live electrical element.'

'Certainly not.'

'... him for the position,' came a voice from behind them.

Siri turned to see Tao attempting to write down the governor's words.

'Officer Tao,' Siri said. 'This isn't an article for the *Pasason Lao* news. I think it would be sufficient for you just to summarize the things that *I* say.'

'Very well, Doctor.'

'We'll have to assume then,' Siri continued, 'that once Comrade Say's big toe touched the surface of the water, he would have received a jolt powerful enough to send him flying across the room.'

'I would imagine that's true,' the governor agreed.

'Why then is he sitting submerged in the bath?'

'I don't know.'

'I would have to guess it's because the water heater was placed in the bath after he sat in it.'

'But that would be ...'

'If Say wasn't of an unsound mind and dunked a live element in his own bath, we'd have to say premeditated murder, Comrade Governor.'

'That's outrageous. Are you getting all this down, Tao?'

'Almost, Governor.'

'As the police officer handling this case, what would your next step be?' Siri asked Tao.

'Next step? Er ... interrogation, sir.'

'Of whom?'

'Everyone. Anyone who had a grudge against the deceased and all his house staff, friends, and relatives.'

'Good,' Siri interjected. 'But that's likely to be a lot of work.'

'It's worth it,' said Katay. 'This was the deputy governor of Champasak.'

'I'm not suggesting there shouldn't be an inquiry,' said

Siri. 'But perhaps I could suggest a method of eliminating the suspects.'

'I'd be grateful for any help,' Tao said.

'Then do you think we could fingerprint the handle of this heater to see who the last person to touch it was? That would certainly have to be the person who put the heater into the water.'

'Excellent idea,' said Tao. 'How exactly would we go about that?'

'How? Surely they taught you fingerprinting at the police school?'

Tao snorted a laugh through his nostrils. 'Dr Siri. I'm just a soldier in a new uniform. Soldiering and policing are interchangeable as far as my bosses are concerned. All the real policemen – I mean the trained ones – either hopped it across the border or they're up with your friends attending seminars. We're hard-pressed just to keep the peace. We're a few years away from doing any actual investigating. Sorry, Governor, but it's the truth.'

Katay shook his head. 'Don't apologize, Tao. These are desperate times.' He squeezed Siri's arm. 'Doctor, can you do anything?'

Siri's emotions were mixed. He bemoaned the lack of expertise in his country and wondered how long it would take to educate its youth to become proficient in even the most fundamental skills. But, on the other hand, where else would a seventy-three-year-old amateur get a chance to play detective as he often did? He had a Maigret mystery right there up his sleeve. The intrepid French detective on holiday in a remote town. A break-in at a small art gallery. No crime laboratory around, so in order to check for fingerprints on a discarded frame, Inspector Maigret turns to basic chemicals: a simple grey powder of magnesium and chalk.

This was how Siri would have gone about proving the identity of Deputy Say's assassin. While the governor's driver was out hunting for magnesium, Siri and a reluctant Officer Tao removed Say's body from the bath and took an impression of the right index finger using a square of carbon paper. All they needed then was to compare it to that on the handle of the heater to determine whether Say had committed suicide and, if not, to start the murder inquiry. Then would begin the arduous business of finger-printing anyone who had access to the deputy's house on the night in question. But the god of unnecessary paper-work intervened. Even before they had the powder, the crime solved itself.

Officer Tao had gone to the home of the mother of the deputy governor's wife in order to obtain the addresses of her staff and close friends. She was an uncomplicated woman. Like many of the nouveau powerful in Laos, Say had gone into the villages and found himself a pretty but uneducated wife to complement his new lifestyle. Tao told her of the magic of fingerprinting and how they would be able to determine the identity of the murderer even without torturing the suspects. To his amazement, the woman burst into tears right in front of him and dropped to her knees.

'It was me. It was me,' she sobbed. 'I didn't realize. "Bring me some more hot water," he shouted. And there he was, all round and ruddy from all them Soviet pleasures: the vodka and the food and the big-boned women I wouldn't wonder. "Bring me some more hot water." What on earth did he want a hot bath for? It's humid enough to bathe standing up with all your clothes on this time of year.

He was just showing off that he'd been given a water heater. That was all. So, I thought, what's the point of having it if you still have to lug heavy pails back and forth across the kitchen? I took the heater out of the bucket, hooked it on the side of the bathtub, and dropped it into the water.'

She sobbed then for a full minute, unable to speak. Tao stood over her with a rather embarrassed look on his face.

'I didn't know it'd kill him,' she went on. 'Just thought it might singe him a little bit and teach him a lesson. But he sort of sizzled and shook and this big grin spread over his face like he was enjoying it. I didn't know what to do. I jumped back and watched him fry. Next thing I knew he was dead.'

It was 11:45 a.m. when Tao related the story to Siri and the governor. Say's wife was locked up in the Pakse police station and the case was solved. The Soviet Union was exonerated, the governor placated, and the widow allowed to purge her demons of guilt all with fifteen minutes to spare before lunch. It was Siri's fastest ever conclusion of a case but he was still a little upset that he hadn't been given the opportunity to eliminate the suspects one by one through the magic of dactyloscopy.

9

FREE LAO

Siri told all this to Civilai under the tarpaulin of a rather special noodle stall overlooking the Mekhong ferry ramp. The lady owner, Daeng, began her day at four in the morning just to have everything perfect by lunchtime. But apart from being a noodle perfectionist she had many other arrows in her quiver.

At the hotel, when they'd returned from the cinema the previous night, Siri had casually mentioned Madame Daeng the cook to the night clerk. Siri held out little hope that his old friend would still be there after all these years. That's why he'd been so surprised by the reaction. The clerk had laughed and told him more people in Pakse knew the name Madame Daeng the cook than they did President Soupanouvong. He'd told Siri where she could be found and, sure enough, here she was.

She still had the keen, all-seeing eyes and the fine delicate features that had fascinated so many young men back when. The look of shock on her face could have drained the river for ten miles in each direction. She'd tossed the noodle sieve into the boiling water, hobbled over to her famous doctor on legs stiff with rheumatism, and thrown her arms around him. Ignoring the stares of the mystified diners, Siri and Daeng could feel the strong beating of each other's hearts as they stood locked together like hands clasped in prayer. From his stool beside the noodle cart, Civilai had timed the embrace at a minute, but for the old comrades it was an exchange of missed decades, of battles and loves and losses, of friends departed and disasters shared.

Siri had first met Daeng thirty-seven years earlier at the southern youth camp where he and his wife, Boua, were serving with the Free Lao movement. Daeng had been their cook. At first that was all the remarkable young woman had done, but she soon demonstrated skills and determination far beyond the wok. In 1940, the French had urged the Lao to set up the youth movement in answer to Thailand's posturing about shifting its eastern border into Lao territory. It was intended as a mechanism to engender nationalistic feeling against the Thais. When Siri and Boua returned from their studies in France at the end of '39, the camp in Champasak had been their first posting. They'd spent two years training young medical interns, teaching French, and moulding young minds. What the French didn't realize was that the youth camps they were sponsoring around the country had a well-hidden and brilliantly conceived agenda. In them the foundations were being laid for ousting the French oppressors. It was from the youth initiative that the Lao Issara – the Free Lao movement – was born, and Siri and Boua had been instrumental in its creation in the south.

When the youth camps were finally closed down by the French for becoming too radical, the Free Lao began its subversive acts of rebellion. Madame Daeng, then a miss, had tagged along with the rebels, cooking, tossing the odd grenade, joining in the campfire plots. She was an inspiration to the young Lao who had grown strong from her noodles, and she was a valuable ally to Siri and Boua. But in the confusion that accompanies a guerrilla war, they'd lost touch. Siri and Boua had gone to Vietnam and Daeng remained in the south. And now, on Siri's first day back in Champasak, they had been reunited.

Siri introduced her to his cousin, 'Pop', and she looked at Siri with a wry smile on her sun-rusted face. She'd always been able to tell when he was lying. She greeted the 'cousin' and told Siri their reunion proper could wait. For the time being, she promised them the best lunch they'd ever tasted in their lives and went to fish the sunken sieve from its tank. Siri knew from experience that this wasn't an idle promise. When the huge bowls arrived in front of them, the aroma was poetry enough to make them lose the threads of their morning adventures. The piquant spices caressed their palates and reminded them how many years it had been since they'd really tasted food. Even Siri in his nullified state could pick out every herb, root, and legume. He forgot Civilai, just as Civilai had no further interest in him, until the last spoonfuls of broth had made the trip north.

It was Civilai who spoke first. 'That … that was …'

'I know.'

'Let's take her back to Vientiane,' Civilai said, only partly in jest. 'She could have a real restaurant there, not sweat out her days for ferry passengers under a grimy tarpaulin for fifty *kip* a plate. She should be rolling in money.'

'Believe me, brother,' Siri said, 'Madame Daeng is the type of woman who could roll in whatever she pleases. If this is what she's chosen it's because it makes her happy.'

'Even so …'

'All right. You've heard enough of men in baths and silly wives. It's your turn. Tell me about the post office.'

'I wish I had a long funny story with a happy ending.'

'No luck?'

'The fellow there looked at the envelope and the post-mark and told me, quite logically, that it could have been brought in by anyone. Some two hundred people a day come in with letters. They pay their money, get their stamps, he cancels them, and throws the letters into a big sack. The sorter goes through them, puts them in smaller sacks, and puts them on the bus.'

'Didn't he recall a customer who came in every fortnight with a letter to Vientiane?'

'Siri, there wasn't even a surname on it. It was a letter to a PO box. What could possibly jog his memory? I prodded him so hard he lost his temper with me and threatened to call the police.'

'Huh, no danger there. But I'm glad you've built up a good relationship with the mail service.'

'Siri, I—'

Daeng interrupted them with two more bowls of noodles. The old warriors were as stuffed as steamed rice sausages but these dishes exuded a scent so erotic it would have seduced a palace eunuch. Daeng winked and they dipped their spoons into the broth. A whole new taste, a whole new love affair.

After several minutes of blissful slurping, Siri managed a sentence. 'Show me the envelope,' he said.

Civilai handed over the letter and watched as his friend studied it.

'I know. You're going to dust it and fingerprint everyone in the province.'

'No, genius. And don't mock. I'm having a remarkably successful run with my Inspector Maigret franchise. What *mon copain* would do is narrow things down by trying to find out where one could obtain an envelope such as this.' He turned it over and noticed something for the first time. 'Well now look at this, older brother.'

'What?'

'In the corner here. It looks like a little cross in pencil. Someone's apparently tried to rub it out but they didn't erase it completely. What do you suppose this means?'

'In the West it's the symbol for a kiss. I don't suppose the Devil's Vagina might have been secretly flirting with the dentist's wife? An affair behind his back?'

'*Ménage à trois d'espionnage*? More likely, the shop that sells them uses the cross when they're counting them out, marking every ten or so. What do you think?'

'I think you're clutching at straws.'

'But it isn't impossible.'

'It once rained tadpoles in Luang Prabang.'

'All right. So that gives us one more lead to pursue. There can't be that many places selling envelopes in Pakse. Then there's the Devil's Vagina himself.'

'Or herself.'

'Exactly. It is rather ambiguous. I think it's worth asking around. See if the name elicits any reaction.'

'Reaction other than taunts and ridicule?'

'Your reticence suggests you'd prefer me to handle the vaginal probing.'

'Not at all. I'll have a stab at it. You can do the envelopes.'

'We can get Daeng on to it, too.'

'Siri, I don't think …' But Siri had already called over his old comrade, leaving Civilai shaking his head and mouthing some unheard warning. Daeng sat with them, wiping her hands with a cloth.

'You two aren't leaving here until every last spoonful of that is inside you,' she said.

'Fear not,' Siri told her. He took her hand. 'We will have completely licked the pattern from the bowls by the time we exit. But, in the meantime, we have a little mystery we would like to get you involved in.'

'Ooh, how exciting. I love a challenge.'

'I know you do. My cousin and I are in search of a devil's vagina.'

Daeng roared with laughter. The late diners looked over at her and smiled.

'Well, I've had some requests in my time,' she said, wiping tears from her eyes. 'Most men your age are looking for something a bit softer, farm lasses straight off the bus, for example.'

'I don't think it's an actual female organ,' Siri said. 'More likely a person's nickname or the name of a place. You ever heard of it?'

She laughed again. It made her face glow like a teenager's. 'The name of a place? No. I'm sure I'd remember it if I'd met someone who was born in the Devil's Vagina.' The thought set her off into another laughing fit and she dragged Siri and Civilai into it with her.

'Don't worry, boys,' she said when the mirth had subsided. 'I'll ask around.'

Siri caught a worried glance from Civilai. He leaned closer to Daeng.

'Just be careful who you ask,' he said.

She didn't need clarification. She seemed to read enough from his tone to realize she was getting into something sticky.

'Siri, my love, you'll never change, will you? Always the dashing hero off on some quest to save mankind. But you'd better put some of that hero time aside for me while you're here. We've got a lot to catch up on.'

Further up beyond the ferry ramp, a man stood in the doorway of a soon-to-be-demolished French villa. His eyes were trained on the two old men sitting at the noodle stall. He didn't need to use his binoculars because his eyesight was keen. His military training had given him the expertise and the patience to fulfil his mission. There was no hurry.

'How's she feeling?' Civilai asked. He was in a wicker chair by the window of his room. Siri had stopped off at the long-distance phone booth at the Bureau de Poste on his way back. He sat on the bed and sighed.

'I don't know. She has a knack of always sounding cheerful, even when the weight of the world is on her shoulders.'

'Do you suppose she's angry that we weren't there for it?'

'No. The one thing you can be sure of with Dtui is that she doesn't hold a grudge. She knows why we're here. If it weren't for the cremation she'd probably have jumped on a bus and joined us already.'

'How did it go?'

'All right, she said. Nice ceremony. The monks got sloshed afterwards. She wonders whether they aren't just Royalists hiding out in saffron till the heat's off. But they knew the chants so nobody complained. A lot of her ma's friends were there, hospital people. Phosy was with her.'

'Any news from him?'

'Nothing about the dentist's wife. A dead end, he says. He managed to get the blood sample to someone at the Swedish forestry project. They promised to take it down to

Bangkok next trip and get it looked at. Otherwise Dtui and Phosy are just sitting around, waiting for orders from us. Dtui did say Judge Haeng was asking why I was still in Pakse.'

'Why? Well, it's obvious. Complications with the case.'

'That's what I told her to say. The possibility of other homicides by domestic appliance. I hinted at an assassination attempt with a vacuum cleaner. I might have to conjure up something more credible if we stay here much longer.'

'We've barely started.'

'Done nothing at all, as far as I can see.'

Their time in Pakse had yielded nothing. The envelope search took longer than Siri had expected. He soon learned that all the shops in Pakse sold pretty much the same things, contraband from either Thailand or Vietnam. There were few stores that *didn't* sell envelopes. But none of the owners recognized the brand or style. The only thing he learned from his search was that the sender probably hadn't bought his envelopes in Pakse. It was frustrating. It always seemed much more straightforward in detective novels.

Civilai's pursuit of the Devil's Vagina had apparently gone no better. As it turned out, his initial fear of being recognized had been grossly overestimated. Without his large black-framed glasses there was little to connect him with the grinning statesman in the grainy photographs in *Pasason Lao*. In fact, it was soon apparent that people in the south didn't read. He didn't once see a coffee-shop patron poring over the week's news or a young office girl hurrying to finish a romance novel on her lunch break. To Pakse, Civilai was just a peculiar old man dressed like a farmer on holiday. Like most outsiders, he was not to be trusted. He asked Siri one evening, 'If anyone knew, do you think they'd tell a stranger in the street?'

No, they both knew it was a waste of time. Civilai busied himself with setting up his network of trustees. He was spending more time by himself. The dentist lead was getting fainter by the day but Civilai seemed to be more occupied. Siri would come back from a day of fruitless detecting to find him surrounded with handwritten notes. He'd always say, 'We might be getting somewhere,' without giving away many details, and for a while, Siri believed there might be hope of an organized resistance. But one day he returned to find his friend particularly flustered and frustrated. The question Civilai asked was confirmation to Siri that they were lost.

'What about your – you know – other friends?'

Civilai had thus far avoided asking the 's' question. The fact that he was pursuing it now suggested to Siri that earthly channels had failed. His confidence crumbled like river salt.

'I seem to have become spiritually impotent,' Siri confessed.

'Oh, I say.'

'I know. I feel like a sinking ship, being deserted. I haven't had any contact with the supernatural for over a week. I've even stopped dreaming.'

'Damn! Isn't it always the way? When you really need a ghost there's never one around.'

And, at exactly that second, like a convenient stage direction in a bad play, there came a loud knock at the door that made the two old fellows jump out of their skins. Civilai scrambled around for his dark glasses, and Siri, laughing, went to the door. The knocking became more intense.

'You'll give yourself splinters,' he called. 'I'm coming.'

With Civilai adequately disguised, Siri opened the door to find a small bony woman of around thirty standing in the doorway. She had on a well-worn green blouse and an oft-scrubbed green *phasin* skirt. Her head was bowed to hide her face, which left him with a view of thinning hair and a broad, uneven parting. Her weather-beaten hands clasped a cloth bag in front of her.

'Are you the doctor from Vientiane?' she asked, without looking up.

'Yes. Can I help?'

'The fat policeman said I should come. He said you knew stuff about dead bodies.'

Siri stepped out to join her in the hallway and pulled the door to. Still she didn't look up.

'Well, it was very nice of Officer Tao to recommend my services,' he said. 'But actually I'm in the south on official business. I'm not sure I can ...'

She looked up into his face. Her eyes were bloodshot and swollen and tight with grief.

'It's just ... my son.'

'What about him?'

'They pulled him out of the Mekhong down at Sri Pun Don last night. He was in his school shirt with the badge. I sewed his name on it.' She paused to catch her breath. 'That's how they found me and let me know. I'd been looking for him for a week. It's just me since his dad ran off but all the neighbours was looking. We went down to get the body. Brought it back today. We all know something's not right.'

'In what way?'

'Our place is on the river, Doctor. We're fishing folk.

Sing, that's my boy, Sing could swim before he could walk. There wasn't no way he could of drowned.'

'Accidents happen, Comrade. Even to experienced swimmers.'

'That's what the police said. That's why they refused to do anything about it. But things ain't right, Doctor. I could take it, perhaps, if I thought he just drowned. I could live with it. But I know something else happened to him.'

'You think he was interfered with?'

'No, sir, not like that. We're all river people. We've all seen drowned bodies before, plenty of them. But my Sing … just doesn't look right. There's something odd about the way he come out of the water.'

'And you want me to have a look.'

'We … we can't pay you much.'

'Couple of fresh fish, perhaps?'

She smiled, tight-lipped. 'That would be no problem at all, sir.'

10

THE DEVIL'S VAGINA

Siri sloshed barefoot through the muddy streets, his old leather sandals in his hands. Twice he'd skidded and landed on his backside, laughing like a fool. The rain fell in a mist so fine and warm it was like walking into a long sneeze. It wasn't a tropical storm by any stretch of the imagination and it wouldn't help the farmers to any great extent, but it certainly felt good to be rained on again. Everything seemed to be going splendidly.

The misty downpour had begun as he sat drinking Lao cocktails (half rice whisky and the other half rice whisky) with Daeng at her humble wooden lean-to. They saw the rain as an omen, a sign that things were going to get better for their country. They'd sat on the front porch that night and talked about the missing years when Siri had fled to Vietnam with Boua. The last time he and Daeng had seen each other was in the sports stadium in Savanaketh on October 12, 1945. It was a date that neither of them was likely to forget, probably the happiest day the Lao had ever known.

The Japanese occupation forces had demonstrated that an Asian nation could match the once invincible West. This created a belief in the Lao that they could and should be running their own affairs. The French oppressor, preoccupied with events in Europe, had let its control of the colonies slip, and on that day in Savanaketh stadium, the governor had stood on the halfway line in the centre of the football pitch and shouted into a wobbly microphone. On that day, Laos had been proclaimed an independent nation with its own national assembly. The cheers could be heard in Paris. There was an impromptu parade and an orchestra of *khen* pipes, gongs, and drums. Householders put up decorations and waved the new Lao flag. The celebrations went on far into the following day.

In fact, the celebrations had lasted almost as long as the independence. Following their rout by the Japanese, the French troops had regrouped, were rearmed by the Americans, and set about reclaiming their colony. The Free Lao movement, the Lao Issara, had suffered horrific reprisals for its audacity. There were massacres and witch hunts and Siri and Boua became fugitives. They escaped from Champasak and fought with a number of scattered Free Lao resistance groups before finding their way to Vietnam and a completely different type of insurgency.

Daeng had stayed in the south of Laos, and continued to sell her noodles by day. At night she coordinated covert Lao Issara operations to disrupt the French occupation. She was the agent they code-named Fleur-de-Lis, and, to the day the invaders scurried back to France with their tails between their legs, her identity had never been discovered. Siri considered her more of a national hero than a lot of the speech givers and hand shakers in Vientiane, and he told her so.

How drunk they became, these two old revolutionaries talking about their victories and defeats, recalling the names of their old allies. And, at the point when they could barely feel their faces, just as Siri was about to begin the long stagger back to his hotel, Daeng had surprised him once more with her resourcefulness.

'Oh, by the way,' she said. Siri had climbed to his feet using the front beam of the porch. Daeng had used Siri to pull herself up. She liked the way rice whisky dealt with arthritis. 'I forgot the most important thing.'

'What could be more important than reviving the Free Lao?' Siri asked.

'I think I might have found your vagina.'

They were both at a giggly stage and it took a while for them to calm their respective convulsions.

'Of course, if you aren't going to take it seriously ...'

'No,' he slurred. 'I'm all right. Tell me.'

'Well, I'd doubted it could be the name of a person or a place so I went for some natural phenomenon. I thought perhaps it was some rock formation or a gully. You know what these country folk are like. The people I asked were wise elders, sons and daughters of the land. They knew all the local myths and legends. And, to my amazement, one old fellow knew right off what I was talking about. Your Devil's Vagina isn't a rock formation at all. It's a tree.'

Siri sat down again, felling Daeng at the same time.

'You don't say.'

'Well, yes I do,' she said. As they were back on the straw matting and the bottles were still there, she filled his glass for the umpteenth time and told him the legend.

'It's all about a Khmer princess. It seems she'd been promised to a king who was a drinking buddy of her daddy's while she was still in the womb. I'm sure worse deals have been made in bars but I can't think of any right off. The girl grew up to be a real looker and the date of her betrothal arrived. Naturally, as you can testify, the ravages of many years of drinking had left her fiancé saggy and bewrinkled, not to mention extremely old, and the princess was beside herself with grief.'

'There were two of her?'

'What? Look, pay attention or I won't tell you the punch line. There was just the one princess, and the night before the wedding she climbed out a palace window and ran off to the jungle. She knew there was only one way to protect her maidenhead, so deep in the forest she ripped off her—'

'Oh, don't!'

'Yes, and threw it high into a nearby tree. In this way she was able to return to the palace asexual and totally unmar-riageable. As if things weren't bad enough, she was banished from the kingdom and forced to fend for herself. Being vaginaless – and thus no longer possessing the soul of a woman – she soon became a devil, and died of old age in a hostel for homeless devils. Actually, I just made that last part up, but good story, eh?'

Siri was blearily silent for a few moments. Finally, he looked up and said, 'Women's souls are in their vaginas?'

'Siri, it doesn't matter where we keep our souls. The point is – are you going to remember all this tomorrow?' He nodded solemnly. 'The point is, the Devil's Vagina is the name of a tree, a real tree.'

'Where does it grow?'

'Mostly around Burirum near the Khmer border.'

'That's Thailand.'

'A plus for geography. But the old fellow said it grows here and there all the way up to the Lao border. He said he's never actually seen one in Laos.'

'No doubt the Department of Culture burned them all

down for having a rude name, corrupting our youth. Why on earth would these conspirators sign their letters with the name of a Thai tree?'

'No idea. But there's more.'

'Thank heaven.'

'The envelope.'

'I showed you the envelope?'

'It was on the table the first day you were here. I couldn't help but notice one of the postmarks.'

'What about it?'

'It was old. They changed that puncher, or whatever it's called, six or seven months ago. They use a round impression now, not a square one.'

'Six months old? How can that be?' Siri wasn't exactly sober now but he was focused.

'That's what I wondered. So I asked the old postmaster. He comes calling from time to time.'

'I bet he does.'

'He told me he'd seen that decommissioned postmark used before.'

'Who by?'

'People in the refugee camps across the border. They want to get in touch with friends and family over here. But they can't just write letters with a Thai stamp and mail it. You know all the letters from outside the country go through the national directorate. It might take six months for a letter to reach its destination and by then it's snipped to confetti and unreadable. So they have a service.'

'What kind?'

'They write their letters in the camps, buy actual Lao stamps there, and get them cancelled with these unused Lao impressions to suggest they were posted in Pakse. They bring the letters to the border, smuggle them across, and put them on the buses to Vientiane. That's the easy part. A few dollars to the driver to take on one more sack.'

'Your postmaster seems to know a lot about all this.'

'Perhaps that explains why he's unemployed.'

'Well, this is astounding.' Siri threw back his cocktail and poured two new ones. The final bottle was empty now. 'This explains everything. The coup's being plotted by the old Royalists in a camp on the Thai side, probably in Ubon. It's the closest. They contact their agents around the country by letter. I wouldn't be surprised if it's all funded with Thai and American money. You solved the puzzle. You're incredible, Daeng.'

He leaned forward to kiss her on the cheek and she pulled back. Even on the wrong side of sixty, etiquette is still etiquette. She stared at him with a disappointed look and started to hum the anthem of the Lao Issara.

'So,' she said, at the end of the first verse. 'Conspirators? There's a coup planned? Feel like telling me about it?'

At last, Siri dreamed that night. It wasn't his usual vividly realistic production. Instead it was more pastel and slightly out of focus. But that might have been due to the fact that he was underwater. He was picking his way – on foot – along the bed of a fast-flowing river. He wondered why he was walking and assumed it had to be because he couldn't swim. Even dreams had to be anchored in reality. He looked up and could see the harsh sun in a cloudless sky high above the surface of the water. On either side of him, two giant catfish floated patiently, like bodyguards.

At one point, they were overtaken by a mermaid. She looked back and smiled at Siri, who was so occupied with admiring her magnificent globular breasts that he almost failed to notice the child riding on her back. The boy's arms were hooked around her slender neck. It was Sing, healthy and alive and happy as a ten-year-old on a fairground ride. He and his mermaid raced ahead and merged into the murky water. Other mermaids overtook Siri, each with a person on her back, each speeding ahead into the gloomy distance while Siri plodded along with his corpulent guard of honour.

When he awoke, the sheet beneath him was uncomfortably damp.

The breakfast area in the Pakse Hotel was an excellent place to meet people and talk about the day's plans. It wasn't, however, somewhere you'd want to have breakfast. The coffee was road tar, the noodles were warm shoelaces, and the menu went rapidly downhill from there. Civilai sat with a cup of weak Chinese tea, tapping his fingers on the tabletop. He saw Siri descending the staircase like a man astounded by the invention of steps. Like Civilai, he was wearing dark glasses. The expression 'the blind leading the blind' entered the politburo man's mind. Siri headed unsteadily toward the front desk.

'Over here, cousin,' Civilai shouted.

Siri obviously hadn't mastered his new eyeglasses because he engaged and temporarily waltzed with a concrete pillar before finding the table.

'Are you joining me in incognito today?' Civilai asked.

'It's the daylight,' Siri said. 'When I woke up I felt like I'd landed my spaceship on the surface of the sun. Couldn't see a damned thing. It is particularly glary today, isn't it?'

'Have a few drinks last night, did we?'

'Older brother, you know me, just a small aperitif before dinner.'

'Really? Then why did you wake up so late?'

'I'm a slow sleeper.'

'Come on. What time did you get in?'

'I had to wake up the watchman to open the door. I almost came directly to your room.'

'I'm a married man.'

'You'll see me in a completely different light when I tell you what I found out.'

'I doubt that, but I'm desperate enough to believe anything. Tell!'

Before Siri could begin, the cook came over and asked if they were ready for breakfast. To Civilai's disappointment, Siri ordered them fried eggs, bread, and coffee.

'We're going to need something solid inside us today,' Siri told him.

'Well, we're in the wrong place for that. How did your visit to the fishing village turn out?'

'Oh, heck. How could I have forgotten that? It was amazing. The whole community was mourning for the boy. I've never seen anything like it: marvellous spirit, lovely people. Poor as river mud yet devoted to each other. Remember the way country life used to be? No, perhaps you don't. Of course, I'd arrived there thinking the mother was overreacting. A drowned child is a drowned child. But once I saw the body I knew she was right. Something very abnormal had happened to that boy.'

'How so?'

'Well, first, yes, he had indications of a drowning: some froth in the bronchi, water in the lungs. Nothing conclusive really, as he'd been in the water for so long. It was the other inconsistencies that made it so odd. I don't really know how to describe it. It was as if there were two parts to him. As if the maceration of the bottom half of his body had happened faster than that of the top half.'

'That doesn't sound very logical, Siri.'

'I know. I immediately understood why the river people were unhinged by the sight. His arms and face were covered in mosquito bites but there were none on his legs. Then there were the splinters.'

'Wood splinters?'

'Yes. There were these enormous splinters, about ten of them, in his back and the backs of his legs. I can't imagine how they got there.'

The cook appeared and plonked down two plates and a basket of grey bread in front of the guests. The eggs seemed to float like flat tropical fish in pools of grease.

'Coffee's coming,' the cook said. To Civilai's ears, it sounded like a threat. He pushed his plate away and turned to Siri.

'Tell me, didn't this boy wash up in Muang Khong or somewhere?'

'Sri Pun Don.'

'All right. So what? A hundred miles from his home after I don't know how many hours of being thrashed about by the river. Surely he would have brushed against submerged logs, tree trunks?'

'I thought of that,' said Siri, spooning the egg goop into his mouth as if it were food. 'So had the family. But think about it. The flow of the Mekhong hasn't yet built up any pace. Logs that have been submerged for months, years? They're soft wood already. You need dry timber to get splinters. And if the damage *was* caused by the river, surely the splinters would be all over, not just on his back.'

'What are you going to do about it?'

'I don't know. Obviously, our priority here is the fact that our country may soon be plunged into anarchy. Nonetheless, I've promised the mother I'll do a little rooting around. The community gave me half a dozen mud carp for my troubles.'

'I love mud carp.'

'Me, too. That's why Daeng and I ate them all last night, sorry. As I say, we have bigger fish to fry, and, to that end, we've made a breakthrough.'

Civilai had managed to spear his fried egg with his fork and was holding it above the plate, watching the grease drip. 'We have?'

Siri told him everything: the Devil's Vagina tree, the refugee camp connection, the mail service. Yet even as he was telling it, he realized the story lacked the same certainty it had held the previous night. Civilai echoed his thoughts.

'Your friend Daeng did a good job. But don't you think you might be a little too desperate to make a link between all these spare parts? Myths and legends and postal networks don't necessarily spell out a camp-based insurgency, Siri.'

'I know, but we've been here almost a week. Do we have anything better? Has all your clandestine networking actually turned anything else up? Be honest now. I've seen how frustrated you're getting. You haven't achieved much, have you?'

'Not a lot.'

'Then this is better than nothing. What do we have to lose?'

Civilai gave up on his egg and let it splash back onto the dish.

'Nothing at all. Let's go with it. I'll get in touch with my contacts in Vientiane and see what they can dig up. I imagine we have people placed in all the camps keeping an eye on things.'

'Spies, you mean?'

'Observers. They'd know if there was a major plot being arranged. Lots of gossip in the camps. Don't forget we have to be careful who we share this with. I think your friend Daeng should be the end of the grapevine.'

'Well ...'

'What?'

'Daeng and Phosy.'

'How on earth could you get word to Phosy between last night and now? You've only just crawled out of bed for heaven's sake.'

'I was excited. I wrote him a note. Daeng said she could have it on the 6 a.m. bus to Vientiane. She knows the conductor. She was going to get him to drop it off at the morgue when he arrived.'

'The morgue? So Dtui's in the loop as well.'

'Come on, old brother, if we can't trust them, who can we trust? They've been involved in this from the beginning.'

'It's not their reliability I'm concerned about. It's their safety. This is a nasty situation, and they have a not-unwarranted reputation for acting recklessly. Let's just hope they don't do anything silly.'

11

SOMETHING SILLY

The refugee couple waited until dark before attempting to cross the ink black Mekhong to Thailand. The ever-present cloud had obscured the moon, so only one or two pricks of light from far downriver gave them any sense of space or distance. Without them the couple would have been suffocated by the darkness.

The journey from Vientiane on the dusty, potholed road had left them bruised and parched and particularly grumpy. Of course, Phosy had been in a mood long before the couple had climbed onto the bus in the capital. He'd already been fuming while he waited for the fake *laissez-passers* at temporary police headquarters. He was a man used to getting his own way and somehow he'd let himself get talked out of his own hare-brained scheme and into someone else's. He knew it was madness. He was sure to lose his job. But then again, if they failed in this mission, there might not be a job to lose. There might not be a life to ruin.

As far as that went, Dtui had been right. And, yes, she'd been right, too, about the fact that a couple would draw less suspicion on the Thai side than a single man. Refugees escaped in family groups or in large numbers. A man on his own might be a spy, a communist infiltrator. Alone, he was far more likely to be shot by the Thai border patrol. In fact, Dtui had been right about everything, which was the main reason he was sulking. She'd acted so smug as she ticked off all the logical reasons she should go with him to Ubon, and he couldn't argue against one of them. All she'd left him with was the perennial policeman's fallback: 'Because I say so.'

She'd laughed at him then, laughed in his face, made him feel as small as the roaches that scurried around their feet in the cutting room. She'd shown him the letter again: scrawled writing, almost incomprehensible to anyone who hadn't spent a year deciphering her boss's notes. It was garbled, as if he was on medication, but there was no doubt to whom he had written:

'Dear Dtui,' it said and 'Please pass this message on to Phosy.' Siri and Civilai obviously saw her as the senior contact. Wasn't that humiliating as well? He really had no choice. The letter hadn't exactly told them they should go to the camp; in fact, it told them not to do anything until they received further instructions. But just how long were they expected to sit around waiting?

So here they were, dressed in their simplest clothes with no possessions other than a small pack containing hurriedly collected paperwork. The house documents and wedding certificate had belonged to Phosy and his wife. Phosy had been an agent of the Pathet Lao long before the communists moved into Vientiane. With the takeover complete, he'd been sent to the north-east for specialist training and to reassure his employers that the soft life in the Royalist capital hadn't distorted his ideals. He'd maintained his cover identity in Vientiane and pretended he was being sent for re-education. When he returned to his home six months later, his wife and children were gone. She'd taken them across the river with no word of apology. He'd heard nothing from her since. After eighteen months of hoping she might come back or get in touch, he filed for divorce on the grounds of desertion.

Now Dtui was to take the woman's name and become the wife of a temple craftsman, a carver of teak door reliefs. It would provide them with the perfect cover: a career frowned upon by the agnostic socialist authorities. He was an ideal candidate to seek refugee status in Thailand, and Dtui had all the makings of a typical wife.

'You're going to have to get over this, you know?' Dtui said, her feet dangling in the refreshing river water. 'We have to get into our roles soon.'

'Don't tell me how to do my job,' he said, ripping the bark off an innocent sapling.

'You're in a mood.'

'So what? We're a married couple, aren't we? This is what marriage is like.'

'I'm sorry.'

'Now what?'

'If your marriage was like this ... Well, it's a shame, that's all.'

He clammed up again.

They were at a spot forty miles downriver from what used to be the ferry crossing between Savanaketh and Mukdaharn. It had closed when the Thais blockaded Laos to prevent socialism from seeping into their country. But eight hundred miles of Mekhong River served as a border between the two, and short of filling it with oil and setting light to it, the Thais knew they could never really police the banks of the river. Phosy and Dtui sat in a spot that was nowhere in particular on the Lao side, directly opposite nowhere in particular in Thailand. It was ideal for discreet crossings. Local entrepreneurs had set up a lucrative business to take advantage of the already disadvantaged. For an extortionate fee they'd row refugees across to where a truck would pick them up and drive them to a main road. Then they were on their own.

Had Phosy been by himself, he would have swum across and saved the money. Dtui was a nonswimmer. On the bus ride he'd suggested someone her shape should be able to float across. He'd immediately regretted saying it but wasn't about to apologize. Dtui, for her part, had ignored him and pretended to sleep most of the way south.

They both looked up when they heard the splashing of oars. It was so dark they didn't spot the skinny craft until it had almost passed them. The oarsman couldn't see them at all.

'Anyone there?' he called.

'Over here,' Phosy said. The pilot steered the long boat toward the bank and crashed against the rocks. It was all he could do not to overbalance into the water. His thick, greasy spectacles slipped down his nose.

'Are you sure you'll be able to find Thailand, brother?' Phosy asked.

The oarsman laughed. 'No problem. I just row toward the smell of money. I know I'll hit it eventually.'

Getting Dtui into the craft wasn't an easy matter. She refused to let the men touch her. It wasn't until they were both standing in the water, holding onto the gunwales to stop the boat from rocking, that she managed to lower herself onto the narrow wooden seat. There she sat, holding her breath and looking directly ahead. The men climbed in and they headed off. It was no more than a three-minute boat ride, and like all good businessmen, the oarsman waited until they were midstream and completely at his mercy before revising the fare.

'This is where you pay,' he said. 'Thirty thousand *kip*.'

Phosy laughed. 'Don't give me that,' he said. 'I could buy the state ferry for that.'

'That's the price, brother. Take it or leave it. It includes the truck pickup on the other side. If you don't pay up, we turn back.'

'We don't have that much with us,' Dtui told him.

'Yeah, they all say that.'

'Is that so?' Phosy asked. He edged closer to the man. Dtui felt the boat rock perilously for a second or two, then heard Phosy's voice as a menacing whisper floating on the water.

'I'm sure you can feel what's pressed up against your neck,' he said. 'Either you take us across for the fee we agreed on in Savanaketh, or I slit your gullet from ear to ear. Do they all say this as well?'

'Yeah,' said the oarsman. 'Some of 'em say that.'

'And?'

'And I tell 'em it's twenty thousand.'

'Good.'

The oarsman's cousin looked undernourished and smelled of fish. He had a beaten-up pickup truck that crunched and putted its way from the river along a dirt track. He drove with the headlights off, somehow negotiating the narrow trail by the illumination provided by the dim cab light above his head. He tried to impose a petroleum surcharge but he didn't put a great deal of effort into it and wasn't too disappointed when Phosy told him to take a hike.

'Some of the rich ones just hand it over without a fuss,' he said. 'You can't blame me for asking.'

The driver eventually reached a paved road, swung left, and turned on his headlights. They didn't do a much better job of illuminating the road than the overhead light. They soon passed a signpost in Thai that said UBON RACHATHANEE EIGHTY-FIVE KILOMETRES. Most literate Lao could read Thai script. Phosy knew they wouldn't make it as far as Ubon. He wondered where the driver planned to let them off to make their own way to the city, and he didn't have to wait long for an answer. Three miles from the sign, a well-lighted border-patrol police hut loomed up ahead. Jutting into the road was a red sign that told vehicles to HALT TO CHECK but there was nobody around to force them to stop. They could have kept going, but the cousin slowed down.

'What the hell are you doing?' Phosy asked, reaching for the gear stick, but the truck was already coming to a stop.

'No problem, brother,' the cousin said. 'All's normal. Just have to stop here for a second.'

He rolled onto the gravel in front of the hut and beeped his horn. From the rear a man appeared, digging a toothpick between his gappy teeth. As he passed the hut he reached in and produced a fearsome-looking M16 assault rifle. He was followed by a second man, this one in uniform, who'd already shouldered his weapon. There was no urgency in their movements. It was just another night at work. They walked to the truck, levelled their guns at the passenger window, and motioned for the latest batch of refugees to get out.

'Come on, both of you,' one said. 'Don't try anything. You're under arrest. Come out with your hands in the air.'

It was a flat non-emotive rendition that Dtui guessed the man had given every night that week and for many months before. As she and Phosy were climbing out of the truck, the second guard went around to the driver's window and handed him a small brown envelope.

'Thanks, Dim,' he said. 'How's the wife?'

'Still a pain in the arse.'

Dtui could hear the laughter behind them as she and her 'husband' were marched at the end of a gun into a small unlit shed.

'Well, damn it, stop them then.'

'Can't! The telegram got here after they'd left already.'

'They're insane.'

Siri smiled and nodded his agreement. 'But didn't we do things like that when we were young and our balls still swung proudly before us? You have to admire them.'

'Do you admire a moth's courage at flying into a candle flame? God, Siri. I thought you liked them.'

'I do. And I'd be sorry to lose them. But they've set out so there's no point in grieving. We can't alter events, so we should take advantage of them. This way, we'll have our own spies in the camp.'

'If they aren't shot getting there. And if by some miracle they make it, how are you proposing to communicate with them?'

'They'll find a way.'

'You still see this as one big adventure, don't you?'

'The alternative being to get frustrated and angry and worry myself into a not-so-early grave?'

'The alternative being to take the situation seriously.'

'What's the difference?'

'The difference is quite fundamental. I'm in a position to affect the situation, so I take it seriously. You know you can't change anything so you treat it like a joke. I can't afford to do that.'

The vacuum that followed wasn't even a Lao silence. Sound had been erased from the room. Siri could feel the pulse throbbing in his wrists. He could feel the weight of his heart. So many thoughts and emotions rushed through his mind he couldn't begin to reckon with them.

'Look, I'm sorry,' Civilai said. 'I didn't …'

'Yes, you did.'

They sat staring at each other, both smiling, neither happy. Siri stood and squeezed his friend's shoulder on his way to the door. Fifteen minutes later he returned, carrying a tray. On it was a bottle of whisky, a bucket of ice, two small bottles of soda, a jug of water, and a packet of prawn crackers. He put the tray on the coffee table and sat back in his seat.

'You think I'm that easy?' Civilai said, his smile now sincere.

'It's never failed before. You've hardly touched a drop since we got here. It's obviously what you're lacking.'

Civilai took up the role of barman. 'I'm sorry about what I said, Comrade. It's just that I'm desperate. I'm not really me these days,' he said, making ice music inside the glasses.

'All the more reason to get pie-eyed.'

And pie-eyed they got. They'd had a frustrating time in the south, but both men understood there was little to be achieved by returning to Vientiane. The whisky went some way towards easing the tension that had been growing between them. It reminded them of what they'd been through together, but it didn't help bring Siri back into his friend's circle of trust.

Siri walked into the room carrying a tray. On it was a bottle of whisky, a bucket of ice, two small bottles of soda, a jug of water, and a packet of prawn crackers. He put the tray on the coffee table and sat back in his seat.

'I'm suffering déjà vu,' Civilai confessed.

'That first time was just an illusion,' Siri said. 'This is the real thing.'

'You do recall I'm supposed to be convalescing? I'm suffering from chronic haemorrhoids, you know.'

'Then I won't let you sit on my lap. Pour!'

Civilai prepared the first two drinks of the second act and the old soldiers sipped them as if they were tasting whisky for the first time.

'A good year,' Siri said.

'Nineteen seventy-seven, I'm tempted to say.'

'Know what I think, old brother?'

'Nobody ever knows what you think.'

'I think we should go take a look at the Champasak palace.'

'What, now?'

'No, I mean in daylight.'

'Whatever for? It's derelict.'

'It isn't derelict. Derelict is when something used to be functional but it gets old and falls apart.'

'Like us.'

'Exactly. The palace can't be referred to as derelict because it's not even finished yet.'

'And never shall be.'

'You can't be sure. Someday the country might be overrun by capitalists and they'll transform it into a five-star hotel.'

'The fat prince would turn over in his grave.'

'I don't think he's dead.'

'Then he'll turn over in his king-sized bed and crush three or four serving wenches.'

Siri put his finger to his lips.

'Shh. You do realize it's against the law to mention the fat prince in Pakse?'

'So it should be, the scumbag. You knew him, didn't you?'

' "Know"? What is "know"? I met him a few times. Our youth camp wasn't too far from his estate in Champa. He'd stop by from time to time and shake hands with the boys and squeeze the rumps of the girls. He'd do his Prince Charming routine.'

'Didn't he know what you lot were up to at the camp?'

'All he knew was the official itinerary: the skills training and the sports. He didn't have a clue we were getting the kids ready to oust his beloved French. He was le Grand Empereur down here in those days. He wouldn't have dreamed of an uprising among his underlings. When the Lao Issara won our independence he was shocked, but he made all the right noises. He said he was proud again of being Lao. Then, at the first opportunity, he was back in bed with the Froggies and driving all the patriots out of his kingdom. Next thing you know, the French decide he's the most suitable choice for prime minister and there he is running their colony for them. I think it was around then he designed for himself that big ugly birthday cake he called a palace.'

'Then why on earth would you want to go and see it?'

'To remind myself why we're here risking our lives for the republic. To see how his kind spent our money. To give myself a little shot of anticapitalist adrenaline. I don't want to go back to those days, old brother. Here, you're looking ponderous again. We can't have that. Have another drink.'

He re-iced Civilai's glass and splashed the cubes with whisky.

'And now,' Siri continued, 'there he is, living the life of Louis XV in a luxury bachelor pad in Paris, spending all the money he made from looting our treasures. He's even having my coffee-and-cognac breakfasts overlooking the Seine.'

'He'll never be happy there. He'll die bitter.'

'Are you serious? He's got everything.'

'That's not true, Siri. He doesn't have everything. In France he'll never get respect. His money won't make him a god on earth. He'll be the odd Asian chap living in the corner apartment. You know how it is there, how they looked down on us.'

'They just felt sorry for us because we weren't born white. I can sympathize with that.'

'Siri, they despised us. I went through the archives of the early French settlers here. They talked about "the disease of Laoness". They said that even French nationals who stayed here too long tended to become lethargic and lazy like the natives. They had grand plans to repopulate Laos with Vietnamese so they could get some work done. We weren't a people at all; we were a substandard slave colony. They disliked us because we didn't have the gumption to do their work for them and make them rich.

They talked of educating a few of the more affluent classes to act as foremen and minor project managers. I laughed when I read that, but then I realized they were referring to me. They were doing me the favour of educating me, so I could go back and control the lazy proletariat for them.'

Civilai was getting worked up. His voice carried along the timbered corridor and into the street. *Samlor* cyclists parked down at the hotel entrance were roused from their backseat slumber.

'In their reports they called us passive,' he continued, 'not given to uprising. Well, we showed them. We saw through their little scheme. Every part of the show – the token Lao managers, the scholarships, the mission schools, the plantations – was orchestrated to make us as poor as possible and them wealthy. God, I hated them for that.'

He slammed his drink down on the flimsy plywood coffee table and his glass cracked neatly into two parts: a napkin ring and a small petri dish. The whisky splashed in all directions. Blood oozed from his finger.

'Shit.' He looked at the mess and started to laugh. 'Is there a doctor in the hotel?'

'Whisky's an antiseptic,' Siri said. 'It'll fix itself.'

'Not if I bleed to death.'

Civilai clenched his fist and walked, laughing, to the bathroom. He emerged wrapping toilet tissue around a wound from which angry blood flowed eloquently. 'They called us the lotus-eaters,' he went on, even before reclaiming his seat. 'Did you know that? The lotus bloody eaters. When did you last eat lotus?'

'Hmm, let me think,' said Siri, observing the distorted

Nordic stag through his glass. 'It's been a while. However, I did have several dandelions for breakfast this morning.'

'Just how condescending could they be?' Civilai had arrived at a stage where Siri was irrelevant. 'Lotus-eaters! How would they feel if we called them snail-eaters?'

'I've called them worse than—'

'And there were the damned Royalists fighting with them against our people. How on earth could they?'

Civilai was sitting on the edge of the bed now. He had a wad of paper tissue the size of Singapore around his finger. He held the empty cardboard roll proudly in his uninjured hand. Siri was impressed by his friend's emergency first aid.

'Well, you have to admit,' Siri said, 'the Royal Lao Army weren't the most fearsome of foes.'

Civilai smiled. 'The president used to say the RLA rarely put fear in the heart of the enemy, but they frightened the living daylights out of their own commanders.'

The two old communists laughed at this lore as they had hundreds of times before. Siri had one of his own.

'I seem to remember,' he said, 'that their few pilots used to drop their bombs in the rivers, miles from the targets, so they wouldn't have to go near the anti-aircraft guns. There was always a bumper harvest of prefried fish for the locals.'

The mood lightened and laughter became more prevalent as they recalled their favourite RLA stories. Civilai drank his whisky from an old teacup until there was no more whisky to be had. There was no third act. This drunken political flashback had drained them both of memories and sense. Siri meandered to the door.

'I am for bed.'

'Don't forget to say your prayers.'

'Prayers? In a country with no religion and no money, it's hard to know what to pray for any more.'

There had been a fine, of course. Officially, any Thai government employee coming across illegal Lao immigrants on Thai soil was obliged to ship them off to one of the camps. But where was the profit in that? A healthy brokerage business had mushroomed along the border. It helped that the Thai junta of the month refused to recognize the people fleeing Laos as refugees. It called them 'temporary visitors' and, as such, they were expected to meet the legal immigration requirements. Those without visas (all of them) were subject to fines. If they could pay up, they were escorted to the camps. If they were too poor to pay, their names would be forwarded to a camp and posted on a board. Family and friends would then be expected to scratch around for enough money to cover the police fine. Those with neither money nor friends were of no use to anybody. They were invariably encouraged to escape police custody and find their own ways to the nearest camp.

Phosy and Dtui spent just one night in the police lock-up at Bok. They were able to pay for their release with a small gold bracelet Dtui carried with her. It looked a lot more valuable than it actually was. They were dispatched the following day to Ban Suan Lao, a sprawling refugee camp in the northern outskirts of Ubon. It was Dtui's first trip out of her own country and, despite the gravity of their mission, she looked out through the wooden slats of the open-air truck like a child on vacation. They passed directly through the centre of the city and, even though

Thailand was just a more affluent version of Laos, she marvelled at the exotic shop signs and the variety of goods on display. She looked at the busy traffic, the foreign cars, the nice clothes worn by the girls who walked along the paved footpaths. Food was for sale everywhere, the scents briefly catching a ride on the truck: frying chicken, freshly baked cakes, sliced fruit on handcarts, strawberry syrup on shaved ice. There was a different feel and pace about Thailand that she instantly fell in love with.

Phosy sat across from her and could see the wonder reflected in her eyes. She didn't seem to feel the danger of what they were doing. To her it was like some holiday trip. It was as if only he knew how much could go wrong, how many perils they faced. More and more he regretted her presence here, doubting his own ability to protect her. She was a distraction and he resented her for coming.

The truck arrived at an open gate manned by two unarmed military guards. It wasn't what Phosy and Dtui had expected. Their imaginations were full of Nazi prisoner-of-war camps from the movies. They'd expected high mesh fences topped with barbed wire, machine-gun turrets, and spotlights. Instead, people strolled in and out through the open gate, pushing carts and wheeling bicycles. The perimeter fence was made of bamboo: one huff and puff and it would have tumbled.

One guard signed the driver's clipboard chit and told the new arrivals to go and register at a large open hut a short walk along the driveway. There were twelve of them in this consignment: three couples with children, Dtui and Phosy without. They'd exchanged nods on the truck and asked a few fundamental questions, but none of them were prepared to share intimate details with strangers.

Suddenly everyone was suspicious. They walked in silence now along the paved road, anxious and apprehensive. They'd been separated from their world, from the devil they knew. Even Dtui and Phosy felt it, that sensation of reaching a point of no return, that the next document they signed would be a contract for their souls.

12

THE FIRST SNEAKY MALEVOLENT
SPIRIT ATTACK

As many counter-revolutionaries would have you know, when in the midst of diverting a national crisis, there's always a case for taking a little time off for tourism. So it was that Siri and Civilai, heads heavy from a serious whisky night, found themselves in possession of a sturdy black Willys jeep for the day. It belonged to the old postmaster. Daeng had somehow talked him into parting with it. Siri had somehow talked Civilai into joining him and assigned him the role of driver.

'I'm not at all sure we should be doing this,' Civilai said, 'given that—'

'Oh, shut up,' Siri shouted above the growl of the engine. 'What else would we be doing? Sitting around waiting for information to drop into our laps? We've got good people on our side doing all the legwork. What difference is one day going to make? Let's just think of ourselves as the command centre. You're the commander in chief and I'm the commander's travel agent, responsible for his psychological well-being.'

'Of course, I hadn't thought of it like that.'

Before reaching the end of the first street, they dropped into a pothole deep enough to bury a buffalo. Siri reached for his stomach. 'Damn it.'

Civilai stamped on the brake.

'You going to be sick?'

'Worse than that.' Siri reached for the hem of his shirt and caught the white amulet as it dropped to his lap. The platted hair that formed its string had always looked frayed, and finally it had snapped.

'This isn't going to cast us into eternal damnation, is it?' Civilai asked.

'Probably not,' Siri answered without any great conviction. 'I'll have to get it fixed, though.'

'Right. We'll just stop off at the nearest haunted-hair-replaiting centre.' Civilai crunched the gear, lurched a few times, and finally found a happy speed somewhere between walking and running with a stone in your shoe. Siri looked at the unmoving speedometer.

'At this rate the hair will have grown back naturally by the time we get anywhere.'

'More haste, less speed. Remember the hare.'

'I seem to recall the tortoise died of old age before he reached the finish line.'

In a city with so few cars, the green army jeep that tailed theirs was never likely to blend into traffic. The only way Civilai could fail to notice it was by being in a Willys with no rearview mirrors, which indeed he was.

They found the only hairdressing salon open before eight. The waxen-faced girl who ran it assured Siri she could reweave the plait but she'd have to make it shorter by some three inches. The hair string was wound and knotted tightly through the loop of the amulet, and Siri's instructions from the amulet maker had been that the hair and the pendant should never part company. Their blessings were intertwined. He had no choice therefore but to leave both at the shop. The girl told him it would be ready that evening and hesitantly suggested a price of two hundred *kip*. Siri gave her his most charming smile and told her if she did a good job, it would be worth even more.

Ten minutes later, the jeep pulled up into a bush in front of the Champasak palace. What little brake fluid there was had been used up at the hairdresser's and Civilai had adopted the tactic of finding something soft to crash into. They sat in their seats and gazed up at the gargantuan monstrosity that loomed over them: Prince Boun Oum's Disney castle. It was five storeys of would-be splendour: a central block with two ornately tiered wings. It was unpainted, unfurnished, and unlovely.

'It looks like something you could make with playing cards,' Civilai suggested.

'Let's hope it's sturdier than that.'

There was an enormous wooden double door at the top of the front steps, the type you'd expect to find a huge knocker hanging from, but it was unadorned, not so much as a keyhole. Perhaps that was why they were surprised to find it locked.

'Anybody home?' Civilai yelled. In fact, there was no glass in any of the three hundred windows, so if there had been anyone home they would already have heard the jeep chug up the driveway and smash into the bougainvillea. 'Nobody home,' he said. 'Let's go.'

'Let me try,' Siri said. He hammered on the door and shouted, 'We know you're in there. I'm Dr Siri from the Department of Justice and I have a warrant to search these premises.'

Civilai laughed. 'I hope you aren't planning to tell them to come out with their hands up. You don't really expe—?'

There was a subtle click from somewhere behind the huge door and one side creaked open. Standing there in the shadows was a couple, late middle-aged, dowdy, and stooped. Surprisingly, they were holding hands. Couples rarely held hands in Laos unless they were drunk. The man looked as if he'd just woken from several months of hibernation, during which time he hadn't eaten. His features seemed to be draped loosely on his face. The rest of him was built like a wire coat-hanger sculpture. The woman's skin was the colour of ash; her eyes no more than hyphens.

'Sorry,' she said, 'we were out the back.' She had a voice like someone with long fingernails sliding off a tin roof.

'You're the caretakers?' Civilai asked.

'Sort of,' she replied. The male simply glared at the two old men, grinding his teeth.

'We look after things,' she continued. 'When it was empty, a lot of the stuff … disappeared. All the tiles went, the balustrades. If we hadn't moved in when we did there'd probably be nothing left at all by now.' Siri wondered whether that would be such a bad thing.

'So you're the government then,' she said.

'Not all of it,' Civilai replied. 'We've just come to have a look around. Won't keep you long.'

They edged warily past the glaring man and found themselves in an empty vestibule. It was impressive that such a large edifice could make so little of space. It was a building site that didn't make any promises of better things to come. They walked up the wide staircase to the open-air second and third floors.

'They didn't get around to putting in rooms, I see,' Siri said.

The woman was at his shoulder, still holding on to the hand of her partner.

'The prin— I mean the original owner— wanted it like this, no rooms, just wide open spaces,' she said. 'Just five big areas like the palaces in Europe. It would have looked so beautiful if they … if production hadn't been halted.'

'Who pays you to look after it?' Siri asked. 'The local government?'

Her laugh scratched hell out of the tin roof. 'No, sir,' she said. 'They wouldn't care what happened here. We're volunteers. We have friends who put a few francs together to help us out.'

It was clear to Siri that supporters of the old regime were funding this preservation project. It wouldn't have surprised him if they expected the good old days to be restored and Prince Boun Oum himself to come riding back into town on his white elephant. Royalists were eternal optimists.

They'd reached the fourth floor, where wide terraces opened out to the elements on all four sides. At the rear, the Se Don River brushed the skirt of the building before joining the mighty Mekhong. In the distance were the Champasak plains and the slopes of the Bolaven Plateau.

'The view's grand, I'll give it that,' Civilai said, leaning on the balcony. Below them were grounds that would look spectacular with greenery, the makings of a tennis court, a huge water tower, and accommodations, presumably for the menial staff. 'Even the gardener's cottage is bigger than your house, Siri.'

'Everything's larger than life,' Siri said. 'A reflection of the man's ego.' He thought he'd spoken softly enough but the woman had bat's ears.

'He was a good man,' she snapped. 'A kind man.'

Siri wasn't about to get into a fight with Royalists. He fumbled around for a change of subject.

'Your husband doesn't have a lot to say, does he?'

'He doesn't have anything to say. He's dead.'

Siri and Civilai looked at one another. Even to a coroner, this was something of a revelation.

'He ...?'

'He's been dead for seven years. This here is my brother. He has problems.'

'Of course.' A second change of subject was in order. 'What's up there?'

He pointed to the top floor. The building had tapered to a single round room, the size of a small observatory.

'Nothing,' she said, too briskly to be true.

'We have to take a look anyway,' Civilai told her, and started up the exterior stairwell.

'It's locked,' she shouted after him, but he continued to climb. The first door he tried proved her wrong. He disappeared inside and Siri followed close behind. The two of them stared transfixed at the domed ceiling. It sported painted scenes from the Ramayana and jungles teeming with badly drawn, wooden wildlife. Around the margin an infinite procession of deformed elephants marched. Their mahouts were wearing hard hats and carrying sledgehammers.

'They did that,' the woman spat, following them in. 'Your people. Beautiful it was, country people riding their elephants to pay respect to the prince. Then your lot came in and painted on the helmets and the blue-collar uniforms. They said it was too bourgeois; it didn't represent the workers. What, may I ask, is bourgeois about a man riding an elephant? Ruined it, they did. Ruined it.'

They left the eerie round room, all but Siri. He found himself alone, following the procession of elephants with his eyes, incapable of turning away from them. He stood in the centre of the room rotating slowly at first, then faster and faster, the elephants and their proletariat jockeys galloping around the room. The pelmet above the windows took on a life of its own. It became a *naga* – an unholy serpent. It curled down from the wall as Siri spun and wound itself slowly about him. It curled around his neck and he could do nothing. Tighter and tighter it squeezed until he could no longer catch his breath. He pulled at the thick scaly skin of his attacker but had no effect on it. He choked and gasped for air that wouldn't come. He dropped to his knees and felt his skin pulling tight against his skull.

'What in hell's name?' Civilai had come back to collect his comrade. 'Siri?' He hurried to the centre of the room and took hold of the blue-faced doctor. Siri's hands were clawing at his neck.

'Get it off,' he wheezed.

'What?'

'The ...' Siri blinked and looked around him. His breath slowly returned to normal and the dizziness cleared. Once he was in control, he smiled and looked at his friend. 'The *naga*,' he said.

'You're seeing *naga*?'

'Yes, but it started with pink elephants.' He laughed and used Civilai to help himself to his feet.

'Brother, if I had hangovers like yours I wouldn't touch another drop. That I promise you. Are you all right?'

'Fine. Just feeling a bit peculiar. It's this room.'

'I know. I felt it, too.'

'You did?'

'Bad paintings always make me nauseous.'

'They are awful, aren't they?'

Siri let it go at that and led Civilai to believe he'd had an attack of vertigo from the five-storey climb. But he knew the feeling only too well. The *Phibob* had cornered him without his talisman and, if he'd been alone, they might very well have suffocated him. They had the ability to bluff him to death. He was exposed. His evening hairdresser's appointment couldn't come too soon.

'They took away my livelihood, just like that,' Phosy said.

He was sitting cross-legged in a circle of ten men. It was a common enough sight, old hands at the camp latching on to the newcomers, getting the latest gossip from back home. They drank Thai rum from mismatched glasses and waited for their food.

Dtui, being a woman and a wife, was with the other wives at the back of the meeting shelter cooking the food. The women drank, too, but their conversation was about babies and hair and the cost of washing powder, and then more babies.

'So, Dtui, you and Phosy haven't managed to get around to it?'

'No,' she said. 'You know how it is. Phosy always said he wanted us to be secure, know what I mean? Be sure our kids could go to school and get a decent education.'

'Right,' said one woman whose skin was like tree bark. She had a cheroot hanging out of her mouth and the ash dropped onto the cabbage she was deleafing. It wasn't easy to catch her words. 'And you believe that shit?'

'What do you mean?' Dtui said. She wiped the onion tears from her eyes.

'Are you sure he's not just using that as an excuse is what I mean. An excuse not to have kids.'

'Why would he?'

'Easier to run away from a woman that's by herself than from one with a couple of babes in arms.'

'Leave her alone, Keo,' said a pretty chicken chopper.

But Dtui was on the defensive. 'My Phosy's a good man,' she said. 'A decent man ...'

'He wouldn't ever leave me,' Keo said, aping Dtui. This drew laughter from the other members of the lunch detail. 'Right. I've heard that one before.'

'You don't know him,' Dtui said, indignant now. 'He's not like other men.'

The sound of women's laughter interrupted the man talk and caused a few smiles in the front room.

'They're never happier than when they're together cooking,' opined the senior section representative, Bunteuk. He was a good deal younger than Phosy. But America's President Carter's recent attack of guilty benevolence had led to the making of an agreement to accept a large number of displaced Lao, his former allies, into the United States. This had emptied the camps of many of their longer-term residents and forced younger men into positions of responsibility. Bunteuk had moved up several notches and was now expected to share his wisdom. Phosy smiled at the thought of Dtui in the kitchen discussing vegetables. She'd help serve the men soon, then retire to the back room to wash the dishes.

That'll teach her, he thought.

The camp was a lively place. Thai vendors plied their wares in an attempt to relieve the refugees of the last of their savings or the few dollars they earned by working part-time for the aid agencies. Bored Lao with nothing else to do strolled here and there, chatting, staring, puffing out their cheeks. The International Refugee Committee sanitation trucks kicked up the dust and panicked chickens. Ubon residents with children at their sides wandered up and down the regimented lanes of wooden shacks whispering warnings. 'These people are from Laos, darling. This is what communism does to you. Never forget it.'

Westerners with lists and large sweat stains under their armpits hurried somewhere, always flustered and muttering. The churches and the nongovernment organizations had coordinated their efforts to some extent and created a semblance of order in the Ubon camp. The latrines were sanitary for most of the year, there was always plenty of rice, and a hierarchy of order – from camp liaison officers down to area and street representatives – kept lawlessness to a minimum.

Money arrived from time to time from relatives who'd already made it to Australia or Europe or the United States, where they were working three shifts cleaning offices or scrubbing grease from Italian casserole dishes through the night to earn enough to restart their lives. For some camp dwellers this pocket money meant a splash of luxury: a bottle of whisky every now and then, an ice cream for the kids, an incentive to the evening guards to allow a visit to the nightspots of Ubon. There were certainly worse places than this old US Army weapons dump in which to be displaced. But even though you could get used to being there, you could never belong. And it was belonging that the refugees at the Ubon camp desperately craved.

Phosy stretched out his well-fed body in front of the open-air meeting shelter of Section 36. He liked his neighbours.

The men had warmed to him. The most difficult part – settling in, being accepted – had been taken care of on this, the first day. All he needed now was to keep his ear to the ground and discover how he might get an introduction to the inner core. He already had an idea. He sidled over to Bunteuk and stood beside him, looking up at the ripe clouds.

'More rain?' he asked.

'Looks like it,' said Bunteuk. 'You'll hate it when the rainy season sets in proper. This place turns into chocolate mousse, mud up to your knees. All your bedding turns to mildew.'

'You sound like you've been here a while.'

'Eighteen months next week.'

'You don't say? How come you didn't get on the bus with the last batch of refugees to the US? I hear they took most of the old-timers.'

'Yeah, they did. Not that easy, though. They did offer us a place but we have to get things settled over there: jobs, community, place to stay. You see, we haven't got family in America to take us in. I've heard of new arrivals starving to death on the street, getting killed by gangs – horrible stuff. I don't want that for my children. I'm waiting for a placement to Australia. It should come this year. I know people there; it's safer.'

'I see. Can't say I blame you.'

'Anyway, welcome, Phosy. It's nice to have you in our section.'

'Thanks for lunch.'

'No problem.'

They shook hands and Phosy watched him walk away. A confident gait; tall, muscular frame: a soldier. A soldier who'd refused the opportunity to get himself and his family out of Thailand and on a plane to freedom. A soldier who wanted to stay close to his homeland.

It was a long drive to Khong on a dirt road apparently engineered by rodents. It was a disaster fittingly numbered Route 13. The drizzle of the previous night had made it slick, so much of the journey was spent travelling sideways. Fortunately, it didn't have much in the way of hills, so the missing brakes were only an issue on the ferry crossing to Wat Phu. The ferry pilot had apparently lost a few vehicles in the past, so he had two blocks of four-by-four ready to chuck under the front wheels just before the Willys vanished off the end and into the muddy water. Siri and Civilai shook his hand with relief.

It was lunchtime when the old black jeep rolled into Khong, where the name of the Mekhong River had originated. The Mother – the '*Me*' of Khong – dwarfed the little town. It rolled past triumphantly, making its last stand as a watercourse before being shredded by the four thousand islands of Sri Pun Don. From there, twisted and confused, it was sent tumbling over the Khone Falls. Not even the intrepid French explorers had found a way to blast the river through an obstacle course such as that.

So here it was, the end of the shipping route. It had once been an impressive city where cargo boats would unload and transfer their wares onto elephants or donkeys to continue down to Cambodia. The colonists had even gone to the trouble of building a short railway line to bypass the falls. But there was little evidence of development now. The train lines lay rusted and overgrown. Modern-day Khong was a huddle of wooden shacks, of fishermen and boat pilots and the odd depressed shopkeeper. Civilai found a good stack of bamboo fish traps in which to park.

'Do we really need to stop here?' he asked. 'I thought we were heading for the falls. Don't forget I have to drive this thing back.'

'I could drive if you want a rest,' Siri said, showing remarkable patience at his friend's constant grumbling.

'You can't be serious. I've seen how much damage you can cause with two wheels. I dread to think what devastation you could create with two more.'

'It doesn't work like that. Cars are safer. You can be lizard-faced drunk in a car and still not fall over.'

'I rest my case. So, remind me. We're here because …?'

'Because we're just briefly going to find out where they fished young Sing out of the river.'

'I knew you had another motive. I should never have believed all that Southern Lao historical heritage bull. I thought we were just here to see the ancient Khmer ruins and the mud-covered capital of the old kingdom, and all the time there you were rushing me through my sightseeing so you could come and show off your do-goodism.'

'Come on. You enjoyed it.'

'I would have, under other circumstances.' He killed the engine and climbed down from the jeep. 'Come on, let's get this over with.'

They found the man who'd recovered the body. As was often the case, pulling a drowning victim from his nets had plunged the fisherman into a deep depression. It was a curse that could only be lifted by several days of shouting at one's children and being unreasonable to one's wife. Mr Keuk was into the fourth day of his penance. His chocolate leather skin was baggy from inactivity. For some reason, he took a visit by two old men from Vientiane as a good omen. He rose from his bamboo litter for the first time since his gory discovery and sat at the back of the jeep all the way to his allotment.

It was a simple setup. The deep nylon nets were strung from bamboo posts sunk into the riverbed. The principle was that the fish would come hurtling towards the net and score themselves like soccer goals. They'd be too trauma-tized to swim against the current to get free and would tangle themselves in the netting. With so many traps dotted around the islands, a fish would have to have the luck of the Lord Buddha himself to make it through.

Keuk took them to the net that had trapped the body of Sing. It still hung wrapped around the post and split, not catching a thing. Siri, Civilai, and Keuk squatted on the bank, looking at it.

'You come to collect the fish every evening?' Siri asked.

'Used to,' Keuk answered with a long face.

'And on that particular evening, you found the body tangled in your net?'

'That's right.'

'What state was it in?'

'You want me to describe it?'

'Yes, please.'

Keuk slowly and deliberately described the body exactly as Siri had seen it in the house in Pakse.

'Where's this line of inquiry leading?' Civilai asked.

'I've just lost another theory. I wondered if the splinters came from the back of the truck they shipped him home in. It appears they didn't. I can't figure it out.' He looked at Keuk. 'Has this ever happened to you before?'

'Not to me personal. It's not uncommon, though. The

old-timers tell me there was times when there was more bodies than fish. Like when the French was getting their own back on the Lao Issara. They say they fished a mountain of patriots out then.' Siri and Civilai looked at each other. 'But not recent, no. I did have a catfish once – it broke the net – and a *pa kha*.'

'You don't say.'

Something sparked in Siri's mind. *Pa kha* was the Lao name for the river dolphins that once played in the Mekhong from China all the way to the delta. There were well-worn tales of *pa kha* saving the lives of drowning boatmen and guiding longboats through rapids. But overfishing and pollution had since wiped out the dolphins from most of their old habitats. The myth that killing the *pa kha* would bring catastrophe to a family had never been as strong as a villager's need to feed his children. She had become a menu item, the *pa kha*: the mermaid of the Mekhong.

'What did you do with the dolphin?' Siri asked.

'Rescued her, of course,' Keuk said. 'You could bring a curse on the whole town if you let one die. There's them don't believe it no more, but I do. I took her downriver to the depths beyond the islands. That's where they like to be. It's safe there.'

'Before the falls?'

'Want to see?'

13

MERMAID RODEO

The path down to the river had been too narrow to drive so, ever grumbling, Civilai had parked in a patch of tall lemon grass and the three men made their way to the river-bank. It was quite a trek and they stirred up nests of hungry insects on the way. At one point they disturbed a small flock of black-hooded river terns.

'Them's *sida* birds,' said Keuk. 'They go where the dolphins go. The *pa kha* are here for certain.'

Finally, they reached the broad, slow-moving expanse of river at the end of the trail. The sight was oddly cathartic to the old doctor. He seemed to recognize it from a different life. It was one of the Mekhong's few secret places. It made him feel slightly stoned: a few-good-puffs-of-ganja buzz.

'So,' said Civilai, sitting on a smooth rock, watching the hornets hover above the silver-grey surface of the river. 'We're here to visit the river dolphins?'

'Yes.'

'And that's going to help you solve the mystery of the young boy's death?'

'No. Yes. Look, I don't know, all right? Don't ask me things like that. I had a dream.'

'Oh, marvellous. You can't dream up how to save the

country but you can make a few fishermen feel a little better about their clumsy son.'

Siri looked at Civilai in surprise. 'That wasn't very nice.'

'I know.' He sighed and looked to the heavens. 'I'm just feeling … all these detours are making me a bit irritable. Oh, Siri.' That was the moment Siri understood. Several heavy realities fell on him one after the other like thick leather-covered tomes from a shelf. He could tell from his friend's expression that he was more lost than Siri could ever have imagined. The world he'd built was, like the palace, being taken apart by looters, and there was nothing he could do about it. Siri knew this diversion was doing him more harm than good.

He went to sit beside Civilai. 'Brother, I'm sorry,' he said.

'Now what have you done?' Civilai didn't look up. His watery eyes stared at his hands. Siri had never seen him looking so old.

'Sirs!' Keuk was standing beneath a hairy mistletoe tree, his arm extended toward the river, his eyes as round as Indian roti.

The grey-green sheen of some large creature had become visible just above the surface of the river at the far bank and was moving now directly to where the old men sat. The dolphin's head emerged not far from their feet. Its mouth was curved into a smile. It looked up and blew a spout of water from its long pointed snout that hit Civilai square in the chest. The politburo man looked with amazement, first at the animal, then at Siri, and burst into laughter. Siri joined in. The *pa kha*, sensing a receptive audience, belly flopped back and forth in front of them. Siri put his arm around his friend's shoulder and enjoyed the show.

'I've never seen nothing like that,' Keuk said, stepping

out from the shade of his tree. 'That's something. That's really something.'

'You know what?' Siri said. 'I think she wants us to join her.' He walked to the water, kicked off his sandals, and rolled up the legs of his trousers. The clay bank dropped suddenly downwards and he sat on its edge with his feet dangling in the passing Mekhong.

'You won't forget you can't swim, will you, Siri?' Civilai shouted.

The *pa kha* came immediately to the bank and rubbed herself against Siri's knees. Then she floated on her back in front of him, looking expectantly.

'I've never in all my days ...' said Keuk.

Siri threw caution to the current and leaned over to stroke the dolphin's belly. It was like running a hand over a large wet pickle, but not altogether unpleasant. The dolphin tossed back her head, meowed, and rolled onto her front.

'I think she likes me,' Siri said with a big smile on his face. Hooking one arm over the animal's back, he slid slowly into the water.

'Siri?' Civilai shouted and walked hurriedly down to the bank, where his friend lay embracing a large waterborne mammal. 'You do understand what you're doing, don't you?'

Siri looked up at Civilai and his smile turned to astonishment as the dolphin set off into the river with him on her back.

'Siri!' Civilai was more anxious now. 'Remember the Sirens. Get back here. Your life is in the hands of a fish.'

Siri gave an uneasy smile in response. He was almost at the deepest point of the river. 'It's all right, old brother. I've never felt safer in my life. This is—'

And at that moment the dolphin dived, taking Siri down

into the water with her. So swift was their descent that within a second or two, the surface of the Mekhong had erased all evidence that the national coroner and his mount had ever existed.

The rain beat so heavily on the tin roof of their single-room home that Phosy and Dtui had given up trying to speak. Odd scents tangled together in the pitch-blackness and made Dtui's head swim: the musty chemical smell of the creosoted plank walls, the bitterness of the banana-leaf matting that covered the raised-earth floor, the wholesome rain, and the sweet smoke of the mosquito coil. She lay, fully dressed, atop the inch-thick foam mattress. The hammering rain made her shudder but her side of the one double blanket remained beneath her. Although she was temporarily blinded and deafened by Mother Nature, she knew that Phosy lay covered in that same blanket just six inches from her side. Like most men, he wore only a gingham sleeping cloth knotted at his waist.

They couldn't have slept separately. There were no locks on the doors and windows, and the cracks between the wooden slats were wide enough to poke a finger through. They were a married couple. They had to fit in, play their parts. She'd done well enough, convincing the other women she was just one more faithful wife following her older husband to a new life. She'd even made Phosy believe she was strong and courageous. Made him think she didn't need his protection, she could do just fine without him. But on their first night alone in a camp on foreign soil, all her doubts found their way to her stomach. She wasn't trembling from the cold.

There were many reasons she'd been unable to escape

into sleep that night. She was hopelessly awake and alert. The timpani on the roof contributed, the strangeness of the camp, the potential dangers. But even if these factors could be wished away by a well-placed prayer, she knew she'd still hear the morning cockerel with her eyelids wide open. She felt a tenseness she'd never be able to explain to anyone, a tenseness that only a twenty-five-year-old woman who had never spent the night in bed beside a man can feel.

14

SIRI GOES TO HEAVEN

The same range of clouds that was currently drenching the camp in Ubon was undecided as to how seriously it should rain on Khong across the border in Laos. It had dropped one serious deluge, then dribbled embarrassingly for several hours. The black jeep had benefited from the wash. Its daytime coat of red earth lay in ruddy puddles around its tyres. It stood sleek and proud beneath Khong's only street-light, but its confident look was all bluff. The old American war wagon had carried its last general, fled its last conflict. A lack of oil, an overheated piston, a small imploding crunch, and suddenly one of man's most brilliant inventions, the internal combustion engine, was no more than four hundred pounds of solid scrap metal.

If 'lucky' was a fitting word to describe their plight, they had been lucky. It could have happened in a more isolated spot far from help. But Civilai had just dropped the enlightened fisherman at his shack and the jeep was passing through the centre of Khong on its return journey to Pakse when everything seized up. Fortunately, the town had a guesthouse, and, as luck would have it, that guesthouse was a short wrench toss from the dead jeep.

Siri hadn't suffered at all from his brief dip beneath the surface of the Mekhong. He'd had the good sense to hold his breath and not let go of his hostess. He had a feeling she'd soon have him back breathing oxygen. But during his five-second dousing, Siri had been afforded a vision – or, more accurately, a sensation. Just for a moment, he'd been young Sing – cold, shuddering, and alone. It was night-time and above his head hung a huge circle of light as if a UFO were hovering over him. That was all. This told Siri that the boy's soul had continued down the river and come to rest in the *pa kha*. To the fisherman, Keuk, this was tremendous news. Now he could be civil to his family and return to the drudgery of catching fish. But it didn't get Siri any closer to solving the riddle of the boy's death.

They lay side by side now, Siri and Civilai, under a huge tent of mosquito netting in the guesthouse bedroom. It wasn't the most lavish of accommodations. There was a coffee shop and small reception area downstairs and one bedroom above. Luckily, it had been unoccupied. Civilai's mood had sunk to new depths since the demise of the jeep. It was the final straw. He had gone to bed at seven, refusing food, drink, and conversation. Siri had walked around in the mud for an hour, enjoyed a slow delicious fish supper, and finally retired at nine thirty. He knew his friend was only pretending to sleep when he climbed onto the creaking bed, but something told him he was better off joining the charade.

Guilt kept him awake: the feeling that this away-day had been more than an excuse to relax. Perhaps it was an escape. It had entered his head as he stood looking at the somnambulant Mekhong that perhaps, just perhaps, he'd lost the will to fight. What if the rebellious young man had slowly deteriorated into a cantankerous old coot with nothing to offer but complaints and sarcasm? He wondered if the lime had been too long on the tree. With so many negative thoughts going through his head, he should have avoided sleep. He should have known that the dream world might be hostile if one entered it with a self-inflicted inferiority wound. But he was powerless to avoid the drop.

He was walking in a beautiful place. Everywhere were crystals of ice, like blossoms frozen in a mystic frost. Beneath his bare feet was a thick carpet of snow. A Nordic elk stood on the horizon watching him. Siri wore only his old Thai boxing shorts and he could see the few white hairs on his chest were frozen stiff, but he felt no bite from the cold. He was invincible, a warrior of Laos braving the extremes of Scandinavia with no ill effects.

He crunched onwards through the snow until he reached the edge of a vast lake of cotton wool cloud. He recognized the picture. He'd seen it before in temple scrolls. Although he was surprised to find it in northern Europe, this was Nirvana. Across the clouds he could see the green and gold roof – the sun glinting off the glass ornaments. It was a place where all his suffering would end – where the inexplicable would become clear. This was the peace he craved.

He stepped gingerly onto the cloud. It looked as if it might cave in like meringue but it took his weight. Another step and his confidence grew. Just a short walk across to ...

The clouds parted and he dropped like a stone into water. His consciousness altered. He could feel the cold now, feel the water against his face, but could see nothing. He gasped and suddenly his lungs filled with liquid. It was too uncomfortable to be fantasy. He gagged and took in another bitter mouthful. Panic. He thrashed his arms and legs, wanting to expel the water inside him, but knowing it was impossible.

Knowing he would instinctively take another breath and that would be his last.

He'd reached the bottom now. His feet plunged into soft, warm mud. If this were to be his last moment, he decided he would go in peace, enjoy the feel of the clay oozing between his toes. His last thought should be one of pleasure. His watery chest felt heavy, and, as his eyes began to close, as he gave in to his fate, a grey shape loomed before him in the murky water. He thought he felt a probing hand against his face, imagined he saw eyes glaring into his. There was a grab at his wrist, a yank, and then everything stopped.

When Siri was finally restarted, he found himself spewing out river water and coughing up phlegm. He felt strong hands on his chest and looked up to see the smiling face of the tight-skinned military man.

Stuck for a funny line, Siri resorted to the predictable. 'What happened?'

'You walked into the river, sir,' said his saviour.

Siri heaved again and produced bile but very little water. 'Why did I do that?' he asked.

'I thought perhaps you might know that yourself, sir.' The soldier had a hold of Siri's wrist and was looking at his watch. 'But it looked like you were sleepwalking.'

'You didn't just happen to be here in Khong waiting for a suicide attempt, did you?'

'No, sir. I followed you here.'

Siri worked himself onto his side and coughed several times. His chest felt like the engine of their jeep. 'Under whose instructions?'

'Comrade Phosy, sir.'

'You're one of his men?'

'Used to be, when we were in the north-east. I'm based in Vientiane these days. The colonel and I have been through a lot together. We help each other out. He asked me to keep an eye out for each of you.'

'Well I ...' Siri vomited violently and the soldier wrapped his jacket around the doctor's shoulders. 'I can't say I'm disappointed. Presumably you didn't follow us here on foot, my friend.'

'I have a jeep, sir.'

'Then I think I need to ask for one more favour.'

'I'm at your disposal.'

'This little adventure's made me a prime candidate for pneumonia. My lungs aren't at their best any more as it is. I need to get to the hospital in Pakse as soon as possible.'

'Should I wake up Comrade Civilai?'

'Yes, but be careful. You might want to wear a helmet.'

Dtui was at the watering tank filling her buckets. In her head she was calculating how many bucket trips she would have to take to lose twenty pounds. There was a formula to calculate weight loss in one of her books, but it had gone completely from her mind. She'd been through all the medical texts, English and Russian, and memorized great chunks of them. She read through them every night so the facts would stick before her trip to Moscow in the new year. And here she was, just a few days away from her studies, and she'd lost a formula she'd taken a personal interest in: calories burned per second, over body weight, times ... What on earth was it? If she couldn't remember this, what hope did all the unimportant facts have?

Her thoughts were interrupted by a voice from behind her. 'Leave some for me, sister.' And then a giggle.

It was no coincidence. Dtui had watched the pretty young wife of section representative Bunteuk and studied her habits. Dtui knew this was the time she collected her water. They fell into a shallow line of chatter and laughed a lot, with Dtui being especially careful not to say anything too intelligent. They delivered their water to their respective house tanks and regrouped at the corner stall for coffee. Coffee chats were a habit they'd picked up from their husbands, and, after a few tentative sips, they both admitted they secretly hated the taste of the stuff. They poured their coffees onto the street mud and ordered warm red soda, Dtui's treat.

They had half an hour to spare before they were expected to prepare lunch. Dtui couldn't bring up the topic that was burning in her mind unless it occurred naturally in the conversation. But no end of steering brought them around to it. With only five minutes to go before the resumption of women's work, Dtui was certain she'd missed her chance. Then the girl said, 'My sister wrote that every home over there has an oven. Even the slums.'

'Over where?'

'America.'

Dtui held on to her deadpan expression. The woman's husband had told Phosy they had no relatives in the US. She knew she was on the right track. 'Well, that's good. You'll be going soon, won't you?'

'I don't think so.'

'Why not?'

Her tablemate looked at the water dripping from the corrugated roof. 'It's just ... it just isn't convenient.'

'Ha. You don't have to tell me about "not convenient". I've got brothers in Australia and I'm not even allowed to tell the Australian Aid people I have connections there.'

'Not allowed? Who by?'

'By ... no, it doesn't matter.'

'Come on.'

'No, really. I've said too much already.'

'Your husband doesn't want to leave the camp, does he?'

'I promised him I wouldn't say anything. Damn my big mouth.'

'It's all right. You can tell me. I understand.'

A tear came to Dtui's eye. 'Just promise me you won't spread it around. My life wouldn't be worth living, really.'

'I know exactly what you're going through.'

'I doubt that.' She looked around at two old men who cowered over their coffees like undertakers. She lowered her voice. 'Because if you did, you'd know what torture it is to be married to a man so single-minded. Phosy's fixated on getting the Pathet Lao out of power. He'd do anything. When he was with the RLA, he—'

'I thought he was a carpenter?'

'Oh, shit. My mouth.' Dtui really seemed to be crying now. 'He'll kill me, I swear he will.'

'Dtui!'

'I just wanted to get out of here, go to Australia. Find some peace.' The girl took Dtui's hand and smiled for her to continue. Dtui spoke in a barely audible whisper interspersed with sobs. 'Phosy was with the Central Command. He trained under General Ouan. He was one of the undercover agents on special duty around the central region.'

'Why didn't he just tell everyone when he got here?'

'Are you kidding? He knows for certain there are over a hundred PL sympathizers spying here at this camp. How could he be certain who to trust? He's waiting to catch sight of one of his old RLA mates, someone he knows. But most of his senior commanders and colleagues are overseas already. He's getting desperate, but I have to give him credit, he's a patient man, is my Phosy. He'll wait months if he has to until he's sure who to confide in.'

'What about you?'

'Me? Of course I'd prefer to be in my own country under a safe RLA government than off catching lunch with a boomerang. But until that can happen, I'd sooner be sitting it out in a suburb of Sydney than stuck here. But not Phosy, he's driven. He can't settle until he wipes out every one of the bastard Reds with his own hands.'

Dtui's friend suddenly remembered the time and rushed off, but not before swearing on the soul of her grandmother that she wouldn't divulge a word of what she'd just heard. As soon as she'd run off to shuck her peas, Dtui smiled to herself. She knew Granny was doomed to eternal damnation.

15

THE INSURGENT VOLLEYBALL CLUB

Siri sat, wheezing, on the balcony of the Pakse hospital. He was whiter than anything else in the town but he was headed for recovery. Dr Somdy, his allocated physician, was evidently the region's authority on near drownings. She told him she'd pumped so many fishermen back to life and earned so many fish in lieu of payment, she'd started to check the mirror every morning for gills.

She was an eight-shaped middle-aged lady with a Chinese face. She'd been hired initially by the French and had stuck with Pakse hospital through all the conflicts. She'd avoided communist re-education only by being indispensable. At the end of her shift she sat drinking tea with Siri on the balcony. They watched two policemen corner a boy of about sixteen on the street below. One of the officers grabbed the youth by the arm while the other produced a pair of scissors and proceeded to give him a haircut. It wasn't a particularly professional cut – he looked more scalped than groomed – but they didn't charge him for it.

'Do they do make-up and give fashion advice as well?' Siri asked, straight-faced.

Somdy laughed. 'Isn't it this silly in Vientiane yet?'

'I haven't seen them actually resort to hairdressing,' he said. 'They've issued a number of edicts: no long hair on boys, no short hair on girls, no holding hands, no female trouser wearing, all that kind of thing. And I think they're all still paranoid enough up north to do what they're told. I can't recall seeing the authorities do anything about miscreants, though. That was quite impressive.'

'You know television watching is illegal here, don't you?'

'How can they stop it? Go door to door with big-eared dogs listening for Thai soap commercials?'

'They don't need to, Doctor. At five every evening they bring down the antenna.'

'Bring it down?'

'Literally. Ten men with ropes lower the reception tower to the ground. In the morning they hoist it back up. It's the only way they can be sure the locals aren't feasting on Thai entertainment. Pakse's a crucible for every silly rule the people in Vientiane come up with. I think it's punishment for Champasak being a renegade province for so long. The effects are so concentrated because the administrators only actually control a twenty-mile circle around the city. They over-regulate everything in town as compensation because they can't regulate anything at all outside.'

'You do realize you shouldn't be talking like this to one of the elders of the Red Revolution?'

'Oh, Siri.' She smiled and put her hand on his arm. 'You think it's every bit as ridiculous as I do. I know you too well. You have no idea who I am, do you?'

He looked more closely at her broad, content face, but nothing registered.

'No.'

'I was one of your kids, Dr Siri, at the camp. I did the basic medic training with you and your wife. I sat in your tent at night and swelled with pride listening to you tell us of the great things my countrymen had done. I was there on the parade ground punching my fist into the air, swearing allegiance to the Lao Issara and destruction to the French. You were my idol. I became a doctor because of you.'

She saw tears forming in the old man's eyes. She squeezed his hand.

'Dr Siri, I know deep in my heart that everything you've ever done and whatever you believe today is for our benefit: me, my husband, my children. You don't see any more sense in these petty regulations than I do. This isn't the system you fought for. I know you'd never compromise your ideals. You taught us to say what we believed without fear and fight for the right to do so. When they wheeled you in this morning, all that pride came flooding back to me. I felt like a disciple at the feet of Jesus.'

'Somdy,' said Siri with a smile on his face, wiping away the tears with his hand, 'I don't think Christian symbolism really applies in this situation, particularly as I failed to walk on water. Did you find God after I left?'

'I found lots of them, uncle. If you want to survive here, you believe in them all. A little bit of Catholic aid here, a little bit of Zen medical assistance there. After a while you learn how to convert to all of them to keep your patients alive. In a way that's what you're doing with politics. Am I right?'

'Nice to see some of my cynicism rubbed off on you, too. Just be careful. The big Reds in Vientiane don't take kindly to religious zealots. But thank you. I can't pretend this little chat hasn't done me as much good as your medical care.'

When she left to sleep off her busy night, he sat alone on the balcony, fingering the newly plaited talisman around his neck. Phosy's friend, Kumpai, the soldier, had gone to collect it from the hairdresser that morning. Siri couldn't risk being exposed to the wiles of the malevolent ghosts for any longer than was necessary. They'd almost finished him last night, almost dispatched him and his resident shaman spirit to a watery grave. They were becoming more malignant, and Siri wondered how long it would be before he needed to upgrade his stone amulet to a more powerful model.

He watched the schoolchildren sliding in the street mud, turning their white shirts dark red like the naughty before and after kids in Thai Fab detergent commercials. He wondered how long it would be before they lost their happy innocence. Who would the role models in their lives be? And he thought about what Somdy had said: 'I know you'd never compromise your ideals.'

He wondered what his ideals were exactly. He wondered if he could define his moral stand or his beliefs any more, wondered how many times he had in fact compromised for selfish reasons since those idealistic days at the youth camp. One time sprang to mind: Tuyen Quang.

It was the conference of aligned Lao resistance groups in Vietnam. The day he'd sold out. The day they'd all sold out. It was supposed to have been a great event, the gathering of all the disparate Lao Issara units who'd fought to the last bullet in their resistance against the French invaders. Old warriors were reunited and cooling embers of rebellion were stoked once more. These were survivors – hunting rifles against howitzers and armoured vehicles – and somehow they'd stayed alive. There were enough of them left for a rousing party on the eve of the conference. Good food, free-flowing drink, soft beds, and rekindled dreams of a free Lao homeland.

In the morning the mood had been high and hearty, even though only the senior Lao Issara officers had been invited to the opening ceremony. Siri, a major general in the Free Lao Medical Corps, was seated four rows from the rear. His generals and senior advisers sat in the row in front of him. On the raised platform far in front, only the Red Prince, the renegade royal once of the Lao Issara, was familiar to them. The other men at the table sat stony-faced and anonymous. The veteran at Siri's side had turned to him and asked, 'Who are the spooks up on the stage?'

Siri had shaken his head. He had no idea. 'Vietminh? Senior Vietnamese?'

But it turned out the men at the raised table were Lao. Civilai was one of them. It was they who'd organized the conference. They called themselves the Lao Patriotic Front, and to the assembled fighters they announced the launch of the Lao Resistance Government. Siri and his colleagues were still pumped up with the adrenaline of the previous evening. They cheered and looked forward to the vote that would piece together a united command of true patriots. This was to be a great day for their country.

But there was no vote. The men on the platform explained that with Vietminh financial aid and expertise, a strong Lao resistance had been trained in the north of Vietnam. Through cooperation between their two great countries, the Gallic invaders would be driven from the borders of Indochina. They read the names of the men who would form the central committee of this great alliance and there was not one Lao Issara name on the list. Not one. *Not one*. Siri had been speechless for one of the few times in his life. He'd looked along the ranks of Lao Issara to see mouths open on either side of him. The Lao resistance that had been fighting and lobbying unaided for nine years had been hijacked.

That was it. That was the moment when all the Free Lao men and women at the meeting should have jumped to their feet and heckled and remonstrated. There should have been a commotion that left the strangers on the platform no choice but to hear their complaints. But that was neither the Buddhist nor the communist way. The Lao Issara had brooded quietly, perched at the rear of the hall, and meditated. 'Was it such a bad thing, this powerful alliance? Perhaps we don't deserve a leading role. We've struggled and failed for so many years. Perhaps this is our destiny.'

So that was how Buddhist fatalism had allowed the powdery Lao Issara to dissolve. The bond had been formed that would eventually lead both countries to socialism, the end proving the means to be justified. Those Free Lao who didn't abandon the fight and flee to Thailand were absorbed into the giant guerrilla war force. Siri, with a different uniform beneath his white coat, worked on his Vietnamese language and his wife gladly indulged her passion for communism.

'They pumped all the fish out of you yet?' Siri was snapped out of his reminiscences by the voice of his best friend. 'You look soulful.'

'Good timing. I was just thinking about the old days.'

'All our days are old days. I've heard living in the past is a sign that you don't have long to live.' Civilai sat in the chair vacated by Dr Somdy.

'Well, it's nice to see you're back to your old cheery self. What's put you in such a good mood?'

'We're getting news from the front line.'

'What do we know?'

'Your men Phosy and Dtui have reached the camp in one piece. They're safe. I have someone keeping an eye on them.'

'You didn't tell me you had a contact in Ubon.'

'I just found an old ally at the camp. I got word from him this morning. They'll be looked after now.'

'What date is it?'

'Come on. You were under water three minutes, not three days.'

'Just answer the question.'

'It's the twenty-sixth.'

'Then we have four days to stop whatever it is from happening. I think it's time to step it up a notch or two.'

'Siri. I'm not trying to sound condescending here, but, despite what you believe, you aren't Bruce Lee. You're just an old fellow with a lung full of river water.'

'I'm glad you steered clear of condescension. I might have been insulted if you hadn't.'

'Well, all right. Let's just say in your present condition you aren't going to be much help.'

'I'll be out of here tomorrow.'

'Oh, good. So we can look forward to what? A guided temple tour? A visit to the museum?'

'All right. I agree my tourism day wasn't that well thought out. But I'm serious now. We'll locate Phosy's soldier friend and ...'

'There you go with the "we" again. Siri, it's all being taken care of. I'm on top of things. Rest your lungs. Go and visit your fisher family. Solve your mystery. It's what you do well. I'll take care of the political stuff. OK?' He stood and put a bag of fruit and sweets on the chair in his stead. 'I'll let you know everything as it happens, I promise. You can wipe that nasty look off your face. You know I'm right.'

'We don't have the concept of nasty on my planet,' Siri growled.

'Good boy. Eat your fruit.'

And Civilai was gone. Siri sat sulking. He deserved this after his Chaplinesque exploits of the past forty-eight hours, but that didn't make him any less resentful. History had repeated itself: the big communist bully had overwhelmed the honest fighting man. He opened the bag and started on a banana. He ate it skin and all, just to show he could. It was awful, of course.

'More breakfast, sweetie?' Dtui said loudly so the neighbours could hear. They wouldn't hear her poke out her tongue and pretend to spit in the rice.

'OK, but don't make it so salty this time,' Phosy replied from his perch on the wooden doorstep. 'God, I miss my mother's cooking.'

Dtui smiled, mumbled under her breath, and took her husband his second helping. She leaned down to fill his plate and put her mouth close to his ear.

'Do you know what the Thais call this place?' she whispered. He shook his head. 'Suan Lao. That's Lao Field in English. Ubon Lao Field. ULF – from the note.'

'Looks like we're in the right place then.'

When she turned back into the house he squeezed her bottom.

'Do that again and they'll have to pull your pants down to find that spoon, mister.'

'Why'd I ever marry you?'

' 'Cause nobody else would have you.'

Their morning sport was interrupted by the arrival of a small boy in a T-shirt that reached his feet. He was about six.

'You Phosy?' the boy asked. He had a smoker's voice.

'No. I'm *Mr* Phosy.'

'That supposed to be funny?'

'No. It was supposed to be a lesson in politeness.'

'You want this note or not?'

Phosy looked up and down the lane, then nodded. The boy had nothing in his hands but somehow he managed to make a note drop to the ground from somewhere inside his shirt. He kicked it toward the step and ran off. Phosy put his plate down, collected his cup, some orange rinds, and the note, and took them all inside. Dtui was relaxing with a Thai magazine.

'Who was that?'

'Just some kid wanted to know if I had any errands for him to run for five *baht*.' He held up the note and she stood beside him to read it.

Dear Phosy,
The sports committee members have looked over
your application for a tryout with the volleyball
team and we are impressed with your experience.
We are delighted to invite you to our training
session on Court Four, Area Sixteen, at ten o'clock
on August 24.

Yours sincerely,
Minmong Yotha, team captain

'You apply for the volleyball team?' Dtui whispered.

He shook his head. She raised her eyebrows and nodded. This was it. The walls had been breached.

At nine thirty, Phosy was walking alone through the camp, asking for directions to Area Sixteen. It was a decent walk across the sprawling base, and the rain had been falling constantly for an hour. It was a bad day for volleyball. What the nearest family assured him was Court Four turned out to be a rectangle of mud. No net, no lines, no players. He wasn't sure why he'd expected to find an actual volleyball practice going on. It just seemed like a fitting way to round out the subterfuge. He sat on a plank nailed to two stumps that probably served as the bleacher, his back to a bamboo fence. Twenty minutes later he was still there. The rain had soaked through his clothes and was working its way through his skin. A camp dog had joined him. Live dogs were always a good sign in a refugee camp, proof that there was enough to eat without getting desperate.

The dog looked up at the sound before Phosy heard it. Ten yards away, three lengths of bamboo fence tilted forward and a dark face peered through the gap at the bottom. The man looked at Phosy.

'You the carpenter?'

'That's me.'

'Come on.'

Phosy ran to the gap, got on his hands and knees, and crawled under the pivoted slats. The dog came out with him. On the outside of the fence three men stood looking down at him. One was Bunteuk, the area chief.

'Good morning,' Phosy said, straightening up.

'Good morning, Comrade,' Bunteuk replied.

Phosy laughed off the address. 'No need for that here, brother.' He held out his hand but Bunteuk didn't return the handshake.

'I imagine that would depend on how stupid you think we are, comrade spy. You've been recognized.'

With his hand still held hopefully in front of him, Phosy

was hit from behind. Through his life he'd been slugged with various blunt and not-so-blunt instruments, and, as he sank to his knees and inkblots filled in his vision, he was pretty sure he'd been felled this time by a block of wood – about four by four – definitely teak.

16

FORGET THE PLANET – SAVE
THE GARDEN

Siri had arrived at the village in time to attend the official wedding ceremony of a neighbour's son. The soldier, Kumpai, had promised to come and pick him up at the hospital but he hadn't shown so Siri found his own way there in a trishaw. It was eleven o'clock in the morning, an utterly inconvenient hour for everyone involved, except for the government cadre who'd been assigned to officiate. As the regulations stipulated the need for chairs, the fishermen had been obliged to borrow two dozen from the Full Moon dance hall and ship them downriver on a garbage scow.

The official was young and puffy and had no more interest in the union of Gaew and Mon than he had in the average yearly rainfall of Finland. He opened the Party manual and read out seven ways the confused betrothed would be able to benefit society and the nation as a whole by becoming a married couple. He reminded them that Marx had described a socialist marriage as the uniting of two people, making them one, but with the output of three. Siri didn't recall that particular equation from his early readings of Marx, nor did he understand the mathematics of it, but for once he kept his mouth shut. The sweating official concluded: 'The Democratic Republic of Laos is proud to announce your union certified.'

They signed a document, he countersigned it, and handed them the carbon copy as evidence. He put the top copy in his briefcase, shook hands with the moderately happy couple, and left. The whole thing took sixteen minutes. Returning the chairs would take two hours.

Siri managed to waylay the young man before he could head off on his little motorcycle. He held out a note he'd conceived and written during the ceremony but the official didn't take it.

'Son,' Siri said, 'I believe you have a Vietnamese adviser at the town hall.'

'What would that be to you?' the young man asked.

'I need you to give this note to him.'

'Do I look like a postman?'

'No, you look like a very junior clerk who performs whatever tasks he's told to. Don't get clever with me. Governor Katay is a personal friend.'

The cadre was suddenly more tentative about his attack.

'If you're his friend, why don't you give it to him yourself?'

'What do they feed you young fellows to make you all so suspicious of everyone? Listen, the governor and I had dinner together last evening. The Vietnamese adviser wanted some information and, as I speak Vietnamese, the governor asked me to write it down. See? It's written in Vietnamese. That's all. Put it to your ear. Nothing ticking in there. I'm sure the governor will be very grateful.'

The boy took the sealed envelope with its unfamiliar writing on the front. Siri always seemed to have plenty of envelopes of various sizes and shapes in his shoulder bag these days. 'Well ...'

'Tell him it's from senior Party member Dr Siri.'

'You're a doctor?' He looked around at the surroundings.

'I'm on a house call. Run along now. I'll phone the governor this evening and check whether your Vietnamese adviser got this, so don't let me down.'

'No, sir.'

Siri sat with Sing's mother and told her about the river dolphin as well as giving her an abridged version of his own spiritual connections. The woman put both her hands on his and thanked him. There is no greater gift to a bereaved mother than to know her child's soul is at peace. She told him he'd already done too much for them and wondered how she could ever repay him. There weren't enough fish in the Mekhong. Siri told her he wouldn't give up on his investigation and didn't expect anything in return.

'In that case,' the mother said. 'I hope you'll be kind enough to help us celebrate the neighbour's wedding ceremony tonight.'

Siri was amazed. 'You have another neighbour getting married?'

'Oh, no, Doctor. Same ones. But you don't call what we just sat through a ceremony, do you?'

'I'm not sure.'

'We don't. That was just to keep the government happy. They like their little speeches and form fillings. Of course, we all know it doesn't mean the kids are really married. Signing a bit of paper doesn't bond you with another person. No, sir. The real thing's tonight. And we'd be honoured if you could make it.'

'In that case,' Siri decided, 'I'd be most happy to accept.'

*

Siri's evening briefing was full of hope. Civilai presently had a core of three national department heads who had proven trustworthy enough to bring in to the ongoing counter-revolution. They were influential men who had agreed to launch discreet inquiries into recent unauthorized troop activities and unscheduled high-level meetings.

The initials PP, set out in the dentist's letter, appeared to be those of the ringleader. But with so few combinations of initial letters equivalent to so many Lao names, there was a seemingly endless list of potential suspects. They ran from ex-Royal Lao politicians and imprisoned dissidents through to Hmong fighters and ex- and current military leaders. There were one or two favourites, but the woman Civilai had working through the list estimated it could be another week before all the potential coup leaders were identified and she could begin eliminating the dead, dying, and departed for foreign shores. It was a huge job.

Siri sat back in a rattan chair, sipping a lime juice and listening to his friend. Civilai was confident and in control now. This was the role for which he was best qualified: the coordinator.

'You're good at all this, Comrade,' Siri said.

'I know.'

Civilai went back to the paperwork spread out across the bed and probably didn't notice when Siri got up and left.

Before heading off to the wedding, the doctor stopped at Daeng's noodle stall, requested 120 orders of thin-strand chicken noodles to go, and sat at a table by himself with a glass of rice whisky and a pout. When Daeng realized he was quite serious, she sent the ferry porters off for half a dozen chickens and extra noodles, and set about filling his order. As she worked, she fired questions at him, and although he answered them all, she could tell he was as flat as paint.

Finally, two large cardboard boxes filled with 120 plastic bags of noodles sat in a pony trap waiting for Siri, but Daeng wouldn't let him leave.

'If I let you arrive at a wedding with that face,' she said, 'they'll be divorced by morning. What's on your mind, old soldier?'

He looked up from his untouched drink. 'Do you remember Somluk Boutavieng?'

'No. What unit was he in?'

'He was a footballer. He scored four goals for Laos against the Thai team in 1952. He was a magician in leather boots. He could trick his way through a six-man defence and break the net with his shot. He was just beautiful to watch. I saw him play in Savanaketh and then at the Olympic qualifier in Bangkok. He twisted his ankle and couldn't play in the return game and we lost.'

'And you're still depressed about it?'

Siri laughed. 'No, not about the game, although it did take me a while to get over it. I was thinking about Somluk. I saw him again when we moved to Vientiane in '75. I recognized him straight-away. You know what he was doing? He was pedalling a *samlor*.'

'And?'

'And a man who'd been a legend, who'd inspired tens of thousands of young Lao men, had ended up scraping together a few *kip* a day just to stay alive. No dignity at all.'

'I have a feeling you're about to make an appearance in this story.'

'I am … you are … all of us old fossils, paraded out on Patriots Day with our medals pinned to our tattered uniforms.'

'Oh, I see.'

'You do? Then at least I'm not alone.'

'Oh, you're alone, all right. I'm nowhere near feeling sorry for myself. I've got a story, too, and it's much better than yours. There's a girl who helps me here from time to time. She was ten when she first came. They didn't let her stay in school because there was some rule about not repeating first grade more than three times. They agreed she was feeble-minded and she ended up kicking around doing nothing for years. People ignored her. She was just a sweet girl with nothing to do. When she first came here I let her serve and I fed her and gave her some fresh clothes. She came back every day. I watched her work, saw how she put effort into getting the condiments lined up and cleaning the plastic tablecloths. And I got it into my head I could teach her to read.

'I'd never taught reading before, and she was painfully slow. She'd take a month to get to know a letter, then forget it. But we kept at it, no hurry: a letter and a letter and then another. We started sixteen years ago and last week she read her first book. It was a grade-two primer but it was a book with a cover and ten pages of text. She cried herself blurry eyed that night, couldn't sleep, went through it ten more times. She finally read herself unconscious just as the sun was coming up.'

'That's nice.'

'Oh, it's much more than nice, Siri. It didn't change the world. It isn't going to get her a job reading the news over the propaganda airwaves. She'll still serve noodles and wipe tables. But she's different inside now. She has a new love in

her life, and I gave it to her. Me. I did it all by myself, and
I'm every bit as proud of that as I am of anything I did
during the resistance. All right, here comes the philosophy.
You can leave if you like but I suggest you stick it out. You
don't measure your own success against the size or volume
of the effect you're having. You gauge it from the difference
you make to the subject you're working on. Is leading an
army that wins a war really that much more satisfying than
teaching a four-year-old to ride a bicycle? At our age,' she
said, 'you go for the small things and you do them as well
as you can.'

In the back of the pony trap, squashed beside his two
large boxes, Siri still felt Daeng's lip prints on his cheek and
heard her whisper, 'Go for the small things and do them
well.' It would be his new mantra. Forget the planet, save
the garden. He thought, too, about what she'd told him as
he squeezed into the cart. She'd been hearing rumours. The
Thai camps had always been breeding grounds for insurgents, launch points for forays onto Lao soil to cause
disruption and spread propaganda. But over the last week,
all that activity had stopped dead. All the indicators were
that something big was about to happen. But Siri was just
an old doctor going for small things, doing them well,
saving the garden. Civilai could have his planet. There were
more personal issues for Siri to think about, like the fact
that Daeng had kissed him on the cheek.

He arrived at the village to find the place jumping like
spiders on a hot rock. The dancing had begun long before
the wedding. Women, old men, and dogs, all apparently
drunk, were jigging back and forth in front of the main hut.
There was a Buddhist-cum-animist ceremony going on
inside. They'd sneaked the monks in by river and borrowed

a shaman from another village. Such an event brought a lot of spirits out of the woodwork and Siri could feel their presence. Some dispossessed he could see sitting around in the shadows. He knew instantly which were the departed even though some of them seemed to be in better shape than the living.

Inside the hut, the villagers had tied their sacred threads around the heads and hands of the betrothed and were chanting along with the monks. Siri tried to slip in unnoticed to watch, but he was spotted and manhandled to a place of honour in front of the saffron-clad choir. One of the monks read from a sacred Pali text. The shaman unfurled some of the unspun cotton from a grandiose tower of banana leaves and flowers known as a *krooay* and tied together the spirits of the young lovers. Incense and mosquito-coil smoke intertwined in the warm air. From outside came the sound of music from traditional wooden instruments.

Siri smiled to himself. 'Sorry, Comrades Marx and Lenin. This is what marriage is all about.'

Siri's noodles joined the fish and vegetables and sticky rice on the communal table and were gone in under half an hour. Siri was plied with glass after glass of unidentifiable and dubious spirits. Like most guests, he was press-ganged into downing the entire contents of the glass in one go. This was the Lao way and he had no recourse. At one juncture along the winding path to inebriation it occurred to him he'd spent much of his time in the south drunk. Human beings mistakenly believed alcohol was a disguise that stopped real life from recognizing them. In fact, it was just a temporary hiding hole, and Siri knew he'd been fooling nobody.

It was almost ten o'clock when he looked around and realized he was at the river's edge beside a beautiful local girl. She had eyes that would melt even the coldest of hearts and a smile that made Siri wish he, too, were ten years old.

'Do you come here often?' he slurred.

'Used to come here all the time,' she said.

'What stopped you?'

'Sing dying.'

If that didn't sober him up in a hurry nothing would.

'You and Sing were friends?'

'Yeah.'

'You must miss him.'

'Yeah.'

She hugged her knees tightly to her chest. Her naked toes squeezed the mud. What is there to say to a ten-year-old who's lost her best friend?

'You know his spirit lives in a *pa kha* now?'

'They told me. That's why I come over. Can I ... talk to him?'

'Sing? Not with words.'

'How then?'

'You can talk to him with your heart.'

'I don't know how to do that, Grandpa.'

'Of course you do. When you think about him, does your heart sometimes feel like it's being pumped up?'

'All the time.'

'His spirit can feel that.'

'It can?'

'And when you think about him, and when you say his name to yourself, all those times, his spirit's always listening. Sing knows.'

She smiled briefly and looked at the shimmering lights across the river. Then she turned to Siri with the serious expression of an adult and said, 'Do you think it happened because of all the naughty stuff he did?'

'No. Nobody Sing's age could ever be naughty enough to deserve what happened to him.'

'He was a terror, though. He started acting bad after his dad ran off.'

'In what way?'

'He used to sneak – you won't tell anyone, will you?' Siri shook his head. 'He went into temples and scraped the gold leaf off the Buddhas. That's a sin, ain't it?'

'Well … what's your name, love?'

'Mim.'

'Well, Mim, there are those who'd say the temple shouldn't have gold in the first place. But it's true, you shouldn't steal from anybody.'

'And he climbed like a monkey. He used to go up the town offices, the post office and the town hall and all them. He went on the weekends when they was all shut and he'd climb all over them till he found a shutter that wasn't locked properly and he'd pinch stuff.' Her eyes welled with tears. 'And … and I told him. I said, "Sing, if you don't mend your ways …" ' She sobbed and Siri sidled over to her and put his arm around her shoulders. She continued to force out the words. 'I said, "If you don't mend your ways, you'll get yourself killed." I said that, Grandpa. It was me that put the curse on him.'

She shook with tears and Siri pulled her to his chest.

'OK,' he said. 'I understand. And you think because you said those things, it's your fault he died.' He felt her head nod. 'Well, that's the silliest thing I've heard all year. And I have to tell you I've heard some rubbish. Mim, nothing you said could make Sing die. It doesn't work like that. I can tell when spirits are angry, and Sing's spirit knows you had nothing to do with his going. You just said something sensible to make him stop being dishonest. That's what friends do. He understands that. Do you believe me?'

Her nod wasn't convincing. She looked up at Siri and he wiped the tears from her cheeks. 'I knew, Grandpa,' she said. 'I knew he was off to get into more trouble the day he disappeared. I tried to talk him out of it.'

'You saw him?'

'We always walked to school together. The days he bothered to go, anyway.'

'What happened?'

'He just said, "Stuff it, I'm not going." And he turned and walked the other way. I think he'd lost a book or something and he was afraid of the class monitor making fun of him.'

'Did he say where he was going?'

'Into town. We always went there at weekends and played around.'

'Was there some place he especially liked?'

'The city offices.'

'Hmm, right. But that day wasn't a weekend. All the offices would have been open. There were people in them. And if he'd just walked around in his uniform, someone would have stopped him and shipped him back to school, the police especially. Was there some secret place you liked to go? Somewhere you couldn't be seen?'

'Well …' She shook her head. 'No.'

'Mim, it can't be a secret any more.'

'I know, but …'

'Mim.'

'Under the new bridge.'

'What new bridge?'

'The one to the airport. It's not finished yet. They got all these big pipes and bricks and stuff under it. We got a camp there.'

'Do you mind if I go and see it tomorrow?'

'Don't care. I'm not going there no more, not ... not by myself.'

'I know. But don't you forget what I told you. Sing's spirit can tell when you're sad or when you blame yourself. You don't want to get his spirit depressed, do you?'

'No.'

'Because you've never seen anything worse than a depressed spirit. I remember seeing one once. It got drunk and rode its bicycle into a tree.'

She laughed and her face lightened. 'Spirits can't ride bicycles.'

'No? Then that must be why it ran into the tree.'

They walked back to the party hand in hand.

17

BROTHER FRED

Dtui was frantic with worry. When the sun went down she'd started to work herself into a panic, not sure how long was a suitable time for a young wife to wait before missing her husband. There were head counts by the guards some evenings, spot checks on this or that sector. At seven she'd gone to Bunteuk's room and asked whether he'd seen Phosy. The chief was seated on the floor with a circle of friends, gambling. He told her he hadn't seen Phosy all day but that she shouldn't worry, he was probably just caught up in a discussion somewhere and hadn't noticed the time. He reminded her there really was nowhere to go.

But by eight thirty she could stay calm no longer. This wasn't Dtui acting like a wife was expected to. This was Dtui anxious and fearful for her friend's safety. She went to Bunteuk again and insisted they go to the camp authorities to file a report. Bunteuk assigned the duty to his deputy, Kumhuk, who was none too pleased to be dragged away from the card game. On the way to the Thai office, he told her not to expect much.

There was a form, of course, as there was for everything in Thailand. The policeman on duty filled it out reluctantly and laboriously: names, address, times, type of complaint, details, signatory, witness, time received.

Once the form was placed in the in-tray, she'd asked impatiently what the officer planned to do about it. He told her to watch her temper and remember who and what she was. He said her husband would probably turn up drunk at midnight with cheap perfume around his fly like all the other worthless Lao shits.

Her natural response to that comment had earned Dtui a night in the violent residents' cell, a crude cage at the rear of the police station, ten feet by ten, containing only a narrow wooden bench. Now, at six in the morning, pacing and huffing inside her metal cage like a wild boar, she waited for the day officer to arrive. She could see the night-duty clown chatting with two younger men before one walked back to the lock-up. He was good-looking but no less condescending. She took a deep breath.

'Can I go now, sir?' she asked.

'Are you going to cause any more trouble?'

'Tr …? I came to report my husband missing. Is that causing trouble?'

'No. But punching an officer of the Royal Thai Police force could be interpreted as such.'

She smiled. 'I certainly didn't punch him.'

'He says you did. He's got a tomato where his nose used to be as evidence.'

'Sir, the mud on my sandals caused me to slip on your concrete floor. I reached out to prevent myself from falling and your man's nose just happened to be there. An understandable accident.'

The young man laughed and opened the cage door. The bird was about to fly when he grabbed her arm. 'Sign!'

He held a letter saying she hadn't been abused or molested while in custody. It was written in Thai and he didn't expect her to understand it. She took his pen and signed 'Minnie Mouse' in English. He didn't bother to check.

Dtui's cramped legs took her as fast as they could to her room. It was empty, the bedding untouched, nothing had been moved. She lay on the thin mattress and breathed heavily.

'Think, Dtui, think.'

She couldn't act rashly or make accusations because it was possible that Phosy's disappearance was all part of his acceptance by the resistance. She couldn't damage his cover. All she could do was fuss like a wife alone in a refugee camp whose husband had vanished. If her actions brought too much attention to the camp's covert activities she was sure someone would invite her to join a volleyball team.

She walked in the direction of Court Four, stopping at each corner to describe her husband and ask whether anyone had seen him. At the court she sat on a bench, looking out at the soft clay that didn't boast one single footprint. A stray black ridgeback came to sniff at her feet.

'What would I do, dog?' she asked. 'What would I do if I loved my husband? Who would a desperate housewife turn to?'

Twenty minutes later she arrived at the whitewashed facade of the office of the Church of the Christian Brotherhood. Her tears were genuine, her words contrived.

'I lose my husband,' she called in English through the open doorway. When nothing happened she tried again. 'My life is finish. I kill myself.' Again there was an absence of movement from inside and she was wondering whether the office might be unoccupied when a young Western man stepped out of the shadows. He was painfully thin and yellowish like bamboo in a bad year. His hair was an orange mop and he wore clothes that could only have been donated to a charity store.

'What are you saying out here?'

To a Lao whose English had arrived courtesy of dense American textbooks and the odd BBC World Service broadcast, his Irish accent was totally incomprehensible. She enunciated slowly, hoping her clarity would encourage him to improve his own English.

'My husband is loss. Please help me.'

'Do you have an appointment? he asked.

It was Dtui's uncontrollable torrent of tears that made the man forgo his timetable and escort her inside. Brother Fred was just a young man entrusted with the administrative duties of an interdenominational mission. He'd gone straight from the seminary to a church office. Souls weren't his speciality. Technically, Dtui was the first victim he'd had to deal with directly, the first refugee who'd spoken to him without the filter of a local Christian interpreter. But on this day adversity had confronted him face to face and he found himself with an obligation. Despite her tears and his language problem, they were able to piece together the story, and the young servant of the Lord agreed to help her find Phosy.

It didn't take long for Dtui to realize she'd probably have been better off without him. He'd marched her with great bluster into all the Non-Governmental Organization offices and before all the Thai government representatives and told them that this poor woman had lost her husband. But Dtui had noticed their undisguised yawns. So, while he sat in the camp administration centre trying to get a call through to the Vatican or some such place, she backed away and left him fondling his worry beads.

She returned to Area Thirty-four, rechecked her own

empty room, and found Bunteuk's house deserted. None of the neighbours had seen his young wife since the previous day. Bunteuk was off at the weekly camp coordination meeting, they told her. Once more she retraced Phosy's steps to Court Four and sat on the bench by the bamboo fence. Her dog friend was still where she'd left him. He came to sit by her.

'Either he came here,' she said, 'or he was kidnapped on the way. Unlikely in a busy camp at ten in the morning. So let's say he arrived and sat right here. There were no volley-ball players so getting him here had to be a ruse. Why here?'

There was only one logical reason. This had to be an established escape route from the camp. She stood on her bench and was still four feet from the top of the bamboo. Phosy could have made it but it would have taken a front-end loader to get Dtui over. She climbed down and watched the dog scratching at the fence a few yards away. He looked up at her and continued to scratch as if he wanted to be let out. Dtui walked along the fence testing the slats. All of them were nailed and firm until she reached the dog. The fencing there didn't give way exactly but it felt suspended rather than attached. She squeezed her fingers between the slats until she had enough grip to pull them forward. The dog's excited reaction told her he was used to getting in and out this way.

The fence swung forward on some kind of hinge and the dog raced out through the gap at the bottom. It was only three-quarters of a Dtui wide, but a lot of her was soft and malleable and she was able to squeeze herself through it like a jellyfish through a mailbox slot. On the outside she readjusted herself and breathed heavily. She'd just illegally left a refugee camp. Dtui was an escapee. It was all rather exciting. She had no idea what she was likely to achieve through this folly but it felt so much better to be active. It was certainly better than following Brother Fred around. Perhaps a wife would go to these lengths to find the man she loved.

She looked around her. She was in a clearing. Most of the surrounding forest had been massacred to build the camp. She imagined the upheaval this must have caused to the tree spirits and wondered whether Thai *Phibob* were as vengeful as those in Laos. Just one scrawny tree stood in the centre of the cleared land. It was obviously too gaunt and gnarled to offer up useful timber. It was twisted and warped like some haunted tree in a myth. But despite its deformities, its foliage was thick and rich and its seedpods had begun to crack and distribute their booty to the land. The insides of the split pods were bright scarlet, and, from a distance, it looked as if the mother tree had bled to produce her young.

Dtui walked closer and took hold of one pod. It filled her hand. She looked at it with astonishment. It had the most human characteristic she'd ever seen in a plant. The edges of the pod rounded into the shape of the lips. At their convergence, a bud, moist and ripe, formed the clitoris. And opposite, where the pod joined the stem connecting it to the tree, was a dark channel. In obstetrics, Dtui had handled many such organs, but they'd all been attached to females – Homo sapiens females. In her hand she held a genuine …

'That's a *yonee peesaht*,' said a deep voice from behind her. She jumped guiltily and turned to see a smiling old man in a large cowboy hat carrying a slingshot. 'The Devil's Vagina, they call it. Knocks your kneecaps right off, don't it?'

He didn't seem at all flustered in the presence of an

escaped illegal alien. Something about his arsenal suggested he wasn't a bounty hunter.

'It's incredible, she said. 'I've never seen anything like it.'

'It always gives newcomers a chuckle the first time they see one. There used to be a lot more around here. They say the young fellas stole so many pods for you-know-what that there weren't enough seeds left to keep the species going. Don't know if it's true, mind.'

Dtui laughed. 'Uncle, I wouldn't be surprised if you just made that up yourself.'

'I wouldn't be surprised by that either.'

Their language was identical, their bond instant. It was only the Mekhong that prevented the two from sharing a nationality. The river cut through the centre of a Lao community with one history and one culture. It should have been a main artery rather than a dividing line. But rivers are often assigned the unpleasant duty of marking a border. A million Lao awoke one day to find they were Thai. The waterway that had once united now separated families and made them unwilling enemies. There was no going back. Only by draining the Mekhong and filling it in would the Lao race ever be reunited.

'What are you hunting?' Dtui asked.

'Rabbits. Stringy little bastards they are around here, but we don't stand a chance of catching anything better with all them hungry scumbags next door.' He lifted his chin in the direction of the bamboo fence.

'Do you live around here?' she asked. She'd started to walk beside him across the denuded land.

'Over yonder. Just a little hut, but I was born there, so it's home.'

'So, you remember when the Americans were here.'

'*Sure do*,' he said in English, squeezing the brim of his hat. 'Where do you think I got this from?'

'And they say this whole camp used to be their armoury storage ground.'

'Armoury and camp. That's why they needed so much land. They had to keep a space between the houses and the bombs, just in case. All this land we're walking on used to be inside the camp. The fence was once way over there.' He pointed to the far side of the clearing.

'You mean they made the refugee camp smaller?'

'Yeah. Odd, isn't it? It spreads out in every other direction the more it fills up, but they don't touch this bit here. It must be because of the A-bomb.'

'What A-bomb?'

'The Americans had their A-bombs stored here and the radiation killed the land and made it dangerous.'

'Who told you that?'

'The soldiers.'

'American soldiers?'

'No, Lao. They told the wife and me not to come over here after dark. They said the radiation's worse at night.'

'You saw Lao soldiers here?'

'Yeah.'

'In uniform?'

'They didn't need to be in uniform. I can tell.'

'So you don't come here at night. And you believe this radiation story.'

'Not really. But if a bunch of boys with guns tell me not to hang around at night, I'd believe anything they told me. Wouldn't you?'

'One last question.'

'Are you with the radio?'

'Eh?'

'We listen sometimes, when we can get batteries. We listen to the women on Lao radio. They all talk nice like you. Are you a reporter?'

'Kind of. Last question: Did they – I mean the Americans – did they store all their weapons in the open air?'

'Most of 'em. They covered 'em with camouflage netting and leaves and stuff. But some they put in the cellars.'

'You wouldn't remember where those cellars are, would you?'

'No, never seen 'em. I only know about 'em cause my nephew used to porter for the Americans. That's how I got my hat. Like it?'

'It's lovely.'

Dtui sat sweating in the shade of the Devil's Vagina tree. It seemed to give off more heat than it stopped. She'd walked every inch of the clearing stamping her feet – expecting a clunk, but getting nothing. There had to be something here. Siri had mentioned the tree in his note and its name was code for the operation. Phosy had disappeared from a spot just inside the fence. There had to be a connection and it had to be at this place.

She'd been sitting contemplating for an hour when the earth moved. A piece of sod rose from the ground some thirty yards in front of her. It was a foot thick and beneath it was a head she recognized as belonging to Mr Kumhuk, the deputy section chief. He checked in all directions, obviously confused Dtui for a shadow, and threw the block of earth to one side. He pulled himself out of the ground, replaced the divot, and sprinted to the fence, where he vanished through the gap.

Dtui hurried over to where Mr Kumhuk had emerged but she saw no obvious entrance. There were tufts of grass and rocks but no lines or handles. Then she saw it, a slight discoloration of the vegetation, a small area of deliberate landscaping. She grabbed a handful of grass and realized straightaway that it was fake, some kind of synthetic material. She pulled with all her might and was able to lift an uneven area of ground surprisingly easily. She shoved it to one side and looked down. Another black hole in the ground. Hadn't she had enough of those? She seemed to have a magnetic attraction to eerie confined spaces. Earlier in the year she'd almost died from heading blindly down a dark tunnel. Oh, well. *Que sera sera.*

She picked out the steps with her feet and lowered herself down gradually. The stairway was concrete and led deep inside the earth. She was already feeling claustrophobic by the time she saw the breaker switch at the foot of the stairs. She pushed the handle up and banks of fluorescent lights flicked on one by one across a vast concrete silo. There were tables and camp beds and hundreds – perhaps thousands – of enormous crates. Banks of artillery lined the walls as well as uniforms in neat piles. This was the home base for the Devil's Vagina insurgents; there was no doubt in her mind. There was also no doubt that the Thais had rebuilt the camp boundary wall so no prying United Nations officials would stumble across this nest of vipers inside a supposedly neutral camp. The Thais were in on it. No surprise there. The Thai military was riddled with Red paranoia. And there was enough American memorabilia around to suggest the US wasn't about to lose the war gracefully either. Dtui doubted the Americans had merely forgotten to take it all with them.

There were no side rooms or annexes. This was one slab of space. An area had been set aside for planning. Chairs with hinged writing trays stood in rows facing a large blackboard, and various pin boards of maps and charts written in Lao stood on easels. She wondered what the best course of action might be. Grab as many documents as possible and make a run for it? To where? She was forty miles from the nearest point on the Lao border. How far was she likely to get? She couldn't memorize all the names and dates. She couldn't even remember how to calculate lost calories. Perhaps she should just set fire to the place and blow it all to hell. That might slow them down long enough to get word to Siri and Civilai in ...

Her discovery, her euphoria, her dreams of saving her country, her heartbeat were all interrupted by the sound of a deep male throat-clearing cough from just a few yards behind her.

18

THE CARDBOARD TELEVISION

Siri sat in the six-foot concrete pipe section beneath the unfinished Soviet bridge. He was looking at the crayon-and-pencil decorations that turned a lump of sewer connection into a clubhouse for two ten-year-old friends. Cracked coffee cups and glasses and little plates piled with river pebbles, a cardboard box with a hole ripped out of it in the shape of a TV screen, a string-and-sardine-tin burglar alarm he'd tripped when he arrived. These were the evidence of happy childhood fantasies, good moments that should never have been erased so suddenly.

Siri wiped away the tears again and put his hand on the amulet beneath his shirt. It seemed pleased with its beautiful new plaited string but it had nothing to tell him about Sing's disappearance that day. The boy's soul was far away, frolicking with the dolphins, but his death remained unsolved and unavenged.

Siri thought about the little fellow, playing truant from school, sitting here in his clubhouse, looking for mischief. He knew he'd be picked up by some do-gooder if he wandered the streets in his uniform. So, with no choice, he'd hung out here, nothing but a plate of river pebbles to eat, nothing but a cardboard TV to entertain him. How long could a hyperactive imp stand it? Did he get bored and go for a swim, get into trouble? Everyone in the village agreed he could outswim and outdive even the most experienced fisherman. Did he fall and hit his head and drown? There had been no evidence of head trauma or of being snagged on an underwater root or a net. Besides, none of those answers would explain the anomalies: the five-day gap between his disappearance and the discovery, the different rates of decomposition between the top and bottom halves of his body, the splinters, the insect bites.

There was no doubt this was a small thing. It wouldn't make a jot of difference to anyone beyond the village. Judge Haeng wouldn't give him a medal for solving such a case. In fact he'd drag Siri over the linoleum again for wasting his time. But this was one small thing he was determined to do well. Even if the country was crumbling around him he would solve this mystery. He willed himself into Sing's mind.

'Think trouble. Think mischief. How would I get the attention I need to bring my father back home? Just how bad would I have to be? It's midday, Wednesday. I've bored myself into a state of unprecedented naughtiness. I need something to boast about at school. "You lot wouldn't believe what I did yesterday, I ..." Come on, young Sing, tell Grandpa Siri what you did.'

The sun had burned through the midday cloud and was casting a distinct black-and-white dividing line beneath the half bridge. Siri walked out into the dazzle and shouted, 'What can I do to show you all I'm a man?'

As the blinding light slowly cleared from his eyes and the blur of Pakse all around regained its rightful texture, one large shape on the far bank loomed like a challenge. It said,

'I am the symbol of power and affluence. I am better than you and I am invincible.'

And Siri knew where Sing had gone that Wednesday.

Brother Fred was all atwitter. The one case he'd accepted personally had grown out of all proportion to have national – nay, international – repercussions. He hadn't handled it at all well. First he'd lost the woman and then set about finding her. His inborn Catholic pessimism had convinced him she'd met the same horrible fate as her husband. He'd used the collective weight of the organization he represented to have a search conducted. He'd talked by phone for half an hour with the head of his mission in Bangkok. He'd even prayed for their safety. His Thai Christian interpreter had told him, 'I admire your concern, Father. But it's looking more like an affair of the heart than a kidnapping.'

'How so?' Brother Fred had asked.

'The chief of that section, Bunteuk, he's reported his wife missing, too. The rumours on that block are that the new chap had a fling with Bunteuk's wife and they ran off together.'

'Oh, I say.'

'Some believe the fat girl was so distraught she fled the camp, vowing to go home to Laos.'

It was a story that would certainly have placated the young Irishman had the fat girl and the philandering husband not walked into his office some ten minutes after the interpreter had left. The man, bruised and cut about the face, was carrying a large box full of rolled paper and files. They closed the office door behind them, locked it, and despite being already in a refugee camp they claimed refugee status. Brother Fred was flummoxed. He'd never seen his little office as a potential island of diplomatic immunity. But international law wasn't his forte so he made tea for three and listened to what the couple had to say.

Dtui had certainly considered her number to be up when she heard the cough. She'd turned slowly, expecting at the very least to see the barrel of a gun pointed at her, at the very worst to hear it go off. But instead, standing between floor-to-ceiling stacks of white wood crates labelled TOXIC, was an exact replica of the metal cage in which she'd spent the previous night. And sitting cross-legged on its floor was Phosy. He pointed out where she might be able to find the key to his cell, and while Dtui searched frantically for it, Phosy described his meeting with Bunteuk and his henchmen.

'I have no idea why they haven't killed me,' he said. 'It appears someone recognized me. If they knew I was a spy, bumping me off would have been the logical move. All I can imagine is that they needed me alive to find out what we already know about their activities. But, I ask you, why not torture me straightaway and have done with it?'

'I hope you didn't make that suggestion to them,' Dtui said, rummaging through cupboards and shelves. She came across a bunch of keys in a drawer in a wooden desk and smiled. 'Victory.'

Phosy continued as she worked through them.

'It seemed as if Bunteuk would have preferred to blow my head off there and then,' Phosy continued, remarkably calmly given their predicament. 'But something or someone was stopping him. He made no bones about what he thought of me.'

The padlock clicked and Dtui pulled open the door. Their

embrace said everything their mouths hadn't been able to.
Phosy looked over to the stairway.

'Did you pull the tunnel cover back?'

'No, I thought I'd have to get out of here in a hurry.'

'Then we'd better get moving.'

Despite the urgency of their circumstances, they went
first to the office and information corner and looked at all
the documentation.

'Where do we start?'

Everything they'd collected there now sat on the large
meeting table at the back of Brother Fred's office. Dtui's
faith in the young cleric was based entirely on her intuition.
She'd never met an Irishman so she didn't know whether
they were a trustworthy race, but there was something
about his eyes that reminded her of a faithful dog she'd
befriended when she was little. Phosy agreed he was the
best, if not the only, option. They were deep in anticommunist territory. They weren't about to wander up to a
policeman and receive any sympathy. He doubted even
Brother Fred would be too distressed about a plot to oust
the evil socialists from Laos. But they both knew the church
had certain rules when it came to human rights. The only
concern was the current Thai refusal to call the Lao
'refugees.' It was merely word choice but it prevented the
United Nations Human Rights Commission from operating
in the camp. Because of this vacuum, the definition of
human rights in this case was left to the Thai government,
and the Thai military would have every reason to waive the
rights of Phosy and Dtui.

On their march through the camp along the busiest main
thoroughfares to the Church of the Christian Brotherhood

office, they'd gone through the options for Brother Fred. A Thailand that changed its junta more often than Phosy changed his undershorts wasn't about to be embarrassed by international community reaction to a little coup attempt in Laos. The UN would issue a strong written condemnation and someone in Bangkok would light a barbecue with it. No one ever quaked in their shoes when the UN roared.

No. They could forget political channels. Their priority was to get themselves back to Laos with the information they'd gathered. To that end, they needed access to a telephone line and a car. Brother Fred had one of each, but he was a nervous wreck. While Dtui held Brother Fred's hand and calmed him, Phosy made several calls. He finally put down the phone with a large smile on his face. Dtui translated that the governor of Ubon was devastated to hear that his province was being used to launch an attack on Laos. She pointed out how much undeclared revenue Ubon was making from illegal logging deals with the Lao military in Champasak. The financial rather than the moral indignation argument made sense to the Irishman and he had no reason to doubt that the governor might want to see the evidence they'd collected for himself.

Dtui uncrossed her fingers and brought up the matter of transport. Brother Fred had no intention of handing over his mission's four-wheel drive, but he was prepared to drive them. The white Land Rover, with a logo of a benevolent Jesus surrounded by Indochinese children stencilled on the doors, went in and out of the camp twenty times a day. The gate guards at the permanently up barrier didn't stop their conversation, or cast more than a cursory glance at the vehicle. If there were two Lao in the backseat, they were meant to be there.

It was an uncongested ten-minute drive into the city. Dtui gazed out at the magical place and wondered why she couldn't have been born on this side of the Mekhong. There were public telephones in the centre of town just like she'd seen in the 8 mm films of Moscow. Even the sellers of fried grasshoppers looked exotic to her. They'd just passed the teachers' college when she felt Phosy squeeze her hand. At first she experienced a brief surge of joy until she recalled it was her signal.

'Oh, oh, Father,' she cried in obvious distress. The young man's eyes opened wide as they stared in the mirror.

'What now?' he asked.

'I must vomit.' When her pronunciation of the letter v proved too baffling for the priest she put her finger into her throat and mimed for him.

'No, not in the project car.' He slammed his foot on the brake and skidded to the side of the road. Dtui jumped out and ran back ten yards, where she pretended to throw up several times. Brother Fred could see this in his side mirror. He also got a perfect view of her collapsing dramatically onto the ground.

'Oh, my God, man. Look!'

Phosy smiled the smile of a refugee being yelled at in a language he didn't understand. The priest pointed and shouted again, but when Phosy merely stared at the roof of the car, Brother Fred had no choice but to jump out of the idling vehicle and run back to help the poor woman. What a day it was for him. Heaven and hell had descended upon him and he knew it was a test. The Lord was putting him through it. But if it was truly a test, the last few problems were about to get a lot more complex.

He knelt beside Dtui and failed to get any response from

her. He had little idea where her pulse might be or what exactly to do with it if he found it. And then his four-wheel drive left without him. It did a screeching U-turn, headed off in the opposite direction for fifty yards, then vanished down a side street. This was certainly his 'Oh Lord, why hast thou forsaken me?' moment. He hadn't a clue where to turn – a dying woman, a lost car, an international incident. He recalled that before he'd left his home in County Colraine he'd told his grieving mother he'd just be off for a bit of excitement for a couple of years. Of course, he hadn't believed that. He was a clerk. If he'd really wanted a life of excitement he could have joined the IRA. He thought Thailand would be hot and dull. He'd been right about the hot.

There weren't too many people around and those that were gave a wide berth to the foreign devil in a dog collar leaning over a dead girl. He couldn't speak a word of Thai and what he needed very badly right now was to communicate. He recalled the sign in front of the teachers' college. Someone there was sure to speak English. They'd have a phone, maybe even a nurse. After fleetingly considering carrying Dtui to the college, he left her where she was and sprinted off down the street.

As he was entering the college gates he looked up to see a white Land Rover with benevolent Jesus doors shoot past him. The driver waved. Instinctively, he waved back.

19

HALF AN EAR

Siri and Officer Tao knocked at the big wooden door of Prince Boun Oum's half-finished palace, knowing nobody in there would react to a mere knock. At Siri's instructions, Tao shouted, 'It's the police. We don't like to be kept waiting.'

After a minute, the bolt on the other side slid open and the door was pulled back a crack. Eyes like hyphens peered out, first at the uniform, then at Siri.

'It's midday. Haven't you ever heard of a siesta?' came the screechy voice of the caretaker. She opened the door just wide enough for them to see that she was barely awake.

'Hello, sister,' Siri said. 'Remember me?'

'No,' she answered.

'I was here a few days ago with another old gentleman.'

'We get a lot of visitors.' She didn't stand back to let them in. 'I'm sleeping. What is it you want?'

The policeman wasn't as patient or polite as Siri. He walked straight at the woman and into the vestibule, almost knocking her down. 'Just come for a little look around,' he said.

Siri followed him in. 'Where's your brother today?' he asked.

'I told you. It's sleeping time. He's resting. You shouldn't be here when he's resting. You might …'

'Might what?'

She chewed on her words. 'Might wake him up.'

'We'll certainly do our best not to,' Siri said. He was doing his policeman stroll, his hands behind his back. 'You said a lot of fixtures had been stolen from this place.'

'Everything that wasn't nailed down and half the things that were.'

'So you and your brother came along at the right time.'

'Yes, we did. What's this …?'

'You keep a pretty tight ship now, by the looks of it.'

'There's not much left to take, is there?' She reversed toward a door in a makeshift plywood office and carefully pulled it to.

'Right, but there'd still be prowlers? Curious people come to take a look? Souvenir hunters?'

Tao was standing back, observing like an umpire who's slightly threatened by the competitors.

'Some,' she said, walking them away from the office.

'And what do you do?'

'Do?'

'Yes. How do you keep them away? How do you protect this place?'

'We just don't let them in. It isn't that complicated. What are you getting at?'

'Not difficult? You have open windows all over. Anyone with a boat could walk up from the river, and someone who could climb a bit could work his way in.'

'They don't.'

'Why not?'

'They just don't. They know the place is protected now.'

'By an old woman and a softheaded retard?'

Siri noticed the first change in her demeanour. If she'd been a dog, the hairs would have stood up along her spine.

'You … you have no right to say that.' She turned to Tao. 'Tell him! Tell him we have rights.' Tao smiled and kept quiet.

'I see you haven't been keeping abreast of the news,' Siri went on. His tone was nasty; his eyebrows formed a bushy *v*. 'We're an oppressive communist state now. Don't mind if we go outside, do you?' He led the way to the back balcony that overlooked the Se Don. The river had collected runoff from the hills and was flowing thick as chocolate. From the balustrade he had a clear view of the half-completed bridge.

'You see?' Siri continued. 'Now the fat old royals have fled the scene with their stolen treasures….'

'They di—'

'Did you say something?' She looked at her feet. 'No, I didn't think so. Where was I? Oh, yes. Since the corrupt Royalist lapdogs of the French ran away with their booty, the country has changed hands. We now have people like me who can say what we like, when we like, because we have the power now. Do I make myself clear?'

'Yes,' she said, unable to contain her anger. 'More's the pity.'

'I'll pretend I didn't hear that. I'd hate to have Officer Tao here lock you up for antigovernment rhetoric, forcing you to leave your softheaded brother to look after himself.'

'He's n—' She was scuffing gravel beneath her sandalled foot like a flustered mare.

'And I was just wondering.' Siri gave her no time to inter-ject. 'With your brother being as scary as he is, what would little kids make of him? I bet he'd be a good challenge for a dare. Suppose, just suppose one of the local kids accepted that dare and came nosing around inside. Say he prised up one of the floor tiles for a souvenir.'

'They don't.'

'I know. But if one did, how would you and your brother deal with it?' Siri could detect something beneath her anger. She was anxious. A tic had begun in her right cheek and her mouth had risen in to a snarl to counter it.

'I … I'd tell him to mend his ways and … and send him home.'

'Of course you would. But let's not forget – a child isn't necessarily a "he", is it? Could have been a she.'

'Boys are more likely.'

'More likely to climb in through one of these big gaping windows on the river side and mess around unsupervised. Cause damage. Talk back. Real little bastards, some of these local boys. Right?'

'I don't know.'

'My word, yes. And they have no respect at all for the royal family.'

'That they don't.'

'They probably hear in school that His Preciousness was making a mint in stolen goods and protection and drugs. Even that he was selling arms to the communists in Vietnam just to make a few more fr—'

'He never did. That's all rubbish.' Her fists were clenched so tightly the knuckles were white.

'Just to make a few more francs for his retirement. When the kids hear that kind of thing, of course they'd repeat it if they met anyone defending the prince. It's only natural.'

'It's slander – vulgar socialist propaganda. Children shouldn't be told spiteful lies like that.'

'Who was there to put him right? He only knew what it

was like for his family to starve under a Royalist regime while the big honcho got rich and built an obscene palace. He wasn't here to cause trouble. He just came to make sense of it all.'

'He had no respect.'

'No respect for what?' Siri's volume had risen in tandem with hers to the point that they were a yard apart yelling at each other.

'For the centuries of proud and noble royal families that have ruled our lands in the south. For the great battles won to protect its people. For the culture they brought to us.'

'Really? Perhaps he wondered – with all that culture and protection – why he was still living in a wooden hut in the mud.'

'His kind will always be in the mud. That class of people never seize the opportunities they're offered.'

'That class is ninety-five per cent of the population. That's an awful lot of people not seizing opportunities. Perhaps the boy saw himself as their knight. Perhaps he thought by coming here and breaching your castle he could avenge injustices.'

'Or perhaps he was just a foul-mouthed little tyke out for trouble. Have you considered that?'

Siri's volume dropped to a whisper. 'And he found it, didn't he?'

She fell silent and lowered her eyes. Siri looked at Tao and nodded.

'We're going to take a look at your water tower, Comrade,' the policeman said, taking a step toward the looming concrete turret. There was a fire in the woman's eyes that flashed, first at Tao, then at Siri.

'This is private property. Get off our land,' she snarled.

Tao smiled. 'This is the People's Democratic Republic of Laos,' he said. 'There *is* no private property. Perhaps you'd be so kind as to lead the way.'

They let her climb the ladder first. At the top she stood on the small landing that was barely wide enough for one. Siri joined her there and Tao remained on the fifth rung from the top.

'Open it,' Siri said.

The tower was twenty feet deep and had a circumference of about sixty feet. In the wet season it would remain open to the elements to catch rainwater, but in the endless summer a temporary roof was attached to the top. This stopped the water evaporating and kept out thirsty birds who drank so much they often died and rotted right there in the tank. The top of the tower was turreted so that there was a gap of about an inch all around the rim that kept the hot summer water aerated but allowed access to only the slenderest of creatures. There was a hatchway in the roof leading to a removable ladder inside the tank.

The caretaker lifted the lid and sidled around to allow Siri to look inside. The light from the gap reflected on the still surface of the water below. He kicked off his sandals, rolled up his trouser legs, and clambered over the ledge onto the interior ladder. Carefully, he climbed down.

'Not a lot of water in here, is there?' he said.

She looked down through the hatch. 'What do you expect? You bastards stole the pump.'

'So how much would you estimate is in here? About three feet?'

'If you say so.'

When his foot touched the warm water, Siri stopped and looked up at the halo of light filtering in around the edge of the roof – a UFO circling above him – and he knew this was the last sight Sing had seen in his short life. He lowered himself into the water and cringed when his foot met the slime at the bottom. He could barely conceive what torture it had been for the boy. How many days had they left him here up to his waist in water? Hungry, eaten alive by mosquitoes, alone and afraid. Overcome by exposure or fatigue, he'd finally slipped below the surface of the water and drowned.

Siri waded carefully around the wall of the tower until he came to some markings. They were scratched in brown on the grey concrete. Siri visualized the scene: hours of yelling for help, the sounds muffled by the thick walls, desperation, boredom. A river pebble or two in the pocket of his school shorts. Around the second day, trembling from exposure, awful pain in his leg and thigh muscles, he occupies his mind by drawing a masterpiece. The stones aren't soft enough to be manageable, but over the course of the day he etches a lovely picture – a little girl with a smile half the size of her head. She's holding hands with a boy who has horns like a buffalo, or a devil. Beneath them a single word: friends.

The mixed emotions of the previous week welled up in Siri and he leaned his forehead against the concrete and bawled shamelessly. Tao's voice filled the tank twice before he could respond to it.

'You all right down there, Doctor?'

Siri wiped the tears from his face and waded to the ladder. 'No,' he said. 'I'm not.'

When all three were back on the ground, Siri put his face close to the woman's and drilled his meadow green eyes into hers. His voice was a growl.

'I've never in my life shown violence to a woman,' he

said. 'Never. But for somebody like you, I could easily break my own rules. You are ...'

He felt an almighty thump against his back and found himself flying through the air. He landed facedown in the mud, and within a split second some snarling and punching creature was on him. It bit into his ear and Siri felt the sharp pain of the membrane being ripped away. He smelled a vile breath and sensed an uncommon, inhuman fury. Only by rolling slightly to one side and digging his fingers into the attacker's face could Siri make out the identity. The brother, roused and angry, had come to the aid of his sister. His was an instinctive, animal reaction. Lurking inside the frail, silent man was a wild beast. This was the weapon that kept out intruders. They had no need of a gun.

Out of the corner of his eye, Siri could see Officer Tao locked in battle with the woman. She was scratching and spitting like a cat. The policeman was behind her with his arms locked around her chest but she was more than a match for the overweight cadre. There was no hope of his coming to Siri's aid anytime soon. Siri had wrestled in Paris, but in the lightest weight class. If his attacker had been more than a skeleton, Siri knew he'd have had no chance. Yet he prayed to summon just a fraction of his former skill to overcome the man who was beating him black and blue. With his fingers still clawing into the flailing brother's face, Siri rolled and pushed him farther away. The punches no longer landed with their full force, allowing Siri to catch his breath. With one final push he unbalanced the man, who fell sideways onto the damp earth. Siri used this momentum to roll him even further until his back was exposed, then latched onto him. He hooked his arms through the man's and locked his hands behind the man's head.

Pinned but still fuming, the man kicked back violently with his heels. The first blow resounded against Siri's shin and a bolt of pain seared through his body. The blood from his ear flowed down his face now, blinding him. He managed to hook his own leg around his assailant's and neutralize him. And there they lay in the mud, locked together like some Indian stone relief from the *Kama Sutra*. Siri was wheezing painfully, uncertain where he might find another breath.

'Nice show, Doctor,' Tao said, still locked in his own reverse tango with the sister. His mouth was very close to her ear. 'Now, Comrade, if you'd just calm down, we might be able to get some—'

'I'm not your comrade, you dirty Red son of a whore,' she screeched.

'Trying to win me over with flattery won't do you any good now,' Tao said. She back-heeled him and he swore under his breath. To forestall her, he lowered himself to his knees, leaving her in a sitting position. There was a moment or two of peace when only the breaths of the four combatants could be heard.

'So, Doctor,' Tao said at last. 'Any ideas?'

Siri looked over his shoulder at Tao and the red-faced woman.

'He did it, didn't he?' he said. 'Your brother threw the boy into the water tower.'

'I'm saying nothing to you, you communist scum.'

'Listen, you old witch, this has nothing to do with politics. I don't give a hoot who or what you support or believe in. What I care about is the little boy your brother left to die in that concrete tomb up there.'

'You have no proof of that,' she said.

The brother wriggled to free himself but Siri's grip was vice-like.

'Oh, but we do,' Siri said. 'You wouldn't believe what technological marvels are available to us at the Forensic Science Institute in Vientiane. I can match up the stones we found in Sing's pocket with the drawing there in your water tank, for one. Then it wouldn't surprise me if I found his hairs in the water. And you know what? I bet if we went to the back of the building, we'd find that wooden slide the builders used to dump their waste in the river is made of the same wood as the splinters in the boy's back. You found him dead, carried him outside, and sent him down into the Se Don like garbage. You're truly evil, both of you.'

'It was me,' she said.

'What?'

'I did it. All of it. He had nothing to do with any of this.'

'Is that so? In that case, you'd better calm him down before we get to the police station. If you don't, I doubt anyone will believe that particular version of the truth.'

'Will he be … if … when they convict me, will he be looked after?'

'The nice thing about socialism,' Siri said, 'is that everyone – no matter what their physical or mental state – gets treated equally.' He didn't bother to add the word 'badly'.

'All right.' She started to sing. It was an old folk song Siri had heard during his stay in the south. Although the woman's spoken voice was annoying and grating, she sang beautifully. Siri felt the brother relax in his arms and heard him breathe a deep sigh. When Siri released his grip, the man stayed where he was. Music had indeed soothed the savage breast.

20

TOASTING THE SPIES

At Pakse police station, Dr Somdy had ministered to the coroner's wounds and given him some painkillers. Tao saw him to the front gate.

'Two for two,' he said. 'That's a two hundred per cent better record than any of us has ever managed, Doctor. You're quite the detective. You ever considered joining the police?'

'You're just sucking up to me because I threatened to have you transferred to hell.'

'Well, yeah. I probably wouldn't bother saying it if I wasn't a bit scared of you, but it's the truth. I admire what you did. I know you had nothing to gain by solving this case. I get the feeling you did it just to let the mother have some peace. That's a great thing.'

'Concentrate on the small things and do them well.'

'I'll remember that.'

They shook hands and Siri walked through the muggy streets to his hotel. The thick cloud had returned, as mean as ever. It was a fitting overhang to his mood. He couldn't get the thought of wasted life out of his mind. He remembered what Keuk in Khong had said about the bodies they'd pulled from the river after the French reprisals. A mountain of them, he'd said, killed and tortured for loving their country, and what did it achieve? Really, what did those patriots have to show for their sacrifice? Was all this actually worth fighting for? Were his whimsical country-men worth defending? There he was again – thinking. It never did him any good. It didn't surprise him at all that the highest doctor suicide rate in the world was among pathologists.

He took a deep breath before walking into Pakse's best hotel, his home for over a week. The place was about as sophisticated as fried rice. The receptionist was sitting cross-legged on the floor behind the front desk plucking a chicken. He leaned over the counter and she smiled at him. She was in her teens and living proof that guest-relations skills are acquired over time.

'Oy, old man, what have you been up to? Did you fall off your bike? Your cousin's been looking for you all day. He asked me a dozen times where you might be, as if I'd have any idea.'

Siri dispensed with his usual lecture.

'Is he in?' he asked.

She looked up at the key rack. It was empty. 'Must be in his room.'

'Thank you.' He put his hand on the large green tele-phone that sat like a camouflaged armoured car on the desk. He'd never heard it ring. 'Does this thing work?'

'The phone? It's good for local. If you want to call long distance you have to go to the post office.'

'Right. Thanks.'

On the upstairs landing he stopped outside Civilai's door and heard what sounded like a party: laughter, cheering, all the sounds associated with celebration. He contemplated going directly to his own room but somehow forced himself to turn the handle and enter. He was astounded to see the array of guests inside. Sitting on the bed were two people so out of place in Pakse he didn't recognize them at first. Phosy and Dtui both rose to greet his arrival. As they approached him, Siri was able to quickly scan the rest of the throng. Phosy's soldier friend, Kumpai, sat on the floor beneath the Nordic stags. Governor Katay sat on one of the guest chairs with his hands behind his head, smiling like a happy father at a wedding. Civilai was in his usual seat with his fingers knitted together beneath his chin.

Phosy shook Siri's hand and Dtui gave him one of her rapid body-slam hugs before stepping back to look at him. He was bruised and bloodied and his less-than-complete ear was wrapped in a bandage. His clothes were the colour of dried mud.

'Hey, Doc,' Dtui said. 'Who beat you up?'

He smiled at Dtui and finally had a chance to use a line he'd heard many years ago in a movie in France. 'You should see the other guy.'

Dtui clapped and Phosy shook his hand again. There was more commotion and a lot of greeting and laughing, but nobody seemed to want to take the responsibility of telling him what they were celebrating.

'All right, I give up,' he said, taking a seat on the bed between his friends. 'What do you all know that I don't?'

'Between us,' Civilai said, 'it appears we've been able to thwart the coup.'

One of Siri's eyes opened wide. The other remained puffy and closed.

'You what? Why that's great. How? Tell me all about it.'

While Kumpai went downstairs to order as much alcohol as the city of Pakse could provide, Phosy and Dtui told of the events leading to their arrival at the land border at Chong Mayk, where they had slipped through a well-used smuggling trail. Escaping into Laos had been easier than escaping out of it. They were met by Kumpai at a predesignated spot and driven to Pakse that morning. The supposed phone call to the Ubon governor from Brother Fred's office had in fact been to one of Phosy's contacts on the Thai side. He, in turn, had been able to contact Kumpai in Champasak.

Dtui, being herself, often found Phosy's rendition of the facts a little dry so she peppered it with anecdotes to keep the crowd entertained.

'The mission Land Rover was better than a *laissez-passer*,' she said. 'The checkpoint guards all the way to the border just stared at the diplomatic plates and glanced up at my driver Phosy here, and me on the backseat. I was wearing these very Japanese ambassador's wife-type sunglasses I found in the glove box. I looked down my nose at these country boys and they stepped back. Some of them even saluted us. I couldn't believe it. I was heartbroken when our policeman here said we had to leave the car on the Thai side. I wanted to live in the thing.'

The first round of drinks arrived and Dtui made the initial toast of many.

'To our republic,' she said, raising her glass. The toast was echoed with resounding enthusiasm.

As the glasses continued to empty and refill, Siri glanced at Civilai. His friend was celebrating, joining in the festivities and enjoying the jokes. But, like Siri, he didn't seem to have the same sensation of unbridled relief and joy that the others obviously felt. It was as if they were both pretending. He wondered whether his friend was feeling the same frustration and guilt of failure that Siri felt himself. It was a fleeting moment and one that alcohol soon erased. He returned his attention to the party and held out his glass for a refill.

'I'm still missing facts,' he said. 'You're at the border and Kumpai meets you ...'

'Well, I suppose that's where I come in,' the governor said. 'I'd been summoned for a tête-à-tête with my Vietnamese counterpart. It appears the Vietnamese had become aware of an uprising, either based in or being channelled through Pakse. I was encouraged to round up any outsiders staying in town without official documentation. We began that search a few days ago and who should we catch in the net the day before yesterday but one undercover Lao army officer.'

'That would be me,' Kumpai said, putting up his hand. Kumpai had been an erstwhile nondrinker who had decided today was a good time to start. He'd begun to slur his words as soon as the cap was removed from the Johnnie Walker bottle (the real thing, not the Vietnamese rebottled variety). 'I got caught,' he said and slouched against the closet.

'We were able to confirm Captain Kumpai's identity with his superiors in Vientiane, and they insisted he share his knowledge with the Vietnamese security adviser. That's how we learned that Captain Kumpai was in contact with agents in Ubon.'

'That would be us,' said Dtui, and she and Phosy threw their hands into the air just as their drunken predecessor had done. They slapped their palms together and whooped. Johnnie worked a lot faster than rice whisky. The governor, relapsing into his schoolmaster persona, told the two to sit down and behave. They obliged, smiling, as he continued.

'When the captain received his call in regard to Officer Phosy, we sent men to facilitate his re-entry into Laos. He and Comrade Dtui were brought directly to my office. Our two rather amazing friends here had no end of valuable information for our attention.' There was another round of applause. 'During our manhunt for insurgents, we had also discovered that Comrade Civilai was here in Pakse incognito' – another round of applause; Civilai bowed dramatically – 'Captain Kumpai had told us of his purpose for being in the south, and today we coordinated our efforts with his. He was instrumental in pinpointing various government officials we could trust. We had the Vietnamese advisers share our information with them. Thanks to the broken code, a number of key rebels have already been arrested around the country. Following those arrests, more conspirators were implicated and apprehended.'

'Who was the character referred to near the beginning of the note?' Siri asked. 'The PP?'

'It would appear that Phetsarat Ponpaseth was involved in the coup.'

'Damn. And he's a minister.'

'He was until this afternoon. We can assume he was slated to be the head of the revolutionary government. I'm sorry to say the security forces were too slow to pick him up. He and one or two of the generals on the list have disappeared.'

'They probably fled as soon as they heard that the Ubon operation centre had been compromised,' Civilai said.

'So it would seem,' Katay continued. 'But despite that little setback, my Vietnamese counterpart assures me that as far as Hanoi and Vientiane are concerned, the coup threat has been nullified.'

There was a spontaneous cheer in the little room, followed by much hugging and backslapping. It was an easy atmosphere to be caught up in but Siri continued to feel like an observer who'd stumbled upon someone else's victory parade. He didn't begrudge them their celebration. A win was a win. But he was sorry Daeng wasn't there with them. She was the one who'd made the Ubon connection. This was her victory also. He'd sent a trishaw driver to find her but she wasn't in her shanty. He thought back to that last night when they'd celebrated together in Savanaketh in 1945, the night they'd drunk to their country's independence. He recalled how he'd felt then and wondered why he didn't have any of those emotions now. Perhaps it was age.

He would have appreciated some time alone with Civilai. There were one or two things still worrying him that he knew his friend could explain, but through the evening and into the night the old brothers found themselves apart. Circumstances didn't give them a chance to chat. First it was the unflagging conversation, then the trail of visitors from the town hall, and the military bringing ongoing reports and not leaving. Then it was the whisky. With Lao rice whisky there were clear signals that it was time to stop: stomachs evacuating, eyes blurring, bottoms flatulating. But those heathen Scottish tribes had created a brew that seduced a man and forced him to consume beyond the point of logic. He would find himself floating above the clouds on the back of a giant eagle, euphorically stupid. He would be so assured of himself that even when the eagle vanished – *poof* – and he was tumbling down toward the bleak rugged mountains of the highlands, he would still swear he was in control. He might even attempt a somersault or two as he dropped, and then *splat*.

Siri awoke from his own personal *splat* in a damp patch of grass above the ferry port. He had no idea how he had arrived there. Before him, the Se Don, which often gave the impression it was something special as far as rivers were concerned, converged with the magnificent Mekhong like a worm running into a giant cobra. The scene was too vast for Siri's limited consciousness to take in. His brain felt like it had shrivelled to the size of a walnut. When he moved his head he could hear it rattle inside his skull. His ear throbbed, his eyes smarted, and his neck was as stiff as a tree stump. His body was a treasure trove of aches and agonies. The morphine and the adrenaline had long since worn off and he was left with no doubt that he'd engaged in a wrestling match with a younger man. Hoisting himself onto one elbow was a major feat.

With the sky still obscured by grumbling clouds, it was difficult to pinpoint the hour. Something in his inner clock told him it was a quarter past dawn, but there was a thin line between instinct and downright guesses. Down in the river, up to her waist in the rust brown water, a woman bathed. She wore a thin cotton cloth tied above her breasts. The bathing sarong is sewn into a tube and, from experience, Siri knew she would be naked inside it. To Siri's mind, there was nothing more beautiful, nothing in the world as erotic, as a woman bathing in a river.

She untied the loose knot and pulled the cloth forward. She took the soap from its floating dish, reached inside her sarong, and scrubbed. Then she retied the knot and reached up inside from the hem and took great pains to soap even the most inaccessible nooks and crannies. She gave a little spin-drier shimmy, collected her soap dish, and waded to the bank with the cloth sticking to her lean body like a tattoo. Siri was invigorated. It was a sight to turn a boy into a man. It was so stimulating he could momentarily forget the river bacteria and algae that dedicated their short lives to seeking out warm fertile flesh to infest. He could certainly forgive her for polluting a waterway that provided drinking water to thousands of families downstream, and the thought of what might have entered the water upstream wasn't even worth considering. All of that fell into the realm of meaningless trivia when compared to the pleasure to be had from watching a woman bathe in a river.

The sight reminded him why he'd come to this spot in the early hours of the morning. Even before the party had begun to wind down, it had become imperative to see Daeng and tell her the news. In his inebriated state he'd been unable to find her small house along the confusing backstreets so he'd gone to her noodle stand. Not surprisingly, at 3 a.m. it was all disassembled and tied onto her cart, which in turn was padlocked to a six-inch pipe. He'd climbed the bluff to consider his next move and there fatigue and pain had overcome him.

But now the ferry was operating and a lot of hungry people would be passing up and down the ramp. He knew his old friend would be at work, and nothing soothed a hangover like a bowl of noodles. If Daeng's noodle stall had been equipped with rafters it would have been jammed to them. The little plastic stools were all occupied, some by two patrons each balancing on one cheek. Others sat eating on the concrete ramp with their feet dangling over the edge. A long queue of people stood in front of the cart watching Daeng work the noodle baskets – ever in control – always with time to smile and joke with her clients. Siri stood to one side and admired her skill.

After a few minutes she noticed him.

'Brother Siri, what are you doing over there?' All the diners looked up at the battered old man. 'And what on earth have you been up to? No, don't tell me. I hear you were walking the streets at three this morning looking for my bedroom.' An ironic cheer rose from the happy eaters. Siri blushed a deep crimson. She really did know everything, this woman.

By the time he'd hobbled to the cart he still hadn't thought of a witty retort. He merely squeezed her arm affectionately and whispered in her ear that the coup had been thwarted. She obviously knew that, too.

'Yes, good news, isn't it?' she said. She didn't seem excited. This was the same 'ho hum' that he'd felt himself the previous evening. Perhaps she'd already exhausted her ability to celebrate. Quite unashamedly, Daeng told the people in the queue that Siri was her one true love so would they mind if he cut in, just this once? Of course, nobody objected. Love conquers all. He ordered the special, which was the ordinary plus fifty per cent more of everything. As she handed him the enormous steaming bowl she said, 'You're going back to Vientiane today.' It wasn't a question.

'At five.'

'I need to talk to you before then. About two? I'll be finished with the lunch crowd.'

'Should I come here?'

'No, I'll come to the hotel. There's something important you should know and I have something to show you.'

Siri took his breakfast and his spoon and his Vietnamese chopsticks to the embankment and sat like a child, kicking his legs over the edge and filling his face. It was a happy experience. He looked back over his shoulder and gave Daeng an enthusiastic two-thumb salute. He couldn't remember having a better breakfast in his life, and he certainly had no dementia when it came to food. It cleared his head, settled his stomach, and started the rusty old cogs rotating in his brain. A peculiar thought, more like an accidental hypothesis, had been following him for the past twenty-four hours. It was so preposterous he'd tried to shake it off but it kept coming back. He had no choice but to satisfy his curiosity.

21

ALL THAT IS SOLID

The Bureau de Poste opened at eight. He was the first customer. A little girl was manning the counter while her mother loaded letters into the PO boxes. Siri ignored the woman and stood in front of the girl.

'Are you the manager?' he asked.

'No,' the girl said. 'I'm five.'

The mother looked over and smiled. 'She's off from school today.'

Siri continued speaking with the girl. 'I'd like to buy a stamp, please.' She was delighted.

'Yes, Grandpa. What colour?'

'How much is a green one?'

'Two *kip*.'

'Oh, dear. I've only got half a *kip*.' He produced a one-*kip* note folded in half. Since the latest devaluation, the notes had become good-luck tokens for weddings and such, but you couldn't buy a breath of air for one *kip*.

'Then you have to have a white one,' the girl said. She took the note and pretended to be looking for stamps in the drawer.

'And I certainly want one without gum on the back,' Siri added. The girl handed him a piece of paper she'd torn from a telegram. 'Perfect. Thank you.'

The mother laughed and returned to her stool at the counter.

'I bet you have a whole houseful of grandchildren,' she said.

He didn't let the hurt reach his face. 'Not a one, I'm afraid.' He remembered Boua's refrain, played over and over like a scratched record. 'We have a nation to salvage, Siri. How selfish it would be for us to dedicate ourselves to our own children.'

He'd always wanted a family. She would have none of it. Perhaps that was his problem in life now. He had no children or grandchildren for whom to make his country a better place. He had nobody to pass his legacy on to.

'That's sad,' the mother said. 'What can I do for you? Apart from the white gumless stamp.'

Siri smiled and pulled the photograph from his shoulder bag.

After the post office, Siri stopped off briefly at Sing's school to tell Mim about the picture her best friend had drawn for her, how Sing had been thinking about her even at the end. Then there was a visit to the town hall, a stop at the police station to sign the witness report, a detour to Pakse hospital for a morphine top-up, and a call to the city radio station. His last trishaw trip was out beyond the teachers' college to a house that took almost an hour to locate. What he learned there emptied him of all hope. He recalled a quotation from the Communist Manifesto: 'All that is solid melts into air, all that is holy is profaned, and men at last are forced to face with sober senses the real conditions of their lives and their relations with their fellow men.' Until today he hadn't really understood it. His mood on the journey back into town was dour and foreboding.

The sky was like a mauve pudding, threatening to dump its filling onto the nervous townsfolk.

Siri arrived back at the hotel at one. Dtui and Phosy were sitting in the lobby. He took a deep breath and did his best to keep his misery to himself.

'Hello, children,' he said, but his disguise apparently didn't work.

'You look glum, Doc,' Dtui told him.

'It's gravity. You get to an age where everything on your face sags. The only way you can look truly happy is to stand on your head. Want to see?'

'Not now,' Phosy said. 'We've just had lunch.'

'Or at least something on a plate impersonating lunch,' Dtui added.

'Very well,' said Siri, knowing there was no time to introduce the couple to Daeng's noodle stall. 'You seen Uncle Civilai?'

'He's still in his room, I imagine,' Dtui said. 'He wasn't hungry. I get the feeling last night's session took its toll. He hasn't been down all day.'

'I'll go and bang on his door for half an hour.'

'I'm sure that'll make him feel much better,' Dtui laughed. 'Remind him we have to be at the airport at four thirty.'

'I will.'

Siri walked slowly up to the second floor and stopped in front of Civilai's door to catch his breath. Pakse would be the death of him yet. He tried the handle. The door was unlocked. It creaked as he opened it and walked inside. Civilai was still sitting in the same chair, now facing the window. He was looking up at the bruised clouds that gave the room a shadowy evening feeling.

'Should I turn on the light?' Siri asked.

'The power's off again,' Civilai said without turning. 'We have a hydroelectric dam pumping out 150 megawatts of electricity and we still can't keep the lights working. I imagine the man who pulls the lever is off at a seminar someplace.'

'The phone downstairs hardly works even when there is electricity,' Siri said. He sat in the other rattan chair and watched the same heavy clouds rapidly turn to charcoal. 'That would have been annoying for you, considering all that contact you had to make with Vientiane.'

Civilai cast him a brief angry glance. 'I've been waiting for this. Don't play Inspector Maigret with me, Siri. Not with me.'

'What do you mean?'

'What do I mean? Tell me your next comment wasn't going to be something like, "At least you kept in shape running back and forth to the post office to call your people."'

'It was going to be a little funnier, but, yes, something like that.'

'And then I say, "Right, I should have taken a room above the post office", and you jump to your feet and say, "Aha, got you." Am I right?'

'Yes.'

'You've been everywhere that has long-distance phones, haven't you? The radio station, the army?'

'Yes.'

'And?'

'You already know.'

'Tell me anyway.'

'The only place that's seen you is the Bureau de Poste and that was yesterday. You apparently made quite a few calls. The woman hadn't seen you at all before that.'

'Which means?'

'It means a lot of things. It means you've been lying ever since we got here. You weren't in touch with anybody at all. Yesterday you warned all your coup pals to get out of town. It means you've betrayed your country, betrayed me – betrayed us.'

'Betray is a relative term. In your case you could look at it as protection. Does that make it feel any better, little brother? What you didn't know couldn't hurt you. How's that?'

Siri laughed. 'Protection? How nice of you. You give yourself a vacation on the strength of my forging you a health certificate. You pretend you're coordinating some huge undercover counter-revolution and all the time you're – what? – hiding. You're biding your time and making sure I didn't stir up any trouble for your coup mongers. Who exactly do you believe you were protecting me from?'

'From your eternal worst enemy.'

Siri got to his feet and stood between Civilai and his cloud gazing.

'No, this is no time to be condescending. We both know you weren't here for *my* benefit. Damn it, you even got to me. You made me feel ashamed that I was interfering with your "official" work. All the time I've been interpreting your moods as the result of things I'd done wrong. Hell, I even apologized. But I had nothing at all to do with your being a pain in the arse. It was all your doing. What on earth were you thinking?'

He waited for a response but Civilai still hadn't looked him directly in the eye. Siri raised his voice. 'That wasn't intended as a rhetorical question. I really do need to know what the hell you were thinking.' Civilai remained silent.

'Damn it. After all the years we've known each other, you think you can do something like this?'

At last, Civilai's eyes connected with Siri's. But they were wet, vacuous eyes like those of a fish staring from a bowl.

'Marvellous,' he said. 'So you really do have all the pieces. I had a feeling you'd work it out sooner or later.'

'Yes, I have all the bloody pieces. I wouldn't have even considered this discussion unless I was absolutely certain you'd lost your old fool mind. I sat at Daeng's going over things. There were too many questions that didn't seem to fold neatly into how this crisis was resolved. I wondered how you could possibly have been in touch with Vientiane if the hotel phone didn't operate long distance. I wondered why you didn't consider contacting the Vietnamese. You'd said something about not wanting them to have more control over us than they already did. But of all the players in this, they were the ones with a vested interest in keeping the Thais out. It was a last resort but I calculated we'd reached that stage already.'

'So it was you who alerted them?'

'Too true, it was me.'

'You couldn't stop your meddling, could you? Despite everything I said.'

'My meddling might just have saved a lot more unnecessary bloodshed.'

'My hero.'

'Then I went over the note again. There was still one part that didn't make sense to me. Daeng suggested I go to see an old Frenchman who lives here. He spent much of his life as a linguist. He interpreted for the colonists, then married a Lao lass, and settled down. He gave me a brief lesson in transcription.'

'Spare me.'

'Not on your life. I have a lot of ammunition and nobody else to shoot. Suffer it! We Lao don't get many opportunities to see our names in Roman script. The Frenchman told me that most Civilais who work for foreigners or study overseas would spell their name with an *S*. He believes only those who wanted to make a statement about being civilized or a servant of civilization would spell it as you do.'

'Far too deep, brother. The school administrators saddled me with it before they shipped me off to Paris. I couldn't do a thing about it.'

'Whatever you say. But either way the Frenchman was confident that in certain circumstances – for example, if an American-educated Lao transcribed a Lao name into English – your initials might very well be SS.'

'Can we stop yet?'

'Dtui had thrown us all with her translation of 2PM. She'd guessed it was a time reference so we all but stopped looking at it. The Frenchman pointed out that 'PM' could just as well refer to prime minister. Prime minister number two. You were about to become the deputy prime minister in an illegitimate government.'

'And?'

'And I'm back to my original question. What were you thinking? And more important, why did you even begin to think about getting involved without consulting me? I'm your closest friend, goddamn it. I could have talked some sense into you. What was it, blackmail? Did they threaten your family?'

Civilai closed his watery eyes and rested his head back on the chair.

'No.'

'Then what hold did they have over you?'

'What is it we do when we're together, Siri?'

'I give up.'

'How do we entertain ourselves during our long drunken bouts of clarity?'

'I ...'

'I'll tell you. Eighty per cent of our topic of conversation is about the inadequacy of our government, the government we fought for thirty years to install.'

'It's not—'

'The government that should have learned from the mistakes of all the fools who ran the country before it. Instead, we've just given a new twist to inefficiency, made it more creative. We are a socialist administration and socialism is the building, under the dictatorship of the proletariat, of the material base for communism. You had to memorize that, too, remember? Well, I don't see myself under the dictatorship of any proletariat. The people are suffering no less than they always were.'

'That isn't true.'

'It is, and you know it. I'd go home after each of our philosophical sessions, with the firm belief that what we've created is a joke. There were nights I'd lock myself in the bathroom and cry my eyes out because I was part of that joke. My name was up there on the party roster and I hadn't done a thing to change the status quo.'

'You tried.'

Civilai opened his eyes. In the shadows they were deep hollows. 'If I'd tried – I mean if I'd really tried,' he said, 'things would have changed. I dabbled. I let out a few old-man rants, but who listened? I became powerless. I became symbolic in a way that inanimate objects or the dead are symbolic. What made our talks together so hard to take was the fact that everything we said was true. If they'd listened to us, we wouldn't be in the mess we're in now.'

'That's what old codgers in coffee shops all around the world believe,' Siri said. 'There are seventy-three-year-olds somewhere in a bar in London, who believe they have the answers to the world's problems.'

Civilai shook his head. 'But they aren't senior politburo members on the Central Committee. They don't have a real opportunity. I did. The disgruntled politicians and military men contacted me. They needed someone senior, someone respected, who represented change, modernity, freedom to the people. It was as if they'd heard me talking in my sleep. They knew I was a loose cannon, dissatisfied, and resentful. And I said, "Certainly, I doubt it could make things any worse." And that was it. Phetsarat as prime minister, me as deputy. I'd be able to influence decisions and accomplish something at last. Why not? I'd be far less impotent than I am now.'

Siri sighed and sat back down. 'And the reason you didn't discuss all this with me was ...?'

Civilai paused, apparently considering this question for the first time. 'Because there was a slight doubt in my mind as to whether you'd go along with it,' he said at last.

Siri leaned back onto the cushions and relaxed his weary body and mind and soul. He tried to imagine that scenario: Civilai telling him of his opportunity to be part of a coup. Yes, he would have talked his friend out of it. Why would there be any doubt in his own mind about that? Why was he unable to say so right away? Why did no words come to him? The sky began to rumble a warning. The room was so dark that if they'd looked at each other there would have been nothing to see. But neither looked. They each stared at the sky. It was Civilai's hoarse voice that broke the deadlock.

'What are you planning to do with me?'

'Do?'

'Yes, you've obviously considered my punishment.'

'It hasn't entered my head.'

'That's because you know I was right to do what I did. We're of one mind.'

Siri laughed. 'Obviously not. If that were true you wouldn't have been too afraid to share this insanity with me.' Suddenly, the words came to him with perfect clarity. 'No rational person would replace a two-year-old administration with a gang of renegade officers with dollars in their pockets and expect things to improve. Don't you see? All the same old criminals would be back on the bus to Laos. The Vietnamese advisers would be replaced by Thai advisers, and capitalism would be back chewing on us again. It would be a hundred times worse than it was before.

'Yes, we're grumpy old men. Yes, we complain. It's in our blood. But it's only because we're impatient. After all those years of struggle we wanted to remake our world in seven days. We wanted to see everything blooming and flourishing right now because we're secretly afraid we aren't going to be around to see it otherwise. But by the Holy Buddha, you aren't going to be able to make those changes overnight. Lord help us. I want to slap you, I really do.'

'Go ahead.'

Siri rose from his seat, walked over to the dark shape that contained his friend, and raised his hand. But he couldn't. The rain began to thump against the glass of the windowpanes at his back and lightning threaded through the clouds. He returned his hand to his side and looked down at his broken friend. Civilai's head bowed toward his lap. His shoulders shook as he sobbed. The lightning picked out a man as old as the earth. Siri knelt on the floor and put his hands on Civilai's lumpy knees. He had thought of a punishment.

When Siri returned to the lobby, Dtui and Phosy were no longer there. It was just as well because he doubted he'd have been able to fake a sense of humour for them. The front desk and some of the tables held storm lamps whose flames were barely visible in the dark room. He went towards the exit with the intention of walking out into the torrential rain. It was a habit he'd picked up in the tropical storms of Vietnam. They pummelled a man like tin on an anvil, and unless the lightning killed you, they were therapeutic to the point of elation. But before he could reach the newly shuttered door, a voice called him back.

'Dr Siri.'

It was Daeng. She sat in the dark reception area dressed in a nice pink blouse and a neatly ironed *phasin*. Her hair was loose. It hung thick and grey over her shoulders. The shadows had blurred the wrinkles and filled the cheeks and for a second or two Siri saw the young enthusiastic girl cook who'd followed him around begging for errands, hungry for knowledge. She walked over to him, looked at his face, and lifted her eyebrows. She had to raise her voice to be heard above the sound of the rain.

'Goodness,' she shouted. 'I was planning to tell you something important, but it looks like you already know.'

'What gives you that impression?'

'Well, a) your face looks like it's been held over a sacrificial bowl and drained of blood, and b) you were about to go out into a storm that could drown a man. It all adds up to you fighting the devil. I'd say you were just upstairs with Comrade Civilai.'

'What colour underwear do I have on?'

'I beg your pardon?'

'You seem to know everything else.'

'Don't bite me, Siri. It wasn't me, you know.'

'Yes, I know. I'm sorry. Was it Civilai you came to tell me about?'

'Yes.'

'I don't think I'm ready to discuss how I feel.'

She took his hand. 'I know. Never mind. I've brought something much better than bad tidings. Come.'

She led him to one of the lit tables at the rear where her cloth bag sat on a chair. The flame of the lamp danced inside its glass bowl as the storm winds forced their way through the gaps around the shutters. The receptionist was busy mopping back a flood of water that had gushed in with them. It was the type of storm you imagined could lift the hotel and carry it halfway around the earth. The old comrades in arms knelt on the vinyl chairs and let the water flow beneath them. Daeng reached into her bag and produced an album. She lifted it carefully as if it were precious or fragile. She laid it on the bare wooden table and opened it at the title page. This had already been a taxing day for Siri's heart, but what he saw in the dim lamplight almost stopped it beating completely.

Champasak Camp – 1940

'Where on earth …?' he asked.

235

'You don't recall the photographer, Siri? A Marseille-trained boy. The French administration sent him south to document everything from the southern camps. They wanted evidence they were doing something for the souls of the local youth.'

'I do remember. Skinny boy from Xiang Khouang.'

'That's him.'

'But we didn't ever see those pictures. He was with us for – what? – six months? Then he took all the undeveloped film back with him to Vientiane.'

'He promised he'd send me prints.'

'He had an eye for you, as I recall.'

'Didn't they all? All but one, I mean.' Siri felt her glancing at him but didn't look up from the title page that described the camp and its purpose. 'And, to my surprise,' she continued, 'he kept his word. It wasn't the fastest-kept word in history but about fifteen years ago I had a visitor.'

'The skinny boy.'

'Had become a skinny middle-aged man. He'd moved to France, married, et cetera, et cetera. But when he decided to come back to Laos he made this set of prints for me. He found me, and here they are.'

'I hope you thanked him properly.'

'Least I could do, considering what he'd brought me. It was the loveliest gift a girl could get.'

She flipped open to the first set of pictures and Siri's mind turned eleven spinning somersaults into the page. He was back in 1940. There he was standing with his class, B5, all eighteen-year-olds in their group photo, everyone taller than Dr Siri, everyone as happy as lizards in an ant storm. There he was in front of a blackboard, his raven black hair invisible against the black paint, his trim-waisted shirt a little too tight, highlighting his muscles. There he was at a campfire, lit by the light of the flames, deep in discussion, eyes burning with passion.

'Heavens,' he said. 'I was adorable.'

'No argument there,' Daeng agreed.

He turned another page. There he was, there they were: Siri and Boua sitting at a foldable table discussing the curriculum. Him smiling; her serious, young, beautiful – alive. His pulse raced just looking at her.

'You were quite a couple.'

Siri couldn't bring himself to turn the page. 'We used to have pictures,' he said. 'Some from France, some from Hanoi, posed, studio pictures mostly. But they were either lost or destroyed by the elements. This is the first picture I've seen of her for … I don't know, twenty years.'

'You loved her. We could all tell.'

'Still do.'

Daeng looked into his green eyes and smiled. 'There are more of the two of you in there.'

Siri went through the photographs one by one, naming the youths, remembering exactly what activities they'd done on that particular day. But while he was studying them, he noticed something as clearly as if it had been written in head-lines above each picture: enthusiasm. The kids looked at their teachers as if they could see halos. They were eating up every-thing. And these weren't the posed photos the PL set up for propaganda. This was the real thing. These boys and girls were pumped up with national pride. Looking at them made him understand why he'd hesitated to condemn Civilai.

'They look like they're happy to be there,' he said.

'We all were. Two important teachers trained in France, and a qualified doctor and nurse no less. You could have both been off somewhere making a lot of money, but instead you gave up two years to work with poor kids. What did they pay you? Two francs a month?'

'I believe there was a fifty-centime Christmas bonus.' They laughed.

'Of course they were happy to be there,' Daeng said. 'They idolized you both. You were heroes to us. We all loved you.'

And that was something else Siri had noticed in the black-and-white pictures. The attractive cook attending classes, helping at meetings. No, not attractive – beautiful. At the time he'd hardly noticed her. It certainly hadn't occurred to him how lovely she was. An old Lao poet had once written that love was a sharpened spear that gouged out a man's eyes. That had obviously been the case with Boua. He'd never noticed other women, didn't once consider being with anyone else. He'd never observed Daeng's adoring stares, her constant presence. He saw them now.

'You weren't ugly yourself,' he said.

'At last, a compliment. Well worth the wait.'

They laughed again and Siri closed the album and rested his hands on the back cover.

'That was marvellous, truly marvellous,' he said. 'You wouldn't know how much I needed that. Or, yes, perhaps you would. Thank you so much for letting me see it.'

'Oh, I didn't bring it just to show you,' she said. 'It's a gift.'

'No.'

'Yes.'

'I could never expect you to part with such a precious thing.'

'Siri, I think over the past couple of weeks, you've lost yourself. I want you to have this so if it ever happens again you just have to look at the faces of your students.'

He leaned over and kissed her on the cheek and this time she didn't pull back.

22

DTUI PUTS ON WEIGHT

It was September. A good deal had happened in the People's Democratic Republic of Laos but nothing had changed. Perhaps it was because news is only news if it comes to fruition. A THOUSAND PEOPLE NOT KILLED IN AN EARTHQUAKE is hardly a headline you'd expect to see in a national newspaper. The failed coup was news that didn't materialize. The Party decided to keep it to themselves and not trouble the population with it. The people had enough problems of their own. *Pasason Lao* newspaper saw fit not to mention an ex-minister's being arrested and sent to seminar, or one or two generals transferred to posts that didn't exist. In the hands of the Lao Department of Information, something like the Second World War could have ended up as a slight fracas.

The resignation of a senior member of the politburo due to ill health, on the other hand, warranted a full page. It mentioned Civilai Songsawat's devotion to the Party and his long career of faithful service. In the accompanying photograph he looked full of enthusiasm and vim. It was thirty years old. As few people bothered to read the *Pasason Lao*, Civilai's departure, like the August coup attempt, passed unnoticed like fireflies in the midday sun.

At the Mahosot morgue, for the first two weeks, the same could be said. A lot had happened but nothing had changed. Mr Geung, the morgue assistant who wore his Down's syndrome like a fashion statement, was out of the hospital and back at work. He'd laughed at all Dtui's stories of their exploits in Thailand and understood no more than half of them, but it didn't matter.

Dr Siri had betrayed his country but only two people knew that – three if he included the fortune-teller. The shadow behind the wicked man was equally guilty. He'd failed to expose a traitor, settling instead for a compromise. Civilai would leave public office and grow vegetables on the land behind his small house in the old American compound. Being away from his beloved politburo would be punishment enough. Neither of them would talk of the events of the Ubon coup. Siri, after much soul-searching and river watching, decided that he could live with that level of treachery, and got on with his life. Dtui ate, Judge Haeng grumbled, Crazy Rajid walked naked in circles around Nam Poo Fountain. Everything had apparently reverted to the way it was before the blind dentist walked under a Chinese logging truck. But then a day arrived when everything turned upside down.

Siri was in his office, trying in a report to explain an aneurysm of the splenic artery in a way that Judge Haeng might understand. He was referring to Chairman Mao's *Little Red Book* for suitable similes when a most unexpected guest walked into the room. Dtui and Geung and Siri all looked up from their desks when Daeng appeared in the doorway.

'Sorry,' she said. 'There wasn't a front doorbell so I thought I should just come in.' Siri walked over to her with a big smile on his face.

'Well, well,' he said. 'Apart from Dr Kissinger, you're the last person I expected to find standing in my morgue.'

'You know how I am, Siri. I had this impulse, and once I get an idea in my head ...'

He introduced her to his staff and sat her on the guest chair in front of his desk.

'Are you in town long?' he asked.

'It's the funniest thing,' she said. 'I thought it would just be a flying visit, see some old friends, do the sights. And there I was at Chantabouli Temple and I spotted this sad little run-down noodle shop with a sign nailed to the front saying it was for sale. I found the owner and she almost begged me to take over the place. All but giving it away, she was.'

'Oh, I say,' Siri blushed. He noticed Dtui grinning over the guest's shoulder. 'Does that mean ...?'

'Well, if I can get through all the red tape and paperwork, I may be living here permanently.'

Siri was outwardly flustered but inwardly turning cart-wheels. 'Excellent. I mean, at last they'll have some decent noodles in this city. What exactly was the impulse that brought you down here in the first place?'

'Just some historical matter I never did manage to resolve.'

'Is it something I can help with?'

She stood and stretched her old legs. 'Oh, I think your input could be integral, Siri. But look at me chatting on. I have to rush. Don't want to keep you from your ... whatever it is you do here. Be good. Nice meeting you all. Bye.'

Siri walked her to the front door and came back with red cheeks and an indelible smile.

'Is that a wicked grin I see on your face, Dr Siri?' Dtui asked.

'He's got a g ... g ... girlfriend,' Mr Geung posited philo-sophically.

In the face of this onslaught, Siri elected to remain silent. He pretended he was engrossed in Haeng's report and ignored all of Dtui's attempts to draw him away from it. At first, he believed it was her curiosity that caused her to stay after the siren had sounded calling the nursing staff to tend their radishes. It didn't occur to him that she might have a bombshell or two to drop herself. As he was putting the final sentence into his report, her significant shadow loomed over him. She was directly between him and the low evening sun.

'Nurse Dtui, you're causing an eclipse.'

'I've cut back on banana fritters.'

'Nevertheless …'

She stepped away from the window but continued to look at him.

'I have no intention of discussing Madame Daeng with you at this juncture,' he said.

'It's not that,' she replied.

She looked uneasy, most un-Dtui-like.

'Sit,' he said. She lowered herself onto the chair in front of his desk. He placed his pen on top of the report and folded his arms. 'Speak!'

'I …'

It was the first time he could recall her hesitating.

'You …?'

'I've contacted the overseas study committee and told them I … I won't be going to Moscow in January.'

Siri's eyes protruded from his face like golf balls. 'I beg your pardon?'

'I've asked if I can defer for two years.' He was too stunned to react. Getting a placement on the study programme was harder than finding a cold beer in a socialist state. 'They said yes.'

'Dtui, have you gone mad? You've been cramming for this since you got your nursing certificate. It's been your dream to study overseas.'

'I know.'

'What in Trotsky's name happened?'

She leaned forward with her elbows on her lap and knotted her fingers.

'First, there was Ma. I'd always thought if I could go to another country, I'd work part-time and send money back for her treatment. Then she ...'

'That was never the only reason, and you know it. You have a sponge for a brain, young Dtui. You thirst for knowledge. You always have. That was always your chief motivation. You have a unique opportunity here. You've worked ... we've all worked too hard to get you there to just give it up. If there's no other reason ...'

'There is.' She sighed. 'Can I tell you without your blowing up?'

'I think I'm ready for anything.'

'I'm pregnant.'

He realized he'd lied when he'd said he was ready for anything. If he hadn't been sitting he would have fallen to the floor.

'What?'

'You heard.'

'How?'

'I'm sure I don't need to tell you how.'

Siri was too overwhelmed to bother with good grammar. 'I mean – you – how? Who?'

'Now just calm down. I'm not going to give you any details until you start breathing again.'

'I'm not breathless. I'm speechless.'

'Well, thank goodness for that. Perhaps I'll be able to get a word or two in. Don't forget, this is a big thing for me, too. A girl doesn't get pregnant every day. I'm a little bit speechless myself. I'm having a lot of firsts here. First baby, first …'

'Oh my word.' Siri slid open his drawer and fumbled deep inside. 'Who was it? Who did this to you?'

'I hope you aren't looking for a gun in there.'

'If I had one, I'd probably use it on you. But for the present I'm searching for a name card.' He removed the entire drawer and put it on top of the desk. 'I know it's in here somewhere. Come on, I'm waiting for an answer.'

When he looked up he saw her staring down at the tiles. There was a hint of guilt on her face that gave away her secret.

'He didn't?'

'He did.'

'In Ubon?'

'Twice.'

'Then I do need a gun.'

'No, Doc. Really, you don't. I didn't exactly play hard to get.'

'How can you tell so soon?'

'These are the seventies, Doc. There have been great advances in medical science since you went to school.'

'Dtui, this isn't a game. And he's married, for goodness' sake.'

'His wife deserted him. He filed papers for divorce in her absence. It came through last month.'

'Well, isn't that convenient? Here.' He peeled an old throat lozenge from the name card he sought and held it up triumphantly. 'Lucky I kept this. It's a lady doctor I met

through the Women's Union. She's perfectly respectable.'
He handed her the card.

She read it and her eyebrows rose.

'Dr Siri, I'm not telling you all this because I want to get rid of the baby. I'm going to keep it.'

'And raise it by yourself?'

'Not exactly.'

'You don't honestly believe Phosy's going to do the right thing by you? He's a randy middle-aged man who merely took advantage of an opportunity.'

'I'm sure he'll be delighted to hear you think so highly of him. In fact, I'm a little bit offended myself. What makes you think it was he who took advantage?'

'Dtui, what's come over you?'

'I think they call it love.'

'Oh, child. What does he say about all this?'

'He seems OK with it.'

'Seems OK?'

'He isn't a big talker when it comes to feelings and personal odds and ends. But I told him I was going to keep the baby and he said he'd raise it with me.'

'Not the most impassioned proposal I've ever heard.'

'He's a policeman.'

'Right. And you realize, I suppose, that policemen get shot.'

'Only in the movies. Phosy's a sticky-rice policeman.'

Siri tilted onto the back legs of his chair and leaned against the file cabinet.

'Until I met you, Nurse Dtui, I could outstubborn anyone in the country. Once you make up your mind I know a battery of field artillery can't shake you. So I'm not going to waste my time.'

'Thanks.'

'I know it's a terrible decision and it will lead to disaster, but if it's a boy ...'

'Your name's already pencilled in.'

'And I expect to see Phosy here in my office.'

'He's waiting outside.'

Siri didn't expect Phosy to turn up with his hat in his hand, but a little more remorse might have been in order. He walked into the office, shook his head, and laughed.

'Who would have thought it?' he said.

'Not me, certainly,' Siri replied. 'How could you?'

'Come on, Doctor. I'm not all bad. She could do a lot worse.'

'I'm not so sure. You're two decades older than she is.'

'Just numbers.'

'Do you love her?'

'No.'

Siri raised his brows. 'I was expecting you to think about that for a bit longer. Does she know?'

'We've talked about it. Siri, she and I are friends. I respect her. I like her personality, most of it anyway. And she did save my life in Ubon. There's fate connecting us.'

'Gratitude's hardly a fitting motive for committing your life to someone. Besides, your life was never really in danger, Phosy. You had someone looking out for you. He wouldn't have let anything happen to either of you.' Siri knew that Civilai had ensured no harm would come to Dtui or Phosy while they were at the camp.

'Yeah? Who was that then?'

'That I can't tell you.'

'You know I'll get it out of you over a drink.'

'I don't drink any more.'

'Right. And I hear they've drained the Pacific so they can tile the ocean bed.'

'Believe what you want. And stop changing the subject. Dtui's a daughter to me.'

'Look! I loved a woman in my way and she ran off. So, as far as I'm concerned, love's overrated. It doesn't suit me.'

'She loves you.'

'Dr Siri. I made an offer. She accepted it. She knows I'll be good to her. I'll look after our child. We'll grow old together and fight a lot and laugh a lot. I'm not going to invent an emotion I don't have, but I'm a stayer.'

'If you ever go back on your word I'll haunt you for life, and you know that isn't an idle threat.'

'I promise.'

Siri stared into Phosy's eyes and beyond them into his mind. 'All right,' he said at last. 'I believe you.' They shook hands. 'Congratulations, Pa.'

'Thanks, Grandpa.'

'Don't push your luck.'

'Sorry. Now, is all the father–son-in-law stuff over with yet? I have some news.'

'Go ahead.'

'The dentist's wife.'

'What about her?'

'She's a sow.' Siri once again exercised his eyebrows. 'Or, at least, her blood wasn't human.'

'You don't say. The test came back from Bangkok?'

'Pure one hundred per cent pig.'

'So her murder was staged.'

'The whole marriage was staged. I went back to Dong Bang and asked around. The dentist was a bachelor. They said the woman only turned up a few months before his death.'

'When the letters started.'

'Right. And it appears she only came to the village on certain days. The neighbours assumed she was a nurse or housekeeper. On the day we went there, she just happened to still be around. She was probably trying to figure out a way of getting her hands on the latest note. Waiting for the authorities to send his things home.'

'And we brought it right to her.'

'Remember, she took a while to read it? I wouldn't be surprised if she was memorizing it.'

'So she was just a courier, there to pick up the week's code.'

'She just put the old fellow on the bus on letter days and waited for him to bring it back.'

'But why on earth go to all that trouble? Surely she could have just taken his key and picked up the letter herself.'

'She probably would have preferred to do that, but something was stopping her.'

'What?'

'Let's ask your Inspector Migraine. What do they have at post offices?'

'Stamps?'

'Think of something that might stop her wanting to be seen inside one.'

'Being seen …? I know. Wanted posters. Her picture's on the wall of the Bureau de Poste.'

'Very good.'

'What did she do?'

'Espionage. She didn't look it but that lady's caused a lot of trouble for the new administration. I noticed the poster when I went to ask about Dr Buagaew's post box. The Security Division has a file on her a foot thick. The dentist had a little file of his own but only as a suspected Royalist sympathizer. I imagine they didn't see him as much of a threat, what with his disability and all. He'd had the PO box under a false name for over ten years. I can't imagine what he was using it for during the old regime.'

'Sleazy dental material from Europe, I wouldn't wonder. But the woman? Is she still at large?'

'She always seems to be one step ahead of the authorities.'

'How intriguing, an aging adversary. She did a marvellous job of faking her own death to put us off the trail. She deserves a code name. Something to do with the devil, perhaps.'

'Sorry, the Security Division's already christened her.'

'Probably some very dull name. They don't have much imagination up there. "Woman 17B"?'

'They're calling her "the Lizard".'

'Ooh, she must have really upset people in high places. Good for her.'

'Siri, she's the enemy.'

'Oh, right. I forgot.'

23

NEVER HAND MONEY TO A
TRANSVESTITE ON A STREET CORNER

Won't be long
   Wrong sex and wrong gender
      Return to sender
   Killed by tender loving lust
Dirty damned needle jab, dust to dust
   What lethal sin
                  In just
A pleasure tax.

'Very nice, thanks. But, to tell you the truth, what I wanted to talk to you about was—'

'Five thousand *kip*.'

'What? I'm not asking you a question.'

'No. You want a conversation. That's five thousand *kip*.'

Siri sat beneath the Aeroflot sign with a peaked cap pulled down over his face. Auntie Bpoo was wearing a hideous skintight cowhide-pattern dress that rode up her thighs. Fortunately, she had on khaki Y-fronts to preserve what little dignity she had. A light drizzle was falling and the fortune-teller held up a red-and-white polka-dot umbrella. Siri just got wet. Everyone passing along Samsenthai that evening felt sorry for the two crazy people.

'All right, so if I did give you five thousand *kip*, would you indulge me?'

'That was a question. To answer that I'd need another ten thousand.'

'Oh, come on.'

'All right. I'll give you a discount. You can have a question and a ten-minute conversation for six thousand.'

'God, man. It's cheaper to bribe a treasury official.'

'Take it or leave it. And it's "Miss".'

'All right. I'll take it. What I want to talk about—'

'In advance.'

'Look, if you can see the future, you know I'm not about to run off without paying.' Auntie Bpoo looked away and twirled her umbrella. 'All right. All right.'

He handed over two bricks of fifty-*kip* notes. Since the devaluations, people in Laos had dispensed with their purses and wallets and taken to carrying cement bags for their small change. Auntie Bpoo counted each wad and decided he'd given her enough.

Siri considered this to be one of the most foolish investments he'd ever made. He could see her at the morning market buying a new leather miniskirt with his hard-earned salary. But the big female impersonator was good, he had to give her that. He'd even go so far as to say 'gifted'. Siri had so little contact with freaks like himself, he often hungered for company. There were still a million questions he needed answers to with regard to his unwanted and poorly utilized abilities. He hoped Auntie Bpoo might be able to help. Mysticism produced strange bedfellows and there were few stranger than the couple seated on plastic bathroom stools on Samsenthai that evening. Auntie Bpoo took great pains to secrete the money in an enormous handbag. When she

was satisfied it was safe, she said, 'All right, Dr Traitor. You
have eight minutes left.'

'But I haven't ... Very well. What I want to talk about is
... our connection to the spirit world.'

'Our connection?'

'Yes, you see, I receive messages from the dead.'

Auntie Bpoo's eyebrows nearly clinked against the
wooden shop sign above her head before returning to her
face. 'Oh, really?'

'Yes, I get messages that tell me how people died.'

She yawned. 'Look, Granddad, perhaps you ought to cut
back on the MSG.'

Siri laughed to cover his irritation. Why was it that so
many obnoxious and infuriating people were blessed with
gifts? Perhaps one was a counterpoint to the other. But he
was determined to lure this brilliant transvestite into a
discussion on the paranormal. Perhaps she'd respond to
aggression.

'Listen, young man or young lady or both, if you prefer.
I am Dr Siri Paiboun, the national coroner, but of course
you know that. I host the spirit of a thousand-year-old
shaman.' Auntie Bpoo started to collect her cards and
charts and pack them into a number of plastic bags. 'Are
you listening? Through him I am able to communicate with
the dead. I have come to you because—'

'Prove it.'

'What?'

'Prove to me that you can communicate with the dead.'

'How?'

'Tell me what my uncle Sithon was wearing when he
passed away.'

'What he was wearing? I don't know. I don't do tricks.'

'No? You should learn. Even the shadiest mediums down at the old ferry crossing can do that one. They chat with dead people all the time, relive some funny event only departed Granny Ting could have known.'

'Well, I can't.'

'I didn't think so.' Auntie Bpoo stood and nodded in the direction of the other stool beneath Siri. 'Time's up. I have a mud-pack sauna appointment.'

Siri refused to vacate his stool. 'You can't just take my money and leave,' he said. 'That's abuse of a senior citizen. I can bring the Aged Union down on you just like that.'

The fortune-teller leaned forward and squared up to Siri. His scent was a mix of lavender and lighter fluid. 'Look, Granddad. I'll be honest with you. I get a lot of crackpots coming down here trying to elbow in on my action. They think they can get me to show them my tricks. Next thing you know, they'd be setting up shop all the way down Samsenthai, and I wouldn't have any customers for myself.'

'Customers? But you don't charge for your normal service. It's only senile old fools like me you hit up for money. What does it matter how many customers you get?'

Auntie Bpoo put the back of her hand against her fore-head and looked to the puffy heavens. It was an action made famous by a popular Thai screen actress. A gamut of emotions played across her face.

'It's true,' she said in the soft, female version of her voice. 'I don't really need money, you see. I have all I want. But money can't buy companionship. No matter how many kilograms of *kip* you have, it can't bring you true respect. Why else would people come to listen to someone like little me? I need a gimmick.'

'It's much more than a gimmick.'

'No, it isn't. It's just a party trick.'

'It is not. You know things. You knew my name.'

'It's a small town.'

'No. You were able to tell me things nobody else has access to. That's why I'm here. I know you're in contact with the spirit world.'

'Look, it's great that you're in touch with dead people.' Her voice had returned to basso. 'It means you'll have contacts up there when you kick the bucket. That always helps in the first couple of days when you're finding your feet, looking for a place to sleep, somewhere to eat. But don't expect me to say, "Wow, you too, eh? Let's compare notes." Because there is no connection. Get it? I don't want to disappoint an old coot like you who looks like he's had more than his fair share of disappointments in his life. I wouldn't know a spirit if it bit my titties. There is no super-natural. I don't get messages. I just guess. Got it? I just say the first thing that comes into my head. Half the time I haven't got a clue what I'm talking about. But people keep coming back, so I keep doing it. It's just a bit of fun. Nobody buys it. You gonna give me back my stool now?'

Siri stood and sacrificed his little white perch. Auntie Bpoo slotted it together with her own stool and put them in a black plastic garbage bag. She tossed her big mauve handbag over her shoulder and hoisted her other luggage. Siri stood dripping in front of her.

'You know why I've been charging you and no one else?' she said. 'It's because I didn't want you to keep coming back. There's something weird about you, old man. I get a funny feeling in my bladder when you come around. It puts me off. This is just a bit of harmless amusement, but people like you take the fun out of it. Lighten up, why don't you?'

ANARCHY AND OLD DOGS

She turned and headed toward the black stupa.

'Wait,' Siri called after her.

The transvestite turned back with attitude. 'What?'

'You owe me a prediction.'

Auntie Bpoo splashed back to him in her platform sandals.

'After everything I've just told you, you still want me to see for you?'

'Once more and I promise I'll leave you alone.'

'Is that so?'

'Coroner's honour.'

'But you know I'm just going to say the most ridiculous thing that comes into my head.'

'I'll take it.'

24

WILL SHE? WON'T SHE?

There was something static about the Mekhong that
evening. Of course it was moving. It had a thousand
communities to feed downriver, rice to water, pretty ladies to
wash. But to the naked eye it seemed to sit like a long, broad
pond. Already it was beginning to swell from the rains in
China and overwhelm the vegetable allotments along its
banks. As the retreating sunlight cast its shadows, Siri sat
alone on his log and imagined that the mighty river had
stopped. He'd learned all its secrets and it was prostrated
before him, seeking forgiveness for all the lives it had taken.

His feet danced back and forth to stop the mosquitoes
settling on his ankles, and his mind danced in time with
them. He wondered whether there would be any more
lunches here with his best friend, whether Civilai would
survive retirement, whether he'd done the right thing. He
wondered whether he was right to give his blessing to a
pressured marriage, and whether Judge Haeng might allow
him to retire now after he'd helped to rescue the republic
from anarchy. He wondered whether the Odeon might
consider showing the odd Bruce Lee film on special occasions. He would have wondered himself into oblivion if his
thoughts hadn't been drowned out by the sudden screeching
of cicadas.

A sliver of lightning and a groan of thunder across in Thailand made him think of Pakse and this brought him full circle to Daeng. The cream-coloured *champa* flowers sat at his feet in a bunch, wrapped in mulberry paper. He'd performed surgery with bullets whistling past his ears and confronted malevolent ghosts, but neither had made his stomach churn as it did now. Would she have him? He wasn't much to look at, half of one ear was missing, and goodness knows there were a thousand other reasons to turn him down. But Auntie Bpoo had confirmed what he'd already known in his heart. The first part of the fortune-teller's prophecy had already been in his plans: that by the end of the monsoons he'd be married. And there weren't that many prospective brides to choose from.

He took a deep breath and began the walk along the river's edge that would take him to Daeng's new noodle shop. The trumpet trees that once lined the bank had been cut down by the army for security reasons. The trees had obscured the view of their enemies across the Mekhong. If the Thai military had been observing at that moment, they would have seen a nervous seventy-three-year-old shuffling his sandalled feet along the Lao bank, indifferent to any thought of being shot. He had two things on his mind that were more worrying: the first, what words he could use to convince Daeng his intentions were honourable; the second, Auntie Bpoo's other prediction, that by the Lao New Year, Dr Siri and his new bride would have two bouncing baby boys.